WISHES

They stood shrouded in candlelight, snow beginning to fall lightly outside the window. He kissed her. His mouth smoothly staked claim on hers, his tongue invading with an unrehearsed orchestration. He pulled her tightly to his hard body and introduced her to his passion. "It's been a long time for me, Sadie. I need you," he whispered, his voice husky.

Her eyes opened wide as he pulled back to observe her face. Mac smiled at her erratic breathing, and accepted her more fully into his heart because of it.

As he led her to the soft bed, trepidation returned in full. She pulled back, wanting to clear the air. "I'm sorry you were not my first."

His eyes took in her beautiful dishevelment. "I'm not sorry. So what if I'm not your first? I'll be your last, Sadie MacCallister." He pulled her close and added, "I promise to sear your soul so completely that there will never be room for another."

WISHES ON WATER

DANA GEORGE

LEISURE BOOKS   NEW YORK CITY

A LEISURE BOOK®

September 2004

Published by

Dorchester Publishing Co., Inc.
200 Madison Avenue
New York, NY 10016

ISBN 0-8439-5449-3

Visit us on the web at www.dorchesterpub.com.

This book is dedicated with love and admiration to my parents,
David and Nathaline George. Thanks Mom and Dad,
for teaching me to love words, for making books
a magical part of my childhood.

And for my husband, Bob, and sons Bo and Ty—
you are the inspiration for everything I do.

WISHES ON WATER

Chapter One

Wahpekute Dakota Sioux Camp
August 1856

Her ebony hair mingled with the peculiar red locks of the big warrior as Crying Star leaned over her sleeping husband. Her breast brushed his mighty shoulder; her hair trailed across his beloved face. She attempted to memorize his features, for some strange inner voice told her that she would not be with him much longer.

Noting the pock-marked face, a face that had been the target of cruel teasing as a child, she considered how it only added to his awesome appearance. The red hair that had caused some to stare and laugh now made her husband appear more distinctive. Scarlet Point, they had called him. The woman's heart filled with pride as she considered how long that name would inspire respect.

Crying Star ran her hands lightly across her husband's chest, searched his body for signs of age, but

1

found few. This man was a grandfather, but still young maidens turned their heads as he walked by. She'd watched them.

Gasping, she suddenly felt him encircle her wrist, then push her onto her back, and she gladly accepted his commandeering of her body. Unashamedly opening herself to him, Crying Star watched each nuance of her husband's expression, each ripple of his deeply corded muscles, as he sought to surround and inspire her weakening body.

The brawny muscles of his upper chest knotted and strained, and as she watched them, the woman thought of all she and her husband did not say. There had been a time when no subject was off limits, when they'd shared their every thought. But no longer. They did not speak of her deteriorating health, or discuss his life after her death. Instead, this man she loved attempted to make her feel like a girl again, to sing the sweet song he had long ago taught her.

Moving above her, at last he cried out in release. The woman called his name, "*Inkapaduta*." She wasn't sure if he heard as he wrapped his big arms around her, turned, and pulled her atop him.

After so many years, Crying Star knew her husband's soul, had shared his deep pain, and had watched him change. Now, in her final days, the woman prayed that her love would be sufficient to soothe him. She feared what her death would do. She feared what would happen if Inkapaduta were ever to release the pain in his tortured spirit upon those he held responsible.

For just a moment longer, she wanted to hold him. She wanted to remember the daring young man he had been, to chase away the rage that sought to control him. For a moment more she would hold him with all her might, lend him her strength, help him to remember his own goodness. And she would hope that would be enough.

Chapter Two

Ribbons of sunlight clung tenuously to the horizon, jealously guarding the last moments of daylight. The big man squinted over the tree line and mentally calculated how much longer he would be confined to the hard wagon bench. Although he was bone-tired, his body stirred at the thought of being so close to home. He was astounded to realize that the four months he had been gone seemed more like four years. It was with some surprise that he realized that he, Samuel "Mac" MacCallister, had finally found a place to call that. *Home*.

A lone rider approached. The huge quarterhorse with its spotted coat was familiar. "Gardner," Mac called in greeting.

Rowland and Frances Gardner were his closest neighbors on Lake Okoboji, and had proven to be supportive and loyal friends. Although the area had been

4

opened by treaty in 1853, it was still a dangerous land in which to settle. Indians, while mostly friendly, freely visited white homesteads. Storms, illness and wild animals added to the daily risks pioneers faced. It was good to know he had a man like Rowland Gardner nearby.

Mac's chest filled with some unnamable emotion. True friendship was new to him, the feeling of belonging completely foreign. He watched as Rowland rode toward him and, suddenly, uncharacteristically, he had the urge to tease the shy, older man. "Rowland." He nodded. "Maybe I'm more tired than I thought, but you look good enough to kiss."

Gardner pulled his mount to a halt and laughed. "Let's just keep that between the two of us. Frances is the jealous type." The man's eyes settled on the back of Mac's heavy covered wagon. His eyebrows rose slightly and he asked, "Your mission was successful?"

Mac grinned, his darkly tanned face framing the radiant white smile. "Yeah, I'll fill you in later. Right now I just want to get home and settled. It's been a long trip."

Gardner shifted in his saddle, its leather creaking in protest. He removed his dark hat and ran a hand through his thinning hair. He replaced the hat, removed it again, and using his saddle horn beat some of the dust off it. He looked everywhere but at Mac, which immediately worried the younger man.

"What happened while I was gone?" Mac asked. "Everybody okay?"

Rowland grimaced. "Well, they were till now. I'm afraid that when you find out what I've done, Frances is gonna have to press my burying suit."

5

Mac's shoulders tensed. *Please God*, he prayed silently, *don't let anything happen to mess things up. Not now.* Exhaling, he asked, "So, what have you done?" When Rowland didn't immediately answer, Mac found himself holding tight to what was left of his frayed nerves. "Just spit it out, Gardner. What's going on?"

"I sort of lent your cabin," Rowland began.

"You *what?*"

"Just relax, Mac. I told a widow lady that she could stay at your place while her kid recovered from . . ." Rowland hesitated.

Mac's voice was a low growl. "From what, Gardner?"

"Smallpox." The answer was clipped.

Mac valiantly attempted to control his temper. "Let me see if I got this straight. You knew why I was going to Kansas City. You also knew that if I was successful, I wouldn't be gone long. What happened? You decided the best way to welcome me back was to let some strange woman and her kid infect my cabin with smallpox?"

Rowland's expression was pained. "Kids."

"What?" Mac's agitation punctuated his question.

"The lady has two little boys."

"And?"

"Her husband had just died in an accident."

"*And?*"

"Half the wagon train they were part of was infected with smallpox."

Mac paused. "That's rough, Rowland. I'll give you that. But—"

Gardner cut him off. "Look, Mac—her youngest son was deathly ill, and the old man who offered to stick with her when she pulled out of the wagon train came down with the pox and died too. We found them a mile or so from here, this pathetic little group stuck in the middle of nowhere. Harvey and I buried the old man."

"Oh, geez." Mac sighed. He took the hat off his head and hit it against the wagon bench. He did not want to feel sorry for this strange woman, did not want her or her sick kids in his cabin. He sure didn't want to say Rowland had done the right thing. He knew he was being uncharitable, unreasonable even—but he had spent the past four months dreaming of getting home, of getting settled in and starting a new life.

Rowland remained silent, his wise eyes simply watching. Mac's internal struggle grew worse. The hell of it was, everyone in the vicinity knew that Rowland and Frances Gardner would give up everything they owned to help someone else, even a perfect stranger. *Like they helped me*, a tiny voice nagged Mac. Hadn't the entire Gardner family organized the party that helped Mac build his cabin and barn? Hadn't they been there at every turn to give him encouragement and advice?

"You play dirty, Rowland," Mac finally conceded. "Don't worry, I'm not going to throw your latest mercy case out on her ear." Frowning, he added, "But it's only the beginning of August. I'll expect her to make other arrangements, to hitch up with another wagon train soon. Where were they headed?"

"Dakotas, I think."

Mac looked satisfied. "Good. They're almost there. They can join whoever's passing through Granger's Point and be there before the first snow flies."

Gardner nodded benignly. "Well, that's right good of you, Mac. I somehow knew you'd be willing to help." Mac's grunt did nothing to deter him, either; Rowland smiled. "You can stay at our place till the lady's ready to leave."

Mac rolled his eyes. "I don't think so. How many people you have living there now?"

Rowland's laughter was evidence that he took no offense. He shrugged and suggested, "Well, how about the barn? You're welcome to stay out there if you don't like close quarters. Frances would love to cook for you. She's always saying you should put some meat on those bones."

Mac knew he was being cajoled. At two hundred pounds of pure brawn and muscle, he needed meat on his bones like a lion needed more mane. "Thanks, but no thanks, Rowland. If I'm gonna be sleeping in a barn, I'd just as soon it was my own. That way I can get some work done on the place."

"Good thinking!" Gardner said, then he turned his horse and headed for home. His ingratiating tone was getting on Mac's nerves, and he knew it. Trying hard not to laugh, he saluted over his shoulder and rode off. "Let me know if you need anything," he called out as he galloped away.

"Yeah. I need my house," Mac muttered irritably. Then, looking back at his precious cargo, he released a pent-up sigh and headed for home. He had slept under the stars for months; surely he could stand a few nights in his barn.

Chapter Three

Sadie Pritchard stepped from the homey interior of the small, rustic cabin. She walked around to the rear of the house and took a moment to simply steep in the splendor of the view before her. Stretching as far as the eye could see was a lake, the likes of which Sadie had never seen before traveling West. Like a carpet of blue gems fallen from the sky, the water sparkled brilliantly. Okoboji, Rowland Gardner had called it.

The cabin was built on the top of a small rise, surrounded by mighty oaks, poplars and spruce. Sadie was becoming surprisingly adept at identifying the plants and animals that shared this little piece of paradise. She loved this place.

She wondered, for the hundredth time, why the owner of the cabin had chosen to build its lone door on the east side of the home, facing away from the lake. She would have to ask Rowland or his son-in-law Harvey Luce next time one of them came by with fresh game. Sadie knew that, if she were to ever settle in a place like this, she would build the cabin so that every time she walked out the door she could see the big blue waters of Okoboji. Little was as beautiful.

Thinking of Rowland Gardner brought a smile to her face. His family had been so good to her. Not only had they rescued her and her boys from being stranded on the prairie, but they also insisted on providing meat for her table. Rowland assured her that Matthew would recover more quickly with hearty meals. Sadie swore again that she would repay the Gardners for their kindness.

After weeks of worrying about her two precious sons, Sadie was finally tempted to relax. All seemed to be looking up. Rowland had told her about a town just east of Okoboji called Granger's Point. He was confident that she could find a lead on a job there as soon as Matthew healed completely.

Then again, there was the money. Sadie reflectively knit her brow as she considered the cash she'd found folded in the bottom of her dead husband's trunk. The man had never had two coins to rub together, but somehow he'd managed to hide hundreds of dollars at the bottom of his battered chest. Sadie knew Eldon too well to believe the money had been earned honestly; she could only imagine who had been hurt in the process of getting it. Still, she would hold on to it until she could find a way to make things right. If she ever could.

She shook her head, determined to focus on how *well* things were going. Matthew was on the mend and seemed almost like himself. It seemed that with every blister on his body that scabbed, the eight-year-old gained energy. And, thank God, Aaron hadn't come down with the illness. Sadie had kept the boys apart, banishing her older son to sleep under the stars, in the wagon, or in the barn. At the age of ten, he'd handled the separation with the understanding of an adult. *Just like he handles everything else*, Sadie thought proudly.

She had no way of understanding why she hadn't come down with the smallpox herself, caring as she had for her younger son. The disease was as mysterious as a tornado, leveling one life while leaving another intact.

Just that day, Sadie had washed every item that Matthew had come in contact with, scrubbing them with a vengeance. The cabin, which had been full of dust and cobwebs, was now as clean as it was ever going to be. She didn't want to leave any illness behind. Sadie already felt that she owed so much to her unseen benefactor who owned the home; she didn't want to repay him by making him sick upon his return.

And she was keeping a careful accounting of any supplies she used. The soap, canned goods, matches— all of it. She fully intended to repay her host for anything she took. It was indeed fortunate that the man was gone, that the cabin had been available, for Sadie knew that no hotel in Granger's Point would have allowed her to stay with a boy suffering from smallpox. And while she wouldn't have exposed the Gardners to the illness, by the time Rowland had found her, she wasn't sure she could stand another day in the stuffy confines of the wagon.

Sadie gazed at the brilliantly streaked horizon and wondered at its magnificence. It was as if The Artist's hand had dipped a brush in his most dazzling shades of pinks and gold, and masterfully slathered the sky from the ground up.

She wished the boys were awake so that she could share the scene with them. No, she reconsidered with a tired grin. The fact that both children were asleep was a wonderful break for her. Now that Matthew was feeling better and it was safe for him to spend time with his brother, the two were always trying to find ways to entertain themselves. That could be draining for a mother.

The sound of horses approaching pulled Sadie reluctantly around to the front of the cabin. Although cautious, she was fairly certain that a lone man driving an overloaded buckboard probably meant no harm. She wondered if this might be the cabin's owner. Rowland had said that he would be gone for months, but . . .

She could see that he was a big man. A *very* big man. The width of his shoulders reminded her of the story of Samson in the Bible. Sadie's heart beat hard within her chest, and she suddenly wondered if the man was as mean as he was huge.

She decided to take the bull by the horns, and boldly approached him. "Mr. MacCallister?" she called.

"Yeah," the man replied, sounding tired and a bit surly. Hadn't Rowland Gardner told her what a wonderful man Samuel MacCallister was? He sure didn't sound wonderful.

"I'm Sadie Pritchard," she forged ahead. "I know it must be a terrible shock for you to find a stranger in your home, but let me explain."

The voice was low and clearly irritated. "Save it. Gardner caught me a few miles back and told me the

12

whole story. You can use the cabin until your son gets well, then I'll see that you get to town."

It was evident that he had thought it over, and that he believed he was being more than gracious. Sadie was somewhat rankled by his attitude, but she couldn't really blame him; after all, the man had been on a long trip only to return to find his home overtaken by complete strangers. Sadie was determined not to dwell on his less-than-pleasing personality, though. "Well, I can't thank you enough, Mr. MacCallister."

"No, you can't," he replied sourly.

A plaintive wail drifted from somewhere behind the giant, grumpy man, surprising Sadie. Her mouth dropped open. Why, it sounded like a baby!

As she watched, the unfriendly giant stepped down from the wagon bench, lifted the canvas flap, reached over ledge, and from somewhere within the conveyance extracted a baby. In what was a truly incongruous picture, he pulled the tiny being to his shoulder and his massive hand began to pat its back.

"Oh, my gracious," Sadie murmured, her legs moving of their own accord toward the unlikely pair.

She couldn't see much of the man's face due to the huge hat he wore, but she sensed a softer set to his features as he held the tiny bundle. "Yours?" she asked, as she stepped up to inspect the perfect baby.

"Yep." Well, he sure wasn't one for words, this MacCallister.

"What a beautiful little girl."

The big man went totally still, as though considering whether he should speak. Even though he attempted to keep his voice low—for the baby's sake,

Sadie presumed—it sounded like the low rumble of thunder when he spoke. "How did you know?"

Sadie gave him a questioning glance. "Know what?"

"How'd you know she's a girl? People we met up with on the way from Missouri naturally assumed she was a boy. Figured the reason I wanted my kid so bad was because it was a boy."

"First of all, that's ridiculous!" Sadie began. "A parent's love knows no bound for his child, boy or girl. And secondly, it's obvious she's a girl. Just look at that gorgeous face. She's far too pretty to be a boy."

The big man's shoulders relaxed, and Sadie thought she could detect a hint of a smile beneath the wide brim of his hat. So his daughter was his soft spot, eh? That somehow made him seem more human, cranky or not.

It occurred to her then that she was not only putting Mr. MacCallister out of his home, but putting his daughter out as well. "I am so sorry," Sadie apologized. "Your baby . . . I'm going to move my boys back into the wagon, and if you'll oblige us one more night to stay on the property, we'll be gone by morning."

Mac's response was gruff. "Forget it. I'm not kicking a sick kid out of my house just so I can be a little more comfortable. Stay as long as you need," he added grudgingly.

"But the baby—" Sadie began.

"Will be just fine. We've been sleeping on the trail for the better part of two months. A few more nights won't hurt."

The giant walked off toward the barn, the impossibly small child held tight against his chest. Calling back, he informed Sadie that he would make a bed for his daughter, then take care of the horses.

As he disappeared into the dark structure of the barn, Sadie blinked; then she blinked again. It all seemed so unreal. She could almost believe that he was an apparition, that she had imagined the entire meeting. Stifling the urge to laugh, Sadie wondered what new turn her topsy-turvy life was going to take.

Chapter Four

It was hotter than Hades, his stomach was growling and he had a bug bite in the center of his back that was driving him crazy. He wanted to scream out in frustration, wanted to hit something big, kill something small. The redheaded urchin who kept pressing a freckled face to the windowpane immediately sprang to mind. Rotten kid; he was getting a kick out of tapping on the window then diving to hide when Mac looked his way. The last time Mac had been fool enough to fall for the kid's stunt, the guttersnipe actually had the audacity to pop his head back up and stick his tongue out.

Well, that was it! Mac was going to finish gathering the supplies he'd brought from Kansas City and get to work on the barn, which was in desperate need of repair. Sometime around midnight it had begun to rain. Not that light, even rain, which freshens the air and revitalizes the world it touches, but big, fat, mean drops. A maddening *drip*, *drip*, *drip* had hit him square on the forehead in the middle of the night, and that was his first indication that the work could not be delayed.

Mac was mad at the barn (which he had at one time considered well built), at the rain (which he had at one time not been sick to death of), but mostly he was annoyed by the woman and her equally irritating children who had taken over his home.

Scarecrow woman, he called her. She was no bigger around than a scarecrow from a field. Her face was all angles, prominent cheekbones and pointed chin. Beneath her worn dress he could see the sharp juts of her shoulder blades. Her arms looked like twigs. Mac had always liked his women voluptuous, like Cynthia. Not like—

What a ridiculous thought, he sneered mentally, cutting himself off. Who cared what Scarecrow looked like? She and her brats would be gone in a few days, sooner if he was lucky.

Scarecrow had actually emerged from his house an hour or so earlier and offered to make him breakfast. Of course he had refused. So what if his stomach growled all morning? After all, you don't go out of your way to make the vermin who crawl into your home feel like family, do you? No. You get them out as quickly as possible.

Scarecrow had taken his rejection distressingly well. She'd had the gall to return to the house, feed her children, then depart once again—with a load of laundry in her arms and a song on her lips. She was actually singing now! What did she think this was, a holiday? Mac hoped that she could see and feel the way his brow furrowed and his eyes turned to twin slits as he stared after her. He hoped she knew how much she was

17

putting him out. But just in case, he was not going to go one inch out of his way to make her stay pleasant.

He checked his daughter, who was cooing happily in a small bassinet near the front of the barn. He fought the urge to pick her up, even for a moment. He had work to do. He climbed a ladder that leaned against the barn and set out to make repairs. Gingerly, he moved over the roof of the structure and looked for the pesky trouble spots.

A man of two hundred pounds had to be pretty careful when walking on a roof. Not many were built to withstand his kind of weight clomping around on them. It would fit right in with the rest of his day to fall through the darn thing!

"Mister?" a little voice piped.

Ignore it and it will go away, he promised himself.

"Hey, Mister!" The voice was louder and more excited.

Mac leaned over the roof far enough to see the source of his annoyance. A skinny blond boy, all arms and legs, stood at the base of the ladder. He held more of the materials Mac was going to need to make the repairs. "You want me to bring these up to you?"

Mac wanted to say, *No, I want you to go home. I don't care if home is Boston, New York, or Timbuktu, but I want you out of here!* Instead, he just growled, "No, kid. I'll do it myself."

"But—" the squeaky little voice began.

"Look kid, I said no. I can take care of it myself!" he yelled.

Well, he'd taken care of that; the kid was moving toward the house. Mac steeled his heart when he noticed the boy's blond head bent, chin practically touching his chest. He told himself, *I am not going to call the kid back. I am not going to call the kid back.*

"Hey kid," he called. "I don't know what I was thinking. Of course I could use the help."

The speed with which the towheaded boy returned was amazing. He never said a word, just picked up the materials he thought he could handle, stuck what he could in his pockets and the rest in the rear waistband of his plain cotton pants, then climbed hand over hand up the ladder to deliver the supplies. Mac said thanks, and set to work.

Scarecrow returned from the lake, freshly scrubbed clothes in her arms. With eyes so big they practically swallowed her face, she stared up at her son on the roof. Mac's scowl dared her to say anything to discourage the boy, and to her credit she simply smiled before entering the cabin.

Mac and the boy worked efficiently together. The youth seemed to know what Mac would need before Mac asked for it. Mac fought hard to suppress the grudging respect he was beginning to feel for the child. The boy wore an expression of pure bliss. Against his better instincts, Mac's mind began to make a list of other jobs the kid could perform. Heck, if it made him happy, the boy could do whatever he wanted.

"What's the baby's name?" Scarecrow's voice rose up from below.

"Grace," Mac's called in a deep rumble.

"Grace? Why, that's lovely."

"Yeah? Well, it was my mother's name." He dismissed her compliment, then added under his breath,

"At least I think it was." That was what the men who used to visit her in their stinking little cabin used to call her—Amazing Grace. They'd walk away whistling, and his mother would have a new bottle of booze or a few dollars tucked down the front of her greasy dress. Geez, those memories were morbid.

Angry that Scarecrow was causing him to dredge up things better forgotten, Mac grabbed for his hammer. In horrifying slow motion, the heavy tool slipped out of his reach. It slid down the slope of the roof, hurtled through the air, and sped right toward his daughter's bassinet.

With the speed of lightning, a movement practically too fast for Mac to register, Scarecrow snatched the baby from her bed. The hammer landed with a sickening thud right where Grace had been a moment earlier.

It hurt to breathe. Mac hadn't even realized that he was holding his breath. The blond boy scrambled down the ladder, praising his mother for her quick thinking. With labored breath, Mac followed. His hands shook as he reached for his little girl.

Suddenly, it struck him just how difficult it was going to be to raise this child on his own. He had left her in danger while he was fixing his roof. Who would watch her while he worked in the field, while he hunted? He knew that Frances Gardner would do what she could, but Mac couldn't count on her to be there every minute of every day.

And what if something happened to him? Would Grace simply lie alone in the cabin until death claimed her? *What if, what if, what if,* rolled through his

20

head, stubbornly refusing him the luxury of leaving it to be figured out later.

A plan, born of desperation, began to take shape in his mind.

Chapter Five

A mile from Mac's tiny cabin was the home of Rowland and Frances Gardner. The family was beginning its morning rituals. Frances quickly pulled her graying hair to the nape of her neck and, after a few quick twists, secured the style with pins. She looked at her smoky image in the tiny mirror that hung above the homemade dresser, and wondered if she looked as tired as she felt. The dream had come again last night, sucking her into a curiously frightening world.

She'd been standing in her cabin, surrounded by the people she loved. They were entertaining guests. A group of Indians, scantily clad and seemingly hungry, were there. And a woman—a woman whose face she could not see—was standing by her side. Frances and the unknown woman had just served their other guests a meal. All seemed peaceful, benign.

Suddenly, the room began to spin. One by one, the faces of her husband, children and grandchildren spun by her. She attempted to focus on each image, and as she did so Frances was overcome with the intensity of her love for them. Fond memories, special occasions, all joined in the whirl of sentiment that was orbiting around her. Caught up in the ferocity of the emotions she was experiencing, Frances barely noticed the hand of the unknown woman on her elbow.

As Frances continued to watch, her family spun more and more crazily around her. The pressure on her arm grew. Before her horrified gaze, one by one, her family members dissolved into mushy puddles of blood. Frances wanted to scream, to run. But she stood her ground, vaguely aware of the woman next to her who by then squeezed her elbow with painful fervor. With macabre fascination, Frances had observed her world disintegrate around her.

Then Frances herself had begun to vanish, and she'd looked toward the face of the unknown woman. Wordlessly, she'd entreated the stranger to look after what remained of her family, to remember what she had witnessed that day. And although she could never make out the face, Frances knew that the woman was nodding, promising to care for those who survived. Just before Frances completely melted into her own crimson pool, she heard the woman scream.

It had been a strange dream.

Chapter Six

Sadie resisted the urge to slam the plate she held against the battered oak table, and as she glanced down into the innocent faces of the three children waiting to be fed, she was immediately contrite. Regardless of the boorish behavior exhibited by the Giant who owned the cabin, she was still thankful to have a roof over her head and food to offer her children.

It had been six weeks since the surly Sam MacCallister and sweet baby Grace returned to the cabin. Sadie was exhausted from trying to make the big man smile. It was as if any time he found himself relaxing, any time he feared Sadie or the boys might pierce his hard shell of a heart, he pulled away, became gruff and unapproachable. But Sadie *knew* there was a streak of kindness in there somewhere. She'd seen how tender he was with his child, noticed how he'd given Aaron tasks that made the fatherless boy feel important. She'd even seen him struggle to control a smile as Matthew pulled a face or said something completely outlandish. But then he would pull back, find some way of escaping their presence.

Sadie had been shocked when MacCallister proposed the deal: She would care for his six-month-old daughter as he prepared for the upcoming winter. In return, she and the boys would have a roof over their heads while Sadie figured out what to do next. How could she have refused?

Grace was a real charmer, with blond curls and shining blue eyes. Sadie enjoyed every moment with the little girl. Fortunately, Grace had not seemed to inherit her father's cantankerous nature. And as Sadie spooned food onto the children's plates, she forced herself to relax; it would do no good to think about how rude Mr. MacCallister was turning out to be.

Naturally, Sadie understood why the man continued to sleep in the barn—although the nighttime temperatures had begun to plummet. She even admired the way he kept Grace with him at night, regardless of how fatigued he was. But what she could not understand was his obstinate determination to keep his distance from her and her children. Though Sadie prepared meals for them all, the Giant refused to eat anything she prepared. He insisted that her only job was to look after Grace, that he could feed himself.

It wasn't so much what he said, but how he said it. It seemed that the friendlier Sadie tried to be, the pricklier the Giant became. He growled at her, spitting words like poisonous darts. At first, Sadie's life had improved so dramatically that she'd been willing to put up with his piercing words, but her patience was quickly wearing thin.

The man worked until it seemed he would drop

from exhaustion. It wasn't unusual for Sadie to wake to the sound of him working outside the cabin: cutting wood, repairing the barn, or one of the hundreds of other tasks with which he busied himself. By the time she had prepared breakfast, Mr. MacCallister would already be glistening with the sweat of a full day's work. Sadie tried to attribute his surliness to the fact that he was overtaxing himself, trying to accomplish too much at once, but she was beginning to wonder if she wasn't being generous. Maybe he was just plain mean.

Oddly though, the boys didn't seem to be intimidated in the least. The harder MacCallister tried to ignore them, the more tenacious they became about gaining his attention. In fact, ever since the day Aaron had worked with him on the roof of the barn, the Giant and the boys seemed to have developed a system. MacCallister would watch Aaron and Matthew bound from the cabin, then, with absolutely no expression on his face, he would give each of them a list of jobs to carry out.

It seemed to Sadie that MacCallister tried very hard to ignore the boys once they'd been given their assignments, but he was not always successful. Like now. Sadie watched from the window as Matthew picked stones out of the small garden. Mr. MacCallister happened to glance Matthew's way, and he noticed that along with the tiny stones Matthew was disposing of a great deal of rich black earth. With a surprising measure of patience, he moved to the small boy and, kneeling next to him, explained how important it was to keep the good soil.

Matthew's round face lit with the newfound knowledge. He looked at the Giant as though the man possessed all wisdom. He thanked MacCallister profusely, then went back to his job, working diligently, hoping to please the big man. Part of Sadie wanted to stomp out of the cabin, to insist that Matthew not treat the grouchy MacCallister like he was some kind of hero, but she knew that Matthew and Aaron both desperately needed a hero. They needed to look at a man and believe he was brave and true, just like in the books. They needed to have someone to look up to.

That thought alone kept her from acting. Then, as the Giant reached down and ruffled her boy's hair, actually smiling and praising Matthew's effort, Sadie felt her heart stop. He was being kind now? How could God have created such a perfect-looking man, only to curse him with such a moody disposition?

Because Sadie knew that she was no great beauty, herself, she had never given much thought to the physical appearance of others. It seemed such a shallow endeavor. Still, Mr. MacCallister would cause a nun to take notice. Standing a good deal over six feet, his body looked like the stuff of legend. He had broad shoulders, a massive chest and narrow waist. His hands looked like they could crush rocks, his arms were enormous, and his long legs were swollen with muscles that could not be hidden even beneath the rough fabric of his pants. The ease with which he carried that body momentarily mesmerized her. Totally comfortable in his godlike shell, he moved about the yard like a lion overseeing its jungle kingdom.

Sadie didn't even want to think about the flawlessness of his face. Wasn't it enough that the man possessed a faultless body? Was it fair that one human being should be blessed with both perfect face and form? Thick, dark hair fell carelessly to his forehead. His features were definitely male; a strong jaw, prominent cheekbones, a straight nose and a dark brow. Deep-set green eyes revealed his moods (which Sadie knew by now were rarely pleasant). Yet despite his unattractive personality, the man's face was captivating.

Sadie took a deep breath, hoping to dispel the foolishness of her wayward thoughts. She suspected that Mr. Samuel MacCallister knew just how attractive he was. It was probably one of the reasons he felt free to treat her with such disdain—she was so unattractive, so beneath his standards, that he did not care to waste his time with pleasantries.

It was fortunate that theirs was a short-term arrangement. As soon as the beautiful Giant was through preparing for the winter, she and the boys would move to Granger's Point. Suddenly uncomfortable, Sadie thought that day could not come soon enough.

Chapter Seven

He had to push his body to keep from thinking, to keep from feeling. Either Scarecrow's appearance was growing on him, or he'd been alone on the prairie for too blasted long.

Mac pounded a stake into the hard ground. He welcomed the pain that shot along the backs of his arms and into his shoulders. Deciding to build a larger pen for the lone milk cow had been a sudden, irrational decision. But he'd had to do something strenuous to keep his mind off the troublesome woman playing house inside his cabin.

Didn't she know he could see her as she stood at the window, gazing languidly out? Did she think he was blind? Did she think he was made of stone? Surely she knew the effect she had on him as she sashayed out of the cabin and walked down to the lake for water; how the sway of her narrow little hips demanded he watch. She couldn't be fool enough to think that he hadn't noticed as she bent to fill the bucket; then, putting the bucket aside, she stretched her arms above her head, arched her back, and exposed her white neck. Suddenly, Scarecrow had looked anything but. She might be too thin, but her breasts were full and, from what Mac could tell, high.

In the six weeks she'd been caring for Grace, the woman's face had begun to fill out; her expression grew less strained, less tired. She actually seemed to be growing into those huge blue eyes. Not that Mac noticed. Well, at least he tried not to. Every time she tried to speak to him, Mac did his best to send her running. Although the method seemed brutal, it was infinitely kinder than the thoughts that had begun to course through his head.

And those darn kids. He was doing his best to dislike them, and since that failed, to ignore them. It was tough going, though. The older boy—Aaron, his mother called him—spent most of his waking hours trying to be Mac's right-hand man. And Matthew, the redheaded imp, kept everyone in stitches. He was always saying something bizarre or outrageous. Mac schooled his features anytime the eight-year-old came near, afraid that he would laugh. He was trying to distance himself from those boys, he really was.

Tomorrow he would do better, he promised himself. Tomorrow he would pretend that they didn't exist. He would finish the pen he was building, burn the weeds the blond-haired kid picked, and work until he didn't have energy to work any more. He would labor until his mind was too tired to think—about how full Scarecrow's lips were, about how feminine she looked when her riotously curly hair escaped its confines to brush her cheeks, about anything. He would work until his body was incapable of physically reacting to this annoying woman. This woman whose presence was quickly filling every corner of his cabin with her presence.

Chapter Eight

Giving a disgusted glance over his shoulder, Mac muttered to himself, "Keep your eyes averted. Keep working. Don't look up. Don't watch them. Ignore them and maybe they'll go away." It was the next day. His plan was in effect.

"Hi, Mr. MacCallister!" the blond boy shouted as he and his brother descended the hill. His mother followed, Grace in her arms.

Mac rudely continued to work. He desperately tried to pretend that the pair of boys weren't standing there, watching him in wide-eyed innocence. The freckled redhead didn't seem bothered by Mac's obvious attempt to shut them out. "Whatcha doing?" he asked.

Mac lifted his rake to push some blowing weeds and leaves back into the blazing fire. "Sewing a dress," he responded.

Instead of being offended, the two boys laughed. They clearly did not understand sarcasm, or when they were being ignored. "Hey, is all this land yours?"

32

Aaron's blue eyes scanned the flat field on which they were standing.

Mac didn't want to answer, didn't want to open any kind of dialogue. To do so would court danger. If he began to talk to them, he might get to know them better. If he got to know them better, he might begin to really like them. And God forbid, if he began to really like them, he might miss them when they were gone. No, it was far safer to discourage them by not answering their stupid little questions. He'd gotten in too deep as it was.

Mac did not notice the hurt expression on Aaron's face, but Sadie did. Shifting Grace to her left hip, she said, "Excuse me, Mr. MacCallister. Aaron asked you a question." She no longer cared that this man had lent them his home; he was deliberately hurting her children, and she had long ago decided that no man would do that again.

His head snapped up, and his eyes bored into hers. "Can't you see that I'm busy here?"

"Boys, go take a look at those woods over there," Sadie instructed, pointing to the heavily wooded area rimming the field. "Just go to the edge. No farther."

Aaron spared one last look at his hero, then challenged his younger brother to a race. They were halfway to the woods before Sadie trusted herself to speak. "Mr. MacCallister," she began.

"What do you want?" he snapped.

Sadie was so conditioned to recoil that she had to force herself to keep her composure. Fortunately, the days of bowing to the ill temper of a man were gone. With measured words she tightly responded, "I want you to know that I am very grateful for the use of your home. But I think it's important that you also know that I will not tolerate anyone trampling my children's feelings. I'm sure it hasn't escaped your notice that my boys seem to think the sun rises only to be in your presence. It is very unkind of you to play with their emotions. You're kind to them one moment, then rude the next. Make up your mind, Mr. MacCallister. Either like them or hate them, but don't toy with their feelings."

The flashes of ire in Mac's eyes should have burned Sadie with their intensity. He turned back to tend his fire, viciously poking the weeds he was burning, and snarled, "Nothing worse than an overprotective mother. What are you trying to do, make sissies out of them?"

Sadie had not expected that response. She should have, but she hadn't. Mac took advantage of her shocked quiet to continue. He knew that if he was ever going to push these people out of emotional range now was the time. "I bet their father didn't much like watching you turn his sons into little girls. It must have been tough for him to keep quiet while you coddled them to the point where they couldn't be treated with anything but kid gloves. Poor guy, it must have been a real burden to balance out your smothering act."

Sadie's face was beet red by the time the he finished. So angry she could have chewed nails, she fought to control her temper long enough to respond. "Their father, Mr. MacCallister, took sadistic pleasure in beating those children any time they looked at him the wrong way. If they didn't move fast enough to suit him, he would take a switch to their legs. If they spoke out of turn, he would backhand them."

Sadie's voice shook with rage, her lips quivering as she blinked back tears. "If you believe that Eldon Pritchard gave any thought to how his children were developing as men, think again. And if you believe that I am overprotective as a mother, then you've never watched your child cower in fear from his own parent. God forgive me, but the only thing that saved those boys from their father was his death. If he hadn't been so drunk that he walked off a cliff in the middle of the night, they'd still be living in terror."

Turning to walk back up the hill, Sadie called back, "It looks like the boys are done exploring. Please send them back to the cabin when they pass by."

She forced herself to put one foot in front of the other. Were all men complete fools? Why she allowed a virtual stranger to cause her this kind of pain was a puzzle. Had she really believed that Samuel MacCallister could be any different from the other men she'd known in her life?

She had for a moment. Or, she'd wanted to.

The warmth of his big hand on her upper arm was a shock. So was the expression on his face when she turned to tell him to remove that hand. Pain and regret were etched deeply on his handsome features. His eyes showed all of his anguish. "I am so sorry," he said.

It was so genuine, so heartfelt, that Sadie momentarily paused. Resisting the foolish urge to actually forgive the man, she turned and continued up the slope.

His voice chased her. "Stop, will you?" That deep, deep rumbling voice sounded commanding, urgent. He caught her and once again lightly gripped her upper arm. This time she stood still, her back to him. The pounding in her ears caused her head to ache, and Grace's weight was beginning to make her arms go numb.

"Please stop, Mrs. Pritchard," he asked, not unkindly. "Do you think you could look at me?"

Sadie, not wanting to appear cowardly, turned slightly to meet his gaze. Her expression as blank as a fresh sheet of parchment, she stood her ground. Mac let out a deep sigh and suddenly looked years older. The lines around his mouth seemed to deepen, as did the furrow on the bridge of his otherwise perfect nose. "I didn't know," he said simply.

Sadie was unmoved. "How could you have known? You've never so much as engaged us in a simple conversation."

She felt weary. The past few months had been monumentally difficult. She did not need this man adding to her heartache. Tears of exhaustion filled her eyes, infuriating her with their betrayal. Instead of brushing away the renegade tears, she lashed out at the man in front of her. "What is it, Mr. MacCallister? Are we Pritchards too low class, too beneath your station in life to talk to? Are you afraid to encourage us, afraid we won't leave if you ask?"

Color flushed her cheeks. Her blue eyes were practically translucent in the afternoon sun. A slight breeze caused a wisp of hair to dance around her face. Mac was startled by her femininity, aroused by her strength.

Abruptly, he lifted Grace from her tired arms and turned away, "I can't talk to you when you look like that."

Sadie's eyes widened. "Look like what?"

Slowly he turned back to her. Taking a deep breath,

he answered softly, "So pretty. It's difficult to have a conversation with you when you look so pretty."

He tiredly lowered himself to the ground, resting his big frame on the slant of the hill. Sadie looked at him as if he were a coiled snake, then, as if in a daze, sat with him on the ground. Darting a glance in his direction, she decided that the Giant looked almost human sitting with Grace perched in his lap. But why would he comment on her appearance? Why would he call her pretty? Was it his way of catching her off guard?

Her children's return caught her attention. "Ma! You ought to see the fort right inside the woods!" Aaron yelled as he and Matthew raced back across the field.

Sadie did not want her children to be aware of the tension radiating between her and Mr. MacCallister. She smiled at her oldest son and asked, "A real fort?"

"Kinda. There's a big log, all hollowed out. But it's big enough for me and Matt to get into. Can we go back and crawl through it, just once?"

"Aaron," Sadie began, hesitant to allow her boys to do anything that might cause them injury.

"They'll be fine," MacCallister announced. Then, addressing the boys, he added, "Just make sure you throw a big rock through first, so you'll scare out any animals that might be hiding there."

Aaron and Matthew did not wait for their mother to respond; Mr. MacCallister's endorsement was apparently good enough for them. They promised to return as soon as they'd investigated the "fort," and headed back across the field.

Sadie simply stared at the big man seated next to

her. She was too tired to argue about him giving her children permission, but she hoped her expression conveyed her feelings on the subject. The man was not slow to catch on. "Sorry. It's just that I can remember how much fun it was to investigate when I was a kid. I should have made them get your approval first."

She turned her gaze to the scene before her: her two sons joyously running side by side across the sweet, virgin ground. They were so happy that it was difficult for her to stoke the fire of her anger. Quietly, she spoke. "You said that you were sorry for your comments, Mr. MacCallister. I accept your apology. Eight weeks ago I didn't know if my baby boy was going to live or die. Look at him today. I have too much to be thankful for to spend my time stewing over hurt feelings."

Just then, Grace reached out and grabbed a stray section of her hair, wrapping its length around her chubby fist. "Ouch!" Sadie cried.

Before she had the chance to disengage her hair, Mac moved his big body closer, bringing his daughter with him. At this distance Grace wasn't doing nearly as much damage to Sadie's tender scalp. "C'mon, Gracie, let go of the lady's hair," he murmured in the baby's ear.

He was so close that Sadie could feel his warm breath on her cheek. As he gently pried his daughter's hand from her hair, Sadie was conscious of everything about him. Like how his jacket smelled of smoke and his skin of some unnamable, strictly masculine scent. She closed her eyes to the fantasies his nearness summoned, afraid that he might see the truth of her fascination.

"All done," he announced, then pulled Grace to the knee farther from Sadie.

The baby began to whimper, a tiny, I'm-not-very-happy-with-life cry. She threw herself in Sadie's direction and held out her pudgy little arms. Smiling, Sadie accepted the baby into her embrace. Immediately, Grace stopped crying and laid her tired head on Sadie's breast.

The expression on Mac's face was comical. "Well, I'll be a . . . What was that all about?"

Sadie felt absolutely smug. She might not be successful in many things in life, but she did have a way with children. "I think she just wanted to make up to me," she answered.

Mac opened his mouth, then shut it abruptly. He was deeply aware that what he was about to say was risky. As much as he had attempted to shut this trio of houseguests out, as wary as he was of another rejection in life, it simply was not in his nature to purposely abuse anyone. Without giving himself time to back out, Mac spoke. "So do I, Mrs. Pritchard. Want to make up to you, I mean. You seem to be a good woman. I've had no right to treat you poorly."

He seemed sincere enough. Still, Sadie was deeply curious. "Why did you do it then? Why have you gone out of your way to let me know how unwelcome we are—after you proposed that we stay?"

He did not want to tell her. How could he possibly tell her that he'd been left alone enough to teach him the folly of caring for anyone? How could he explain the lengths he was willing to go to to avoid losing another person?

Sadie saw the indecision on his face. "It sometimes helps to talk," she said. Then, smiling, she added, "In fact, I feel much better now that I've told you about the vile man I was married to."

"You can smile about it?" Mac asked, amazed.

"What are my choices? Laugh or cry. He's gone now. He can't hurt us anymore. So I'll laugh about it, and promise myself that it will never happen again."

Shame filled Mac's broad chest. He knew now how deeply his attitude and words must have cut her. And yet she had put up with him for weeks before complaining. "I would take it all back if I could," he swore.

She was convinced. "I know you would," she answered. And her gentle smile declared a truce.

Chapter Nine

"My mother was a whore," Mac began bluntly. "She was hard and tired and soiled, but she was my mother. She never provided me a moment of security, but once in a while she would wrap those perfumed arms around me and I would feel like the luckiest kid on earth. She would give me a nickel and send me into town to buy candy or a trinket. Of course, she was busy entertaining some strange man at home and needed me out of the way, but I thought she was amazing anyway. She was my mother," he finished reflectively.

"What happened to her?" Sadie asked.

"Just disappeared one day when I was around eight. I don't know if she ran off or if one of her customers killed her and buried her body. I just don't know . . .

"I was sent to St. Catherine's Home for Children, and was given a pretty decent upbringing. But I never, ever forgot the feel of my mother's arms." He touched his sleeping daughter's cheek and said, "That's why I called her Grace. In honor of my mother and those wonderful, rare moments when she was there for me."

"Where is St. Catherine's?"

"Kansas City. I spent the majority of my childhood there. Like I said, they were good to me at the orphanage. It wasn't like having a parent, but rather a group of good, kind women who took care of me. I know some people have horror stories about their experiences at an orphanage, but mine was okay. They gave me a safe, warm place to sleep and a good education. I was fortunate."

Sadie was intensely curious about Grace's mother. Throwing out any pretense of politeness, she asked, "Is that where you met your wife?" She only guessed that he had been married. Fortunately, she was correct.

"Cynthia?" Mac laughed. "Oh no, not at St. Catherine's. Cynthia's father, Morton Kendall, is a wealthy Kansas City banker. He and his wife had two children, Steven and Cynthia. Steven was the dutiful son, but Cynthia . . . she was a real wild card. Whenever her father made his semi-annual treks to impress the nuns with a huge donation to St. Catherine's, he would bring his daughter with him."

With a rueful smile, Mac continued, "Little did Mr. Kendall know, but Cynthia had her eyes on us poor, unfortunate orphans. I was thirteen or fourteen when I first noticed her staring at me. She sent me notes, hoping that I would be intrigued enough to take interest. I won't lie to you. I *was* interested, but something in my gut told me to steer clear of her.

"I was old enough to leave the nuns a couple of years later. Headed out to Fort Leavenworth and joined the Army."

"You were in the Army?"

"Spent twelve years protecting the good citizens of Kansas from the menace of the Red man," Mac said sarcastically. "Twelve years was about all I could stomach. You should see what we've done to those so-called savages. Stolen their land in useless treaties, infected them with smallpox-ridden blankets, robbed them of everything they value. Then we wonder why they're angry when more of us swarm in."

Mac shook his head as if to dispel the memories, and continued, "Anyway, an Army buddy was going back to Kansas City with a promise of a job at his uncle's cattle yard. Figured he could get me on too. I had just gotten back into town when I ran into Cynthia again. Saw her sashaying down the sidewalk, and figured she was married by then with a half a dozen kids. Figured she wouldn't recognize me. Damn if she didn't, though. Stopped me to ask how I'd been, where I'd been."

He smiled wryly. "You can't imagine how distressed her father was at Cynthia's resistance to marrying a suitable, stiff-necked husband. She was in her mid-twenties and still playing coy—or so he thought. Old Mr. Kendall would have been *very* distressed to know that his precious daughter was playing the intimate role of wife to whatever ambitious young man she was currently seeing.

"Between appropriate escorts, I guess she thought it might be fun to finally scratch her itch with someone from the poor underclass. I knew she was using me, and I was using her. I'm not proud of it, but at the time it didn't seem like anyone was getting hurt. We met regularly in my rented room."

43

Pain flashed through Mac's deep eyes, giving testimony to the raw emotions the memories still stirred. For a moment Sadie did not think he would continue. When he did, it was with that curt voice that had intimidated her when they first met. "When Cynthia found out she was pregnant with my child, she suddenly decided that a hired hand was not up to her standards. It occurred to her that she could marry any number of her witless suitors and then pass the baby off as his.

"One day in early July, I marched straight into the dining room of the Kendall home, and with Morton Kendall and his perfect little family situated around the mahogany table, announced that his daughter was carrying my child. I know it seems desperate, but I was desperate. I may not have much, but I was not going to allow my child to be claimed by another man!"

Mac wiped his hand across his brow, as if to ease the memory. "Kendall waited for the doctor to disprove my claim, and when he couldn't, quietly demanded Cynthia leave the house. All Cynthia's pleading, all her mother's tears, could not dissuade her father. With no other options, a furious Cynthia became my wife—or hostage, as she called it. Knowing that I couldn't compete with her family in Kansas City, I brought my new bride to this beautiful spot, hoping to build a home for us here."

Sadie could feel the terrible weight of sorrow that had pierced Mac's soul. She knew what it was like to feel unloved, to lose faith in happy endings. "Did she adjust to life here?" she wondered aloud.

He looked at her, not quite rolling his eyes but giving the same impression. "About like a calico cat would adjust to life in a rowboat."

"I'm sorry," Sadie said simply.

He was surprised to see that she truly seemed to be. Perhaps their painful experiences had made them kindred souls of some kind. "Thanks," he said gruffly. "She lasted a few short months. Every day she would sit, as if in a coma, mourning the life she had left. At night she would cry until I was sure she had no more tears. I even asked Frances Gardner to intervene." Mac grimaced. "Cynthia made poor Frances a nervous wreck by the time she was done.

"Nothing I did, nothing I said, made a difference. Worse yet, she began to hate me. For getting her pregnant, for spilling her dirty little secret to her father, and finally, for bringing her here. She considered this the most isolated spot on earth. I began to worry about Cynthia's health and the health of our unborn baby. That much hate and misery could not be good for either of them. In desperation I wrote her parents, asking for their help. It killed me to do it, but that was my kid suffering inside Cynthia."

Sadie wanted to touch his hand, to lend comfort, but settled instead for a commiserating nod.

"Her parents sent Cynthia a letter telling her that they forgave her foolish, youthful mistake and insisting that they wanted to be part of their grandchild's life. They asked if it would be possible to send a few of their men to escort her back to Kansas City, just until after the baby was born. Naturally, they wanted their first grandchild to be delivered by a seasoned doctor."

"She left?" Sadie asked, clearly baffled by the other woman's behavior.

"The moment they rode onto our property."

"You let her? You let your wife leave while carrying

45

your child?" Sadie did not know much about this man, but he didn't strike her as the kind who would let his family go without a fight.

Mac shook his head. "I know it doesn't make any sense. I just knew it was killing her to stay here—killing our baby."

His jaw tensed. He balled his hand into a tight fist, then deliberately relaxed it, self-consciously wiping his palm on the leg of his pants. His voice was laced with bitterness as he continued. "Now that she and her parents were on speaking terms again, she was sure that she could convince her father to build us a comfortable house. In fact, she believed that we might eventually become social pillars of this community. After all, as the child of a prostitute and a ward of St. Catherine's, I could never hope to break into society in Kansas City. Here, nobody knew about my past. We could build our life from scratch."

For Sadie, it was all achingly familiar. She knew how helpless it felt to be looked down upon because of the family she was born into. The stubborn glint in Mr. MacCallister's eyes could not hide the hurt he'd been exposed to. Sadie waited until he was ready to go on. "I repeatedly told her that I would not accept money or assistance from her father. Whatever I built, I wanted to build on my own. And I didn't give a damn about being a social pillar. There are fewer than fifty people living around here. Who do I want to impress?

"So, just like my mother, she disappeared from my life. I might not have loved her, but it brought back the same old feelings. Only this time, I was madder than hell. I had already decided that I would be in Kansas City for the birth of my child. When the baby was able I would return here with her. Cynthia could come or stay, but the baby was mine." Now, that sounded more like what Sadie expected from him.

Her mind spun with unanswered questions. How could a mother allow her child to be taken away from her? Was she still with her family in Missouri? She settled for asking one that seemed less intrusive. "You were there for Grace's birth?"

"No," he answered abruptly. Then, realizing that the woman he was being short with was blameless, he checked his tone and explained, "Winter storms slowed my travel. By the time I reached the Kendall home it was late April. Grace was already a month old, and Cynthia was dead."

Sadie caught her breath. "That's terrible!"

Mac continued as though Sadie hadn't spoken, lost in his thoughts. "Only two weeks after Grace was born, Cynthia decided that she had to get out of the house, had to get back into the swing of things. She dressed as if she planned to attend a party. According to her brother, Cynthia's father stopped her at the door. He insisted that she spend more time recuperating. Neither of them would back down. If there is anyone in this world as mule-headed as Cynthia, it's Morton Kendall. The old man stood his ground and Cynthia stomped back up the stairs. Somehow, as she neared the top landing, her foot tangled in her dress and she fell down the entire flight of stairs, hitting her head along the way. She died several days later."

Sadie felt a pang of surprise and sorrow for the selfish, impulsive woman. "That is truly tragic! She will never know the beautiful daughter she gave birth to."

Mac scowled. "Well, I somehow doubt that she

would have spent much time with Grace. She had never even settled on a name for her. The nurse said that Cynthia had been content to leave the care of Grace wholly to her."

He looked out across the broad expanse of field. His deep voice softened. "I know now that Cynthia would never have returned here. I would have eventually left Kansas City, bringing my daughter with me. As it was, Cynthia was not around to put up even a token fight, and her family was too distraught over her death to protest."

Releasing a pent-up sigh, Mac chanced a look at Sadie. "That is my entire, pathetic life story." Feeling embarrassed at how morbid he had become, he grinned crookedly. "Top that, if you will."

Sadie returned his smile. "Oh, I wouldn't want to do that. How about we take turns? One day we'll say that you have had the most horrible life in history, and the next day will be my turn." There was a sparkle in her blue eyes that Mac found disarming.

"Deal," he said, enjoying her sense of humor. Maybe her idea about laughing at hard times had some merit. He stood and reached down to help her up, watching as she effortlessly cradled Grace in the crook of her arm.

Without hesitation, Sadie took his outstretched hand. "Uh-oh," she observed as she peered around his broad shoulder. "The boys are on their way back, and they look filthy! I swear, Mr. MacCallister, you are going to have the privilege of giving them a dunking in the lake if they're covered with old log slime. I do not want them in my house covered with muck!" Catching herself, Sadie was mortified by what she had said. She had actually called it *her* house.

With surprising sensitivity, the big man eased her embarrassment. "I know what you mean," he said quietly.

Within minutes, they were all headed back to the tiny cabin. Mac made one last check of the weed fire to make sure it had burned itself out. The boys were busy regaling them with stories of their play in the woods, complete with their own private fort.

Sadie couldn't help it; her mind kept slipping back to the little comment Mr. MacCallister had made about her being pretty. The crazy man had actually called *her* pretty! She was sure that he didn't mean it. He'd only said it to shock her into shutting her mouth, but still . . .

And Mac could have kicked himself right then and there. Of course, he'd only end up looking like an even bigger fool. He had actually told her what he was thinking. Stood right in front of her and blurted out that he thought she was pretty. And she was. But she didn't need to know that he thought so. Lord, he sounded like a fourteen-year-old instead of a man of twenty-eight.

She wasn't well-rounded or as blond as Cynthia had been. But she had one of those faces that grew on you, eyes so expressive that they had a language of their own, and a spirit that captivated.

And her face had turned crimson when she realized that she'd called his cabin her home. Mac couldn't help thinking, as he watched the skinny woman walk in front of him, how very at home she did seem in this little cabin on the lake.

Chapter Ten

Wahpekute Dakota Sioux Camp

The silent Inkapaduta was envious of those able to publicly grieve. His own sorrow was too deep to express. Little Dove, the wife of his eldest son, lay dead. He had girded himself for the death of his own wife, but Crying Star lingered. Instead, it was Roaring Cloud's young wife who was now a spirit, and Roaring Cloud the one left alone in grief.

Inkapaduta watched Roaring Cloud walk blankly through the center of camp and mount a skinny horse to ride away from it all. He knew that his son would return when he was able. He himself would see to the burial of his son's young wife.

It was strange. Little Dove had anticipated with glee the birth of her first child, not knowing it would kill her. Let the others worry about the lack of fresh game, she'd said. She'd been so filled with joy at the thought of suckling a son, she'd sworn she could exist on berries and her husband's sweet caresses. For sixteen years she had looked forward to the moment, had lived for it.

When her time came, she'd been not at all concerned. Her mother was with her through it all, was to be the one to carry the joyous news of her son's birth. For hours she'd done as her mother instructed, walked when told to walk, squatted when told to squat. She'd laughed as her mother wiped perspiration from her brow. In her mind's eye, she could see the child who labored to emerge from her body: handsome brown eyes and a smiling cherubic face. She was restless to hold him, to introduce him to his father.

At first Little Dove had been confused as her mother insisted she lie on a soft bed of furs. But hours later, with a shocking clarity, she'd recognized the truth. She was dying. And her child was an elusive dream, slipping like smoke away from the camp.

The young woman had been angry. She did not want to leave the man who was her sustenance. She did not want to become only a vague memory in his tender heart, to have him marry another. She hated the woman who would one day bear her man's children. She hated the white men who frightened away the game, who stole fish from the people's ancestral fishing waters. If they had not come, she would have been strong with health, better able to bear her husband's child.

As her writhing body grew weak, her hatred had grown stronger. The interloping white man had cost her people much and was even now robbing her child of his life, her husband of his dreams. With her dying breath she'd whispered a message to her mother, hate lending strength to her weakened voice. "Tell my husband and beloved father-in-law, the white men must be stopped!"

And Inkapaduta heard.

Chapter Eleven

Sadie snuggled deeper into the thick, feather-filled mattress. Briefly she wondered where Mr. MacCallister, or Mac, as he insisted she call him, had come across such a luxury. Perhaps he had purchased it for his reluctant wife, hoping to provide her with a familiar extravagance. She almost felt guilty about enjoying the lushness of the soft bed while Mac slept in the barn. Almost.

What an interesting man. In the weeks since their confrontation in the field, they had begun to forge a friendship of sorts. He was hesitant as a bear cub being baited away from his mother, but Sadie detected a definite change in his attitude. At first it was most obvious through his interaction with the boys. He was teaching them some of the games he had enjoyed as a child. Simple games that needed few instructions and no equipment, but her children ate it up. The poor man rarely got to sit down without one of them pleading with him to play another game; "just one more," they would beg.

His relationship with Sadie was less easily defined. The first few days were uncomfortable for Mac. He turned red any time she caught him watching her. It was clear that he was embarrassed to have shared so much of his thoughts. Sadie wondered if her revelations about life with Eldon had been the catalyst that opened Mac's own dam. In any case, she was glad he had confided in her. It made him seem more human, more approachable. Still, they circled warily those first few days, each wondering if and when they should broach another conversation, each afraid of the wound that accompanies rejection.

It happened midweek. Sadie prepared dinner for the children, and as was her habit, walked outside to invite Mac to join them. She wasn't sure which of them was more surprised when he accepted. As Mac accompanied the boys in washing up for the meal, Sadie worried about how it would turn out. Would they just sit there, enduring an uncomfortable forced silence? Would it feel like being with Eldon all over again, her worrying about saying the wrong thing? As it turned out, Sadie had nothing to be anxious over.

Mac sat at the head of the small table and bowed his head. The room swam in silence. The boys stared at him, slack jawed. Was he going to pray? Their father had never done that. Eldon had claimed that he couldn't see any use for it.

Mac lifted his head. He saw the look of confusion on the children's faces and smiled. "I'll just say grace," he offered. His blessing was short and to the point.

Sadie peeked up before he was done. Mac's large

hands were folded on the table. She looked higher and was touched by the expression of reverence on his face. That did it for her. However awkwardly their relationship had begun, however nervous she was in his presence, Sadie was determined to become friends with this man. As powerful as his body was, his character was even stronger.

The meal was filling, both physically and emotionally. Without a moment of unease the little group talked. They talked about everything, and nothing; the kinds of banter regular families shared every night. Sadie wondered if someone had looked in the window, would she, Mac and the children be mistaken for a real family?

Mac reached for another biscuit. "Tell you what I'd really like to do," he said. "I'd like to build a supply store, right here on the banks of Okoboji. Someday this area is going to open up, bringing in scores of new settlers. I can even envision a day when rich folks from back east travel to our lake, just for a vacation."

His gaze settled on Sadie as he tore off another bite of biscuit. "I want to be in on the changes that I know are going to make this region spectacular," he finished.

Sadie tried to get caught up in his enthusiasm. But the more Mac talked, the louder that little voice in her head got, telling her that it was time she made plans of her own. She and the boys couldn't stay here with Mac and Grace indefinitely. She had to think about moving to Granger's Point, of finding a way to make a living. After all, she had Aaron and Matthew to think about. There was a school in Granger's Point. Her boys could have a real education. Yet, regardless of how she tried to convince herself that the move to Granger's Point would be a good thing, something inside of Sadie cried out to stay. Even if she knew that in good conscience she could not continue to sleep in the cabin while Mac and Grace slept in the barn.

She reached to spoon another bite into Grace's mouth and tried hard not to think about how difficult it was going to be to leave. Sadie forced herself to remember that she had cared for Grace for less than three months. If she left now, it would be infinitely easier than it would be if she stayed long enough to become even more attached to the baby.

"Ma, can we go outside? Please?" Matthew interrupted her thoughts. She was embarrassed to be caught gathering wool. Sadie looked up to find that she was the center of attention.

"Please?" Matthew pleaded. "It's still really warm outside, and the moon is so bright we can see what we're doing." Sadie nodded absently, then smiled at the whoops of glee from her boys.

Why was it that the moment her children ran out of the cabin, Mac seemed to fill the entire space? Sadie felt scorched each time he looked at her. She busied herself clearing the table, hating the way her hands shook. "Let me get that," Mac's rich voice intoned. Their hands met on a coffee cup. His was huge. Their eyes met and held.

Sadie finally broke the spell. "I . . . ah." She cleared her throat. "I'm just going to wash these dishes up."

She tried to focus her attention on the task. She scrubbed a plate in a bucket of soapy water, then slid it into a bucket of clean water for rinsing.

A warm arm reached around her and pulled the dripping plate from the water. "Wanna trade me places?" Mac asked, then laughed at the expression of surprise on her face. "I know how to do dishes, you know." With practiced ease he dried the plate, then waited patiently for her to wash the next one.

Though shock had slowed her down a bit, Sadie was amazed at the speed with which the whole task was completed. "That was fast!" she exclaimed, looking around the clean room.

"Let's go outside for a bit," Mac suggested.

Sadie nodded, and moved to pick Grace out of her chair. She wrapped the girl in a soft white blanket, then looked up to see Mac holding the door open. "Ready?"

Her heart raced wildly. *This is ridiculous*, she chided herself as she walked out of the door. *He is just being polite.*

They sat on a knobby pine bench in front of the cabin. Grace snuggled on Sadie's lap, thumb in her mouth, and fell asleep. They sat quietly and watched the boys play. It all felt so . . . normal. Sadie wanted to soak in every moment.

From the pen behind the barn a cow mooed contentedly. "Stupid beast," Mac muttered.

Sadie raised her eyebrows and shot him a questioning glance. "You have something against cows?"

"It hates me," he answered sullenly.

"Hates you?"

"Don't laugh. It tried to make my life miserable all the way home from Kansas City. If I hadn't had a hungry baby on my hands, I would have shot the darn thing."

"Why?" she asked. She tried hard to choke back a giggle.

"She did everything to make me miserable. The darn thing would cry to be milked, then refuse to give me more than a few drops when I tried. She refused to budge anytime I tried to stake her to a tree for the night. Take my word for it, that cow has something against me. I'm glad Aaron's taken over milking her. She likes him okay."

Sadie looked away. She wondered how Mac was going to feel about taking back that particular chore when she and the boys were gone.

After that night, it became a pattern: Mac would share the evening meal, help Sadie clean, then sit with her for a peaceful evening chat. Sadie tried not to think about how attractive he was. She would not let herself dwell on what the sound of his deep voice did to her. And his scent . . . Sadie believed that she could recognize his masculine scent with a blindfold on. Unlike Eldon, he was always clean. He smelled of soap and fresh air.

Sadie vowed not to think about it. She would not torment herself. She would not think about how feminine he made her feel, how protected. She did not believe for a minute that Mac saw her as anything more than a caregiver for his child—but being near his powerful body made her feel dainty in comparison.

Sometimes, when she nodded off to sleep in the warm embrace of the feather bed, Sadie could almost believe that she was a part of all this. Mistress of the home, mother to Grace, and to Mac . . . Well, those were the thoughts, the wishes she allowed only in her subconscious mind. She had been taught that a decent woman did not dwell on inappropriate thoughts regarding a man to whom she was not married. But her dreams, her dreams were beyond her control.

"Sadie," Mac said one evening as they sat together on the pine bench.

"Um?" Sadie answered, caught in the warm web of her daydreams.

Mac cleared his throat. "I have a proposition."

Well, he certainly had her attention.

Mac took a deep breath, rubbed his palms over his pant legs nervously, and turned to face Sadie. "I was just thinking that maybe—"

"Ma!" Matthew cried, running toward his mother, blood streaming down his face.

Sadie handed Grace off to Mac and caught her son in her arms. "What happened?"

"It was terrible, just terrible," Matthew cried dramatically.

Aaron sauntered up behind his brother, rolled his eyes, and said, "He ran into a low-hanging branch, Ma. He was pretending he was the sheriff and I was an escaping criminal, and didn't look where he was running. It was just a tree branch."

"Let me get you inside, son. We'll clean those cuts right up," Sadie soothed her hysterical boy.

Sadie and Matthew disappeared into the cabin, leaving Mac alone with Aaron and Grace.

Mac silently wondered what Sadie's reaction might have been to his proposition. He also wondered if he'd ever find the nerve to try to ask her again.

Chapter Twelve

"Shh, shh," Mac crooned in the fussy baby's ear. "It can't be all that bad," he insisted. Grace wasn't having any part of it. She pulled her little legs up tightly and let loose with a shrill howl. Mac guessed it to be around two in the morning. Ten minutes earlier, Grace had awakened him with her cries of pain. He'd immediately picked her up, thinking that she probably just needed a little comforting. Nothing he did seemed to help.

He stood in the center of the little barn and bounced his daughter in his muscled arms, trying to comfort her. A huge gust of wind screamed through the door. Following the gust through the portal was Sadie Pritchard, whom the wind seemed to push into the barn. She fought to pull the door closed behind her. Although she had thrown a blanket over her small shoulders, it was clear that beneath it she wore only a thin nightdress. Mac tried not to notice the way the blast of air plastered the material to her legs, like a second skin. Even as Grace squirmed uncomfortably in his arms, he could not seem to pull his gaze from the sight of her shapely legs and round bottom.

Sadie was beside him before he was completely able to dispel the effects of the image. Immediately she reached for Grace. "How long has she been like this?" she asked with concern.

"About ten minutes." Mac watched her place her dainty hand on Grace's brow, then, satisfied that there was no temperature, pull the baby over her shoulder. Grace continued to whimper even as Sadie paced around the interior of the barn, gently patting her back.

The light emanating from its lone lantern did little to dispel the shadows of the small barn. Sadie continued to comfort the baby. She paced from one end of the building to the other. After a few minutes, Grace's entire body stiffened. With amazing power for one so small, she released a loud burp. Immediately, her little body relaxed and she laid her tired head on Sadie's shoulder.

Sadie and Mac just looked at one another with an expression of surprise. A deep, low rumble bubbled up from the depth of Mac's belly. Before long they were both laughing. Poor Grace was so exhausted that she was unmoved by the adults' noisy antics.

Sadie laid Grace back in the little bassinet that Mac had purchased in Kansas City. She turned to him and attempted to control her mirth. "Well, it looks like the situation is under control."

Mac was still chuckling, "You heard her crying?"

Sadie smiled. "The wind is so strong, I couldn't tell what I was hearing. Once I was sure it was her, I rushed out." Her face flushed as she continued, "I'm sorry, Mac. I know that you had everything under control."

Mac's big body seemed to fill the barn, practically overwhelming the small woman standing before him. He could tell that, now that the crisis had passed, Sadie was anxious to escape. He hoped to ease her discomfort. "I probably would have fed her again. Seems to me that the last thing she needed was more in her belly!"

Sadie wasn't sure how to gracefully make her exit. She felt awkward and unattractive in the presence of a man with Mac's virility. She had no way of knowing how her long curling hair, falling in soft cascades around her shoulders, made her appear in his eyes, how he had grown to find her nervousness endearing.

As she began to move toward the door, Mac's hand stilled her. Without a word, he turned her back to face him and pressed his warm mouth over hers, thrilling in the surprise he felt there.

Cynthia had already become jaded when he first kissed her, worldly and experienced; Sadie was still innocent despite her marriage. She even *tasted* clean, he realized, as he boldly probed her mouth. Careful to keep control, he wanted her to feel what he was feeling.

She did. Sadie's head spun. She placed her palms on Mac's broad chest, if only to retain her balance, and wildly wondered how this had happened. Greedily, she took advantage of the opportunity to be kissed by a man the likes of Samuel MacCallister. Even as her brain screamed that he was simply a man alone, hungry for female companionship, her body demanded that she take the chance. Just once in her life she would like to know how it felt to be held by a man of character, a man she liked and admired. Tomorrow she would sort out the right and wrong of it.

His brawny arms pulled her to his chest as he bent to deepen the kiss. His mouth devoured hers. His lips claimed and drew the breath from her. His tongue didn't dart, but rather leisurely explored the interior of her mouth. It teased her tongue, danced erotically. It caressed the roof of her mouth and lightly stroked her teeth. Sadie sought to memorize each moment of this extraordinary experience, sure that it was a once-in-a-lifetime opportunity. She wanted to remember how his big, strong hands felt gently rubbing her narrow back; to remember the cadence of his uneven breathing. As that breathing became more labored, Sadie felt Mac pull away. *No, come back*, her body screamed. She had waited twenty-six years to feel this kind of physical tenderness, this kind of want. It was ending much too soon.

Mac refused to apologize for the kiss. He somehow knew that the lady did not expect an apology. But if he didn't put an end to this little session right here and now, he was going to end up taking her in a pile of hay, just feet away from his sleeping daughter.

The hurt in her eyes as he separated his big body from hers seared him. How could he explain that she deserved better, that despite the animal she had been married to, not all men would use her cruelly? When she experienced lovemaking in the way it was intended, she deserved to be in a comfortable room, on a soft bed, with a man to whom she was committed.

Sadie stood mute. Her mussed hair and dazed expression made her look like a complete innocent. The lantern flickering behind her exposed the slim lines of her body. With trembling hands, she bent to retrieve the blanket that had fallen from her shoulders and pulled it like a protective cloak around her. Mac could sense her emotional withdrawal.

"I won't say I'm sorry. I've wanted to do that for some time," he said. "I doubt your husband ever told you so, but you *are* beautiful."

Sadie shook her head. He didn't owe her any lies. It was only a kiss (like the sun was only a small ball of fire). "Mac, you don't . . ."

"I know I don't," he responded bluntly. "I don't *have* to do anything. I told you how attractive you are because it's true. I'm not sure what makes you think differently, but you're wrong. You are a lovely, poised, brave woman, and I wanted to kiss you. What I don't want, Sadie, is to disrespect you." His intense green eyes arrested her with their passion.

"Did you know that you are the first female I have ever been friends with? I've been surrounded by women all my life, but I've never taken the opportunity to become friends with one. I've told you things that no one else knows. And do you know why? Because you're good, Sadie. I know that I can trust you with my secrets. You've experienced enough heartache in your life to be respectful of mine." Mac smiled at her. Sincerity laced every word that came out of his mouth.

"You are an incredible lady," he continued. Then, grinning crookedly, he added, "But if you don't scoot your sweet little body out of this barn right now, my resolve to be respectful is going to disappear."

Sadie was not going to give the fickle hand of fate the opportunity to snatch these precious moments back from her. For just a sliver of time, she felt cherished, and she was going to hold on to that feeling like a drowning woman to a rope. She flashed Mac a shy grin and slipped from the barn.

The wind had receded some, not that Sadie noticed. She didn't remember walking back to the cabin, or returning to her bed. Every fiber of her being, every cell of her brain, was focused on the sweet sensation of feeling wanted.

Mac's gaze followed her back into his house. When she was inside, he turned back to his daughter. Looking down at the peacefully sleeping baby, he knew that he would need to get her out of the barn and back into the cabin soon. Like a punch to the stomach, the notion of Sadie, Aaron and Matthew riding out of his life forever brought an ache. And they would have to leave to make room in that tiny cabin.

When did I become such a coward? Mac asked himself. *Why can't I just ask her to stay? Why can't I just run the risk that she might say no?*

Mac had once imagined a little romance and a lot of raw lust to be the stuff of enviable relationships. How was he to have known that this friendship business could be so gut-wrenching—so sweet, yet so potentially painful?

Chapter Thirteen

East Shore, Lake Okoboji

The sun flirted with morning, coyly caressing the horizon with its brilliance. The tall, red-headed warrior knelt beside the ancestral blue waters. Dipping his hands into the cold, clear lake, he allowed the transparent liquid to run through his callused fingers. His thoughts strayed to the interlopers on the other side of the lake.

When had so many arrived? The last time he had passed through this land only a handful had dared to settle here. The few whites who had built their ugly square dwellings had been little more than a nuisance. Inkapaduta had actually found it entertaining to visit the pasty-faced outsiders. They were so intimidated by a fierce warrior, so relieved when he left them unharmed, they'd practically thrown their valuables at his feet. He'd loved to laugh at their cowardly reaction to him; loved the expression on his woman's face when he returned to her bearing food, blankets, cooking utensils, and other items that helped to ease her burden.

Until recently, he had considered these whites little more than pests. But now there were so many.

Inkapaduta was cognizant of the eyes of the braves standing behind him on the shore. They were fixed on his back, wondering what his reaction would be to this latest intrusion upon their land. He wanted to appear in control, yet his mind worked furiously, his heart searched wildly, for a sensible solution to this dilemma.

For years, his hate toward the white man had been focused on the person of Henry Lott. The sins Lott had committed against Inkapaduta and his family were burned upon the warrior's soul. Justly, his mind argued that these people were not Henry Lott. Perhaps they could be convinced of the sacredness of this land. Maybe there was a peaceful solution. There was surely room for all of them in a land so great, so vast.

Inkapaduta suddenly felt his sixty years. He allowed his gaze to tiredly drift to the radiance of the water, looking for an answer that would preserve them all. Pain began to pulse behind his ears, so intense that he closed his eyes against it. When he reopened them, he squinted against the rising morning sun. Again, his eyes sought the tranquil comfort of the sacred waters.

They widened at the image that unfolded before him. Looking into the surface as clear as a white man's mirror, Inkapaduta could see the face of his mother. His heart beat double time, his breath became ragged as he saw the look of anguish on her sweet visage. Her features were set in a terrified mask.

The water was no longer a crystalline blue, but

rather a crimson red—like the blood that had bathed his mother at her death. Her face was now floating upon scarlet, her frightened gaze calling to him. As suddenly as it had begun, a wave rolled in and the image was cleared away.

Inkapaduta stood, dazed, and noticed that the pain in his head had receded to a dull throb. He turned back to the braves on the shore, sure now of what he would tell them.

Chapter Fourteen

Sadie was sick to her stomach. She sat thigh to thigh with Mac on the wooden bench outside the cabin. For weeks she had been putting off the inevitable, but the day had come. It was early November, time for her to make a move. She had finally announced that it was time for the Pritchards to leave. They would stay at the hotel in Granger's Point until Sadie found employment. There. Now, that wasn't so painful, was it?

But it was. Sadie fought the ridiculous urge to cry. She would not make a fool of herself in front of this man! Why should she cry, anyway? Just because this was the very first place she'd ever felt safe? Because her boys were happy here? Because she worried that Grace would feel that Sadie had abandoned her? Because, even though it had turned out to be little more than a momentary diversion, she had felt so good in the arms of the man sitting next to her?

The truth was, winter was breathing down their necks. It was surprising that it hadn't snowed already.

She had to get while the getting was good, or she and the children would be stuck here all winter (oh, banish the thought).

Sadie sneaked a peek at Mac, and was surprised to see the muscles in his lower jaw working furiously. Why did he look so agitated? He had finished preparing for winter. The wood was all cut and stacked, the barn repaired, the grounds in good order. Her job here was done.

Sadie figured he would be especially glad to see them leave now that it was too cold for Grace to remain in the barn at night. But he didn't look glad. He looked . . . angry. And that confused Sadie. She knew that Mac liked her, in fact, liked the entire family. But surely he was ready to have his home back.

"The good news is you and Grace will have the cabin back," Sadie said, in an attempt to lighten the mood. "It's too cold for you and her to stay in the barn any longer."

Mac didn't say a word, just shifted slightly on the wooden bench.

"I have enough money to rent a room in Granger's Point, and with the money I pay you for all you've done for us you'll be able to replenish the supplies the boys and I have used."

Mac turned his head sharply, piercing her with his blue eyes. "I don't want your money," he said tightly.

Sadie was running out of good reasons to leave. "The boys will get to go to a real school," she added, trying to catalogue the advantages of living in Granger's Point.

Mac's response was barely a grunt. *I could teach them*, he thought stubbornly. *I could put some time aside every*

70

day to teach them everything I learned at St. Catherine's. We'll have more spare time than we know what to do with this winter. But he didn't say anything. He just sat there, staring at the toe of his worn boot, wondering how big a fool she would think he was if she knew how he felt. How would it look if Sadie knew that the reason he was mad was because he wanted her to stay so damn much? Would she abandon him anyway, like his mother had? Would she laugh at him like Cynthia?

"I only got to go to school when it struck my pa's fancy," Sadie said. "I always loved it. The smell of the books, the tidiness of the room—I loved it all. But Pa never did think school was very important. When my mother was alive she made sure we all went to school, my older brothers and me. After she passed away, Pa said he'd rather I was home taking care of things. School just wasn't a priority."

"Well, it's not all it's cracked up to be," Mac said gruffly.

Sadie's head snapped around to look at the man beside her. That had sounded just like the Samuel Mac-Callister who had ridden into the yard months earlier, making it clear that they weren't welcome here. Why the transformation back to the tough, belligerent Mac?

And then it struck her. Here she was worrying that Grace was going to feel abandoned when Mac was the one she should be concerned about.

He kept his eyes fixed firmly ahead of him. His entire body was testament to the tension he was feeling. "Mac, look at me," Sadie implored.

He ignored her request. He'd be damned if he'd let her see how much her leaving hurt.

"Mac."

Suddenly, he turned to her, green glints sparking in his eyes. "What?"

"Mac, we . . ." she began.

Hostility laced his voice. Sadie knew him, knew that anger just helped him mask pain. Still, his words were like tiny daggers. "We *nothing*," he spat. "You helped yourself to my cabin while I was gone, then took care of my kid in return for a place to stay when I returned. Beginning and end of story. We both knew that you were only going to hang around here long enough for me to get things done. I'm done, and now it's time for you to go." As he stood, he stuffed his hands into the pockets of his big, bulky coat. He stalked away from her, but added over his shoulder, "So, go! I'll help you get your things back into your wagon."

He turned to Sadie. Gone was the man who had shared his experiences with her, who had listened to her story with compassion and understanding. Standing in his place was the cold stranger she had met in this very yard so many weeks ago. Maybe the kindest thing she could do was to allow him this victory. If he needed this rage to make himself feel better, so be it.

"Tell you what," he said after a moment. "I'll even drive the wagon to Granger's Point for you. Just let me know when." Then he headed for the sanctuary of the barn, head down.

"Mac," Sadie called after him.

"Yeah?" His voice was so distant that Sadie wanted to cry. Already, she missed him. Missed what he had become for her.

"The Gardners' get-together is in a few days. I would like to stay for that. I'll leave early the next morning."

72

"Whatever." he shrugged. Savagely pulling the barn door open, Mac disappeared into its interior.

Her boys played tag in the distance. Grace was sound asleep. The only sound Sadie could hear was her own heart breaking.

Chapter Fifteen

The clouds hung on the treeline, impishly spitting snow. Wet, frozen flakes drifted toward the ground, evaporating as they touched down. Sadie sat next to Mac on the wagon bench, his back board-straight, his features frozen in an expression of indifference. The distance between them was no more than a foot, but it might as well have been a mile for all the communicating he was doing. Sadie had given up on trying to make conversation.

Her chest ached from unspent emotion. If only Mac would say something. Anything. She craved a word from him. It would have been better if he had never been kind to her, if she had never known what it was like to feel close to him. And the kiss—she didn't even want to think about the kiss or the feel of his brawny arms holding her, the smell of his skin. If she hadn't so thoroughly memorized each moment of that encounter in the barn, she might have convinced herself that she had dreamed it. Did he know how his silence cut her?

Mac was trying hard to keep his distance. He could see, out of the corner of his eye, Sadie's occasional glances in his direction. What did she want from him? She had made it perfectly clear that she intended to leave after tonight's party. Well, let her. She obviously did not care that Grace had begun to think of her as a mother, that her leaving was tearing him apart. Couldn't she see that?

Mac knew that his line of thinking was irrational, unfair even. But how the hell was he supposed to deal with her loss? Say "thank you very much, it's been nice"? He felt like a fool for the incident in the barn. Had she felt how tightly he held her, how much the kiss meant to him? He was like a starving man with Sadie as his nourishment. Embarrassment flooded him as he thought of how desperate he must have seemed. The poor woman had simply come out into the night to check on his crying daughter, and he had practically molested her. Thank God he had stopped himself!

All he knew was that he had never known anyone as sweet at her. Sometime, when he wasn't paying attention, she had crawled under his skin, teasing him with her innocence, enticing him with her gentle spirit. He hated it. Dangling from a thin wire over a bottomless abyss would have been preferable to the vulnerability he experienced when she was near. Maybe it was better that she was leaving after all. Eventually he would get over this foolish attraction.

"Mr. MacCallister?"

Mac was grateful for the sound of the little scamp's

voice. Maybe it would keep his mind off his mother. "Yes, Matthew?"

"How much longer till we get to the Gardners'?"

Mac couldn't resist a smile. Matthew was not the most patient of children. Reminded him of himself. "No more than ten minutes." He looked at the children bundled in the back of the big buckboard, and asked, "You guys hungry?"

Aaron and Matthew answered in unison. They swore that they were starving. Even little Grace, who was snuggled against Aaron's chest, wrapped so tightly that only her eyes were visible, got excited. She was obviously ready to be fed.

Sadie kept her eyes on the bumpy road. How could Mac be so kind to the children while continuing to ignore her? She refused to allow it to happen. His little fit of pique was beginning to annoy her. Pretending she couldn't feel his tension toward her, she said, "I'm really hungry, too. We can't get there soon enough!" Her heart was beating like a hummingbird's wings and she felt like a fool. *But better a fool who tried than a lonely fool*, she told herself.

Mac's eyes widened a bit, but otherwise he did a good job of keeping his surprise to himself. He certainly hadn't expected her to be so enthusiastic, so ready for the evening's festivities. With practiced indifference, he responded by shrugging.

"Noontime meal seems like it was days ago, doesn't it?" Sadie asked innocently.

Mac just looked at her. Stared, as though she had grown a third eye. Sadie moved closer and imagined that she could feel his body warmth even through their thick coats. "What did we have, anyway? Gosh, I can't even remember."

Of course she remembered. Rabbit stew. Same as they had yesterday and the day before. And he knew that she remembered. His eyes squinted slightly as he attempted to figure out what she was up to. "I don't remember either," Mac answered. He sounded to Sadie like a petulant child.

"Well, that doesn't say much for my cooking skills, does it?" The smile plastered on her full mouth was as disingenuous as it was irritating.

Leaning so close that only Sadie could hear his voice, Mac hissed, "Stop it!"

"Stop what?" Sadie managed to look confused.

"The stupid questions."

"Why, Mac, I once heard that there is no such thing as a stupid question—only stupid answers."

"Well, that was stupid!"

Sadie had no idea where she got the nerve, but she laced her arm through Mac's and leaned toward him. "Well, so is ignoring me just because you're mad." Smiling benignly, she continued, "So is talking to the children like everything is just fine, then pretending I'm invisible."

As long as she was shooting herself in the foot, she decided that she might as well shoot the whole darn leg off. "So is kissing me two weeks ago like you meant it, then acting as though I have a terrible disease. You, Samuel MacCallister, win the stupidity contest this month!"

Mac didn't say a word, just pulled the cart to a sudden halt. With a warning to the children to stay put, he dragged Sadie from the wagon bench. She never felt her feet touch the ground as he pulled her toward the trees lining the dirt road. Weaving through the pines, he dragged her behind him.

The moment they were out of sight, he swung around and intensely searched her face. She should have been afraid. After her experiences with Eldon's wrath, she should have had the good sense to feel at least a measure of fear. But the only thing Sadie felt was a shot of excitement, and power. She knew now that she could bring a powerful man to his knees, cause him to act like a complete lunatic with just a little taunting.

His massive body pushed her against the rough bark of a mighty oak. It brought welcome pain. Sadie could feel the tree bite into her scalp as her head rested against it. He was upon her like a delirious man. His mouth plundered hers, leaving only long enough to send wild kisses down her neck, softly biting her there. His big hands roamed her body, covered as it was by her coat. Impatiently, he pulled at her buttons until one hand found entrance. He sent his tongue into her mouth as his other hand cupped her head, stroking her cheek with his thumb. More slowly now, the hand inside her coat caressed her, rested momentarily on her breast, then moved down her side, up her stomach, and back to her breast. She ached for him. She knew her nipples pushed against his palms and she didn't care. She wanted him to know what he did to her.

"Mac," she moaned into his mouth.

He answered with his body. Bending his knees slightly, he pushed his lower body against hers. "See what you do to me?" he asked, his voice husky with desire.

She wanted to touch him there, to watch him soar. But of course, she wouldn't. She was leaving soon and this man was not her husband. In a curious mingling of reactions, shame edged its way into her consciousness. All she had was her pride. And here she stood, willing to give herself to a man who didn't seem to know if he loved or hated her. She wanted to leave this place with a little dignity. This was not the way to do it.

"The children . . ." she managed to say.

"Will be fine for another minute."

"Is a minute enough, Mac? Is a minute behind a tree with me all you really want? Would anybody do?"

Mac pulled away, his angry mouth a slit. "No," he answered, "and that's the hell of it." Stiffly he moved away from her, walked back toward the road. "Fix your coat," he commanded as he disappeared from view.

Sadie wanted to slump down the tree and have a good cry. What did he want from her? What could she give him that he couldn't get from any other woman? For pity's sake, Samuel MacCallister was the best-looking man she had ever seen! She knew when she was being used. It had happened before, though not for the same reasons.

As her shaking hands rebuttoned her coat, she realized that she could not get away soon enough. The power of her feelings for this man was beginning to frighten her.

Chapter Sixteen

Aaron and Matthew's eyes were wide with curiosity as the adults returned to the wagon. Grace decided that she'd had enough of being ignored by her surrogate mother and began to wail. Glad for the distraction, Sadie turned and held her arms out to accept the crying baby.

"Thanks, Ma. I don't know how much longer I could have held her. She keeps trying to get out of the blanket," Aaron said.

Sadie could see why. "Good heavens, Aaron. She's wrapped tight as a mummy. No wonder she wants out!"

Aaron sat back against the sun-bleached wood of the wagon. "I was just trying to keep her warm," he muttered. "Besides, it was kinda nice to have her arms inside the blanket. She's always pulling my hair."

Sadie reminded herself that the boy was only ten years old. She expected so much of him already. "You did a fine job, son. I think she just wants a change of view."

Sadie loosened the blanket enough to allow Grace to slip her hands out. The little girl promptly snatched the coarse cap from off her head, and fine blond hair sprung free as a smile lit her little face.

"She is such a beautiful girl," Sadie said.

Mac was irritated by the remark. Since she'd told him she was leaving, everything about Sadie seemed to rub him the wrong way. "She looks just like her mother. I can't look at her without remembering what a beauty Cynthia was," he snapped, irrationally hoping that his words cut Sadie.

It was, of course, a lie. Lately, whenever he noticed Grace's resemblance to her mother, Mac was doubly grateful that Sadie was around to instill a gentle spirit in the child. He did not want her to grow up as Cynthia had.

Sadie felt like someone had sucked the air out of her lungs. It was ridiculous to be jealous of a dead woman, but she was. Tears stung her eyes as she attempted to put Grace's hat back on. So what if Cynthia was the most beautiful woman on earth? Sadie was not competing with her, could never hope to compete with her. She reminded herself that it had not mattered six months ago that she wasn't pretty, and it did not matter now.

The glow of a huge bonfire lighting Rowland and Frances Gardner's neat yard came into view. They didn't even have time to stop the wagon before Frances Gardner glided toward them with words of welcome. Sadie had met the woman long ago, while Matthew was recuperating. Frances had been kind enough to bring food to their lonely family. The warm smile on her face now made Sadie feel like she was greeting an old friend.

Graying hair was the only indication that Frances was a grandmother. Her body was still firm from hard work. A flawless complexion drew attention to dark eyes that sparkled with good nature. Frances was indeed a captivating woman. Sadie guessed that Rowland thought so too, if his continual attention was any indication.

"You're here! I am so glad you were able to make it. I was afraid that this weather would scare people off." Taking a quick look around the crowded yard, Frances laughed. "I guess we were all too desperate for a good visit to let a little cold keep us home!"

Frances walked to the rear of the wagon and put her hands on her hips. She looked at the boys and asked, "What are you two waiting for? There are children of every age here just waiting for you to play. Get going!"

Aaron and Matthew grinned, and with a quick glance at their mother, climbed out of the wagon in search of other children.

Mac's deep-timbred voice announced, "I'll hitch the wagon behind the barn. You go on with Frances."

Sadie looked at the man and noticed that his jaw was still clenched tight. So, he was back to being an iceberg. She did not know what to make of him. "Why don't I just stay with you and help carry the food we brought?" she suggested.

Coolly, Mac met her gaze. "Just take Grace and get out there. Frances will take a dish, and I'll bring the rest." The anger in his voice was confusing. What had she done, other than protect herself and her honor? And that was something he'd claimed to want, at one point.

"But . . ."

"Get out, Sadie."

Sadie knew that Frances stood near, listening to their exchange. She did not want to embarrass Mac, but she'd more than had enough of his moodiness. "Fine," she snapped. "You just take the wagon around the barn by yourself. You carry all the food by yourself. If I knew what was good for me, you would be driving back to the cabin tonight by yourself too!"

She handed Grace to Frances and climbed down from the wagon. She couldn't miss the grin that Frances attempted to suppress. Mac shot back, "Even if you stayed here, I wouldn't be going home alone."

Sadie turned to face the infuriating man, shocked. "What?"

Mac spoke as though Frances was not standing a few feet away. At that moment it was just the two of them, fighting their own private battle. "I have Grace, remember? Even after you're gone, I'll have my daughter with me. I won't be alone."

"More's the pity," Sadie spat. "Poor Grace will have to put up with your moods all by herself! Tell me, Mac—will Grace ever know how you feel about her? Are you going to act like you love her one moment, then hate her the next? Or has that hot and cold act been reserved for grown-up women like me?"

Sadie's entire body shook. She took the baby from Frances's arms. "Let's go, Frances. We'll let Mac be alone for a few minutes. Lords knows, he's not fit company for anybody else!"

Mac's eyes shot darts of fire at her. "Just get your damn plate," he hissed.

Sadie gave a mock salute, but didn't let it go. It had

been building too long. "Oh, yes sir! Frances, would you mind grabbing one of those dishes from the back? We wouldn't want to upset the general."

Frances tried desperately not to laugh. She reached over the side of the wagon for a dish, and Mac and Sadie stared at one another for long, tense moments. It was clear that neither of them was going to back down. Even when Grace began stroking Sadie's face with her chubby little hand, Sadie continued to stare daggers at the girl's father. Finally, Mac gave the reins a snap and commanded the patient horse to "Giddup."

Sadie watched him pull away, her emotions as tight as a bowstring. Frances's arm laced through hers and led her toward the cabin. "I sometimes think I could hate that man!" Sadie fumed.

Frances shrugged. "Love, hate . . . what's the difference?"

Sadie looked at the older woman, exasperation filling her face. Frances smiled benignly, then added in a conversational tone, "He never acted that way around his wife, you know."

"Well, she was lucky!"

"You think so? I always reckoned that a man who didn't feel enough passion for a woman to have a good argument with her, probably didn't feel enough to love her much, either."

"Of course he loved Cynthia! He just finished telling me how beautiful she was." Sadie couldn't keep the hurt from creeping into her voice.

Frances rolled her eyes. "Beautiful like a poisonous flower. You could look at her, but never get too close. Mac knew that. How satisfying do you think that was

84

for him?" With an impish grin she added, "Oh no, I'd say that you're much more Mr. MacCallister's type."

Sadie was shocked, and it showed. "Me? Have you looked at Mac, Frances? I may be mad enough to spit nails at him right now, but even I know that he is handsome. Gorgeous, even. What in the world would he want with me?"

Frances slowed her pace a bit, forcing Sadie to do the same. "Tell me something, Sadie. What do you think is bothering Mac?"

"I have given up trying to figure him out."

Frances gave her a level look. The light from the bonfire danced in her dark eyes. "When are you leaving for Granger's Point?"

"Tomorrow." Suddenly, seeing the direction the conversation was headed, she said, "It's not what you think."

"And I'm a two-headed cow. That boy is grieving for you, missing you before you even ride off his property. I'm not saying he's doing it right, but . . ."

Sadie wanted to tell her how ridiculous the notion was, but she was interrupted by two girls walking their way. "Hello, Mrs. Pritchard!" It was Rowland and Frances's thirteen-year-old daughter, Abigail. Abbie had accompanied her parents the last time they had visited Mac's cabin.

Sadie smiled. The girl looked so much like her mother. "Hello, Abbie. Are you having fun?"

Abbie bobbed her head excitedly and introduced her friend. "Mrs. Pritchard, this is Agnes Mattock. We were wondering if we could play with your baby for a while. We'll take real good care of her."

With a twinge akin to pain in her chest, Sadie said, "She's not really mine, you know, Abbie."

"Well, she will be after you and Mr. MacCallister get married. Ma says so!"

Frances had the good grace to look at the ground as Sadie shot a questioning glance her way. Now was not the time to tell Frances what she thought of the idea. She handed Grace to the sturdy girl, giving an admonition to be very careful, then walked over into the brightly lit yard.

Instinctively, her eyes searched for Mac. She couldn't see him among the men who stood talking in small groups. Finally, her eyes found his big body, leaning negligently against the small barn. He returned her stare. She couldn't see him well from that distance, but knew that he was looking right at her. For a moment, neither of them moved.

Sadie actually put her hand to her stomach, where a knot was forming. He was the most infuriating . . . and yet wonderful man she had ever met. Leaving him, leaving Grace, would take all the strength she could muster.

But that was tomorrow. Tonight she would enjoy the company of all these fine people. Tomorrow she would start all over, again.

Chapter Seventeen

Sadie could see her breath in the cold night air. It was worth it though to enjoy the cheerful company of the Gardners, Maddocks, Howes and other families that were present at the party. She stood behind a long table near the cabin door, assisting the women as they spooned portions of plain but plentiful food onto plates. The children had been served and allowed to find a spot in which to settle.

Serving the children first was a novelty to Sadie. Her father, and then Eldon, had always insisted upon eating before anyone else. Sadie was in favor of this new method. She watched Aaron and Matthew share their meal with newfound friends. Occasionally, laughter would erupt from the tight little group. It was a balm to Sadie's soul.

Four men from the cabin that the settlers referred to as the "bachelors' quarters" were just making their way through the serving line. Having settled in the Spirit Lake region in hopes of founding a town site, they were among the first in the area. Gentlemen to the core, they each accepted the fluffy biscuits and tender beans that Sadie offered, thanking her profusely. Sadie blushed. She couldn't remember the last time any man had treated her with such respect.

Sadie felt his presence before she saw him. His big frame blocked the warmth and light of the fire. Mac stood before her, plate out, wearing a guarded expression.

Frances, who was serving next to Sadie, acted as though Mac was not there. "I swear, Sadie. Did you see the way Bertell Snyder was looking at you? He looked like he wished you were one of the dishes being served!"

Heat suffused Sadie's face. "Frances!"

Frances was not to be stopped. "Don't you deny it! You saw how all those bachelors were paying special attention to you."

Sadie had absolutely no response. She had a sneaking suspicion that she knew Frances's game, but she was not going to aid the woman in getting under Mac's ever-so-thin skin.

Frances feigned surprise. "Oh, Mac, there you are. Hungry?"

"I was," Mac answered sourly.

"I don't know if you heard what I was just telling Sadie, but it wouldn't surprise me in the least if one of these single men here tonight gets it into his head to come courting!"

Mac, who had been moving steadily down the table, stopped. Although he spoke to Frances, he looked directly at Sadie. "She's leaving tomorrow. There's not much chance of anybody courting her, is there?"

Frances's voice was as airy as the biscuits they were serving. "Oh, I don't know about that. I was just thinking that it might be nice to have her around. In fact, Rowland and I have discussed asking her if she would like to stay with us for the winter. I know the place is crowded, but we could always make room for a few more."

Mac gave Sadie one last measured look, then left to join the other men who ate near the fire. Immediately, Sadie pulled Frances by the arm into the cozy little cabin. The door was not yet shut when she turned to the older woman.

"What has possessed you, Frances Gardner? I swear, it appears to me that you enjoy seeing Mac all worked up! I'll thank you to remember that I'm the one who has to ride all the way home with him tonight."

The smile on Frances's face signaled how useless Sadie's tirade was. Mrs. Gardner clearly believed that there was more to Mac and Sadie's relationship than actually existed. Nothing Sadie could say was going to dissuade her.

Exasperated, Sadie threw her hands into the air. "Oh, I give up. Really, Frances, you are the most stubborn woman I have ever met!"

"Funny, that's just what my father says," a disembodied voice intoned from the corner of the room. Sadie turned to see to whom it belonged, and saw a lovely young woman gently rocking a baby.

Frances let out a clipped laugh. "Sadie, this is my oldest daughter, Mary. The gorgeous child she is holding is my newest grandchild, Amanda."

Sadie moved closer to the rocking chair. "Harvey Luce's wife?" she asked.

Mary's smile was beautiful. "Yes, ma'am. Harvey is my husband."

"Well, you know that your husband and father were the ones who rescued my sons and me, who made sure we had a roof over our heads. I'll never be able to thank them enough for all they did."

Mary pushed a stray lock of brown hair out of her eyes with a slender hand. She smiled up at Sadie. "They both thought you were pretty brave, taking care of a sick boy all by yourself. You're kind of a hero around here. And don't worry; if my mother is pestering you about Mr. MacCallister, it's just because she wants to keep you as a neighbor."

"I do not!" Frances insisted, her twinkling eyes belying her words. "As a matter of fact, I was just telling Rowland what a snooty woman Mrs. Pritchard is. As far as I'm concerned, she can't leave soon enough! We were hoping to find a nice, pleasant woman for Mr. MacCallister."

Mary's laughter filled the small room. "Don't you listen to her. Momma falls in love with people easily. She'll probably cry a bucket of tears when she hears you've left."

Sadie thoroughly enjoyed finding someone who would call Frances's bluff. Looking at the woman now, she teased, "Why, Frances—I didn't know you felt that way!"

"Don't you make light of my tender feelings, Sadie Pritchard. I'm only pushing you in Mac's direction 'cause I know how right you are for one another!" Grinning, she added, "Well, that and the fact that I think you would be a wonderful neighbor. But, if you would rather go off to Granger's Point where you don't know a soul than stay right here and live near a friend you will treasure for life, far be it for me to try to stop you."

Sadie couldn't resist a chuckle at Frances's melodramatic words. Really, the woman should have been on a stage.

Their attention was turned by a cool draft. Abbie and Agnes tiptoed into the cabin, Grace sound asleep on Abbie's shoulder. "Look, the baby fell asleep!" Abbie whispered. "Do you want me to put her on the bed?"

"Sure, honey," Frances answered. "You did a real fine job, Abigail Gardner. You're going to be a good mother one day."

Abbie waved off her mother's compliment. "Oh— guess what, guess what?" she gushed. "Eliza was outside giving cow eyes to William Wilson, and Pa walked up behind her and went, 'BOO!' Eliza screamed like a pig gettin' fixed, and Pa laughed and laughed. Eliza was so embarrassed that she ran into the woods. I'll bet she doesn't come out until Christmas!"

"I'm sure your sister appreciates your concern, Abigail," Frances said dryly. She looked at Sadie. "Nothing like a sixteen-year-old girl being humiliated in front of everybody in the territory. I'd better go see if I can find her."

"Of course. I need to get back out there and check on my boys." Sadie smiled at Mary. "It was nice to meet you. I'll be right back to see to Grace."

"Don't worry about it," Mary assured her. "Amanda's feeling a bit poorly tonight. I'll be in here with her anyway. I'll be glad to keep an eye on your baby."

"That would be wonderful!" Sadie answered.

But as she walked out into the chilly night air, she

realized that Mary had just mistakenly referred to Grace as her baby too. Oh, how she wished it didn't feel so true.

The evening passed in a blur. Sadie met so many people that she was sure she would never be able to keep their names straight. She was especially impressed with Joel and Millie Howe's oldest daughter, Lydia. Lydia and her cousin Elizabeth Thatcher, along with their husbands and babies, had followed the Howes to northwest Iowa. Lydia didn't want to be away from her close-knit family, and the Howes were thrilled to have their daughter and grandson so near.

Lydia was a striking young woman with mahogany hair and a ready smile. Her words poured out as if she was in a race, and the first one done with a story was the winner. "And this is Elizabeth," Lydia said. "She's my very, very best friend in the world, so when we decided to move here Elizabeth just *had* to come too. Now we live together. Can you imagine that?" she added with a giggle.

Elizabeth Thatcher seemed to Sadie the flip side of Lydia's coin. Whereas Lydia bubbled over with exuberance, Elizabeth was more subdued; she measured her words more carefully. While Lydia's hair was dark and smooth, Elizabeth had tight blond curls. And just as Lydia carried energy into a room, Elizabeth was the picture of calm. Sadie could see why they were close; Elizabeth's quiet thoughtfulness was a perfect foil to Lydia's more impetuous nature.

"Are you glad you made the move?" Sadie asked Elizabeth.

"Very much." She smiled. "Lydia and I grew up together. Now our children can do the same."

With a pang of envy, Sadie wondered what it would be like to have so close a friend. She hoped that Lydia and Elizabeth recognized how fortunate they were. She could imagine the flurry of activity that took place in the small cabin the two women shared with their husbands, Lydia's year-and-a-half-old son and Elizabeth's baby girl.

"My brother Asa got here too late in the year to build his own cabin, so he's living with us too. *And*, he brought his friend Morris Markham, who's also going to build a cabin. That's eight of us in one house this winter," Lydia reported. "Seriously, can you imagine that?"

"Ready?" Mac's deep voice hummed in Sadie's ear. He had come up from behind. The simple act of his leaning over her shoulder, his breath caressing her cheek, sent a prickle of pleasure up her spine.

Sadie felt disoriented. She had been so deep in thought that she momentarily forgot just what she was supposed to be ready for. "Pardon me?"

"Everybody's leaving. Are you about ready to go?"

She said goodbye to the effusive Lydia and thoughtful Elizabeth, then turned to look up at Mac, startled anew by his handsomeness. Sadie had barely seen the man all night. It seemed that wherever she was, he was somewhere else. Had he been avoiding her?

"Of course. Let me get Grace. She's asleep in the cabin."

"Already took care of it. Aaron's with her in the bed of the wagon." His face was completely devoid of expression, his voice neutral. He gave no hint as to what he was thinking.

"Did you put blankets over the children? They're going to be cold on the way back."

"Yep."

"The dishes?"

"Yes, Sadie. I took care of the dishes. Say goodnight and let's get going."

Sadie looked at this man; so strong, so in control. She had the urge to needle him, to cause him the same kind of turmoil he caused her. "Trying to get tonight over with so you can get rid of me?"

His eyes dueled with hers. For long, tense moments he shared a taut space with her, exhaling the air she inhaled. She could tell Mac fought to control the emotions that boiled just beneath the surface. With a stiff turn, he walked away from her. She knew that it took all of his self-control not to respond.

Sadie stood in the center of the yard for a moment, then gathered her wits enough to seek Frances and Rowland. They stood with the Mattocks, discussing plans for spring. With a lump in her throat, Sadie realized that she would not be here to enjoy spring with these good people. Hoping to speed the goodbyes, she approached the group.

"Well, Mrs. Pritchard, did you have a good time?" Rowland asked.

"Yes. Thank you, Rowland." Her throat was clogged with emotion, and she was finding it difficult to say the final words. "I know that I can never thank you enough . . ."

"Say no more. It was our pleasure to help you."

Looking around, Sadie knew that she was avoiding the inevitable. "We'll be leaving for Granger's Point in the morning. I'll try to find employment. If that's not possible I'm not sure where we'll end up. But wherever it is, you can be sure I will never forget you. Thank you for everything."

True to Mary's word, tears ran freely down Frances's face. She laughed as she attempted to brush them away. "Oh, pooh. I just hate getting to like someone then having to say goodbye. I've had too darn many goodbyes in my life!" Frances pulled Sadie into a tight hug and whispered, "You sure this is what you want to do?"

At Sadie's miserable nod, Frances said, "Well, all right. But you let us know where you end up because we've come to care for you, Sadie Pritchard."

Sadie could not say a word. She just nodded again, then moved toward the sanctuary of the wagon. She refused to look at Mac as she climbed onto the narrow bench, curled her fingers around the edge of the rough wood, then thanked God as they pulled away from the Gardner home.

They rode in silence for long minutes before Mac asked gruffly, "You okay?"

Sadie gave one quick nod as she continued to fight the torrent of tears that threatened. How long would it be tonight before they were back on Mac's property? Before Mac settled in the barn, the boys and Grace in their beds? Sadie knew that she was just holding on to her dignity here. If she were to start crying now, she wasn't sure she could stop.

With a quick glance to the wagon bed, she could see that the children were all asleep. Aaron's blond head rested against the side of the buckboard, his mouth open as he lightly snored. Grace had fallen asleep on a pool of blankets, her head in Aaron's lap. Matthew was cuddled close to his brother for warmth, his head resting on Aaron's shoulder. Sadie vowed to be strong for them. It would do the children no good to watch her fall apart.

"Better now?" Mac asked. Sadie thought she could detect concern in his deep voice.

"I'm fine," she answered, a trifle too sharply. She could not bear his pity.

"I can see that."

Blessed silence reigned again for a few minutes. The wagon seemed to be seeking out every rut in the road. Sadie was surprised that the children could sleep through all the bumps and jolts.

"Tell me again why you're leaving." Mac's voice was low, practically a whisper.

Sadie was exhausted. It had been a long day and she was emotionally drained. Did they really have to go through this now?

"Tell me," Mac insisted.

She responded quietly, her voice as tired as her body. "I can't continue to ask you and Grace to sleep in the barn. I've taken too much from you already."

"And?" Mac asked stubbornly.

Sadie shot a glance his way and answered, "And, Mac, I can't continue to stay with you and not expect there to be some damage to my reputation. It's all I have, you know," she added softly.

Sadie pulled her hands more deeply into her warm coat. "Finally, I need to take care of myself. I've always depended upon someone else, and that someone else always ended up hurting me. It's time I took care of myself."

"Even if you're lonely?"

Sadie didn't answer. She had no answer. Loneliness

was something she had experienced while married to Eldon. Loneliness she could deal with.

He wanted a reaction from her, any reaction. "I guess you won't be alone for long. Judging from the way you teased those men from the bachelors' quarters tonight, you ought to have yourself a new man in no time."

"What?" Sadie had to control the urge to scream. She had barely said two words to any of those men!

"I saw the way you were looking at them in the serving line. And don't think I didn't hear what they were saying about you during the meal."

"What did they say about me?" Sadie demanded

Mac's jaw was so hard, it seemed to be blasted from granite. How dare he start a conversation like this and then freeze up. "Darn you, Samuel MacCallister. Don't you back out on me now! You tell me what those men said!"

When he did speak, his voice was laced with sarcasm, mocking the words of the younger men. " 'Isn't she lovely?' 'Where do you suppose she's from?' 'She doesn't look old enough to have two children.' "

Sadie's mouth dropped open. "In exactly what way am I responsible for their innocent comments?"

Mac pulled back on the reins, slowing the wagon to a near standstill. "Don't play coy, Sadie. I saw the way you looked around that yard, hoping to see one of them."

Her eyes widened. "I was looking for you, you dimwit! Despite my best intentions I just wanted *to catch a glimpse of you.*"

"Oh." Mac's mouth formed the word, then snapped shut, surprise evident on his handsome features.

Slowly, a slight smile transformed his lips. "You were looking for me?" he echoed.

She groaned. "Don't make me say it again. It was hard enough the first time."

His smug smile rankled her. "You know what this means, don't you?"

"I don't think I want to know."

Mac continued as though she hadn't spoken. "It means you don't really want to leave. First, you were looking for *me*. Then, you were crying when it came time to say goodbye to the Gardners."

"I was not crying. I . . ."

"Save it, Sadie. You were crying. And you wanted to see *me*. And, you love my daughter."

"But . . ."

"No buts. You are not leaving. You are staying right here. We'll get married."

It was so matter of fact, so casually mentioned, Sadie was sure that she had misunderstood him. She decided that she had finally lost her mind. She began to laugh.

Mac stopped the wagon completely. He turned to Sadie and scowled. "Do you always laugh at marriage proposals, or is mine the first?"

"Oh, that was a proposal? It sounded so much like a commandment that I just wasn't sure. I didn't hear you ask anything, Samuel MacCallister."

Mac looked pained. His dark brows were drawn together. He licked his lips nervously. "You're really going to make me do this?"

For once, she felt in control. "Yes, sir."

"Okay, will you marry me?" There, he'd asked. Now it was up to her.

"Why?"

"What do you mean, why? Why does anyone get married?"

Sadie took a moment to collect herself. This man could really be frustrating. "Well, Mac, most people marry for love. We don't love one another, so why do you want to marry me?"

"Oh hell," he muttered.

Sadie gave him her profile. Primly folding her hands in her lap, she intoned, "If this is too much for you, let's just continue our journey."

"All right, not so fast. Look at me, will you?"

Sadie shifted her body so that she faced him. She waited patiently, her blue eyes fixed upon his face. Mac finally said, "I know that we had a pretty rocky start, but somewhere along the way we became friends. I told you things I've never told anyone; you told me things that you normally keep buried. I don't know about you, but that is probably the most intimate thing I have ever done."

His words touched her battered heart.

Mac tiredly rubbed one big hand over his face, then continued, "Look, I've slept with women over the years. Some whose names I never knew. I'm not bragging, Sadie. I just want you to know what kind of life I've lived. I've never cared about any of those women, not even Cynthia. I've never felt any connection with a woman outside of bed."

Taking a deep breath, he warmed her with his gaze. "But you're different. Sure we argue, but we also talk. Or we used to. Before you decided to go. I feel like I can say anything to you. Don't get me wrong, Sadie; I think you're amazingly pretty. But the most beautiful thing about you is something that's not immediately noticeable. You have a good heart and a strong spirit. You're beautiful from the inside out."

Without waiting for a response, Mac turned back to the road. He gave the reins a snap and continued homeward. After a strained moment, he added, "Maybe that's not love, Sadie. But in my book, friendship is a whole lot more valuable. Maybe it's even a more solid foundation for marriage."

"I don't know what to say," Sadie whispered, touched by his honesty.

"Say yes." He was afraid to look at her.

A smile lit her face. "Yes," she answered. She studied his profile, tried to read his mind, then answered more enthusiastically, "Yes, I'll marry you."

Again, Mac stopped the wagon. This time he pulled her into his arms, and with soul-searing intensity, kissed her senseless. When he was done, he smiled. "Oh. By the way, I forgot to mention the main reason I want to marry you."

"What's that?"

"You are one great kisser."

Chapter Eighteen

The ceremony was simple, and in Sadie's opinion, heartbreakingly sweet. Performed in the parsonage home of Reverend David Long of Granger's Point, Iowa, it was attended by Rowland and Frances Gardner, the reverend's wife, and of course, Aaron, Matthew and Grace.

Mac was so handsome, so sure of what they were doing, that Sadie's heart thudded inside her chest each time she looked at him. He recited his vows with a strong, sure voice, and smiled at Sadie each time she raised her eyes to his.

Sadie avoided looking at Frances. One glance in her direction would be enough to send Sadie into gales of laughter. Dear, sweet Frances could not resist teasing her with mischievous expressions. At one point, she'd actually raised her eyebrows and wagged a finger at Sadie, as if to say *I told you so*.

Aaron and Matthew had difficulty bridling their excitement. Mac would be the father they had always dreamed of. They would get to stay in the cabin on the lake, play in the woods in their hollowed-log fort, and fish and hunt to their hearts' content.

Mac and Sadie were declared man and wife. Sharing an intimate kiss that hinted of the night to come, they sealed their union.

The new couple was surrounded by hugs and good wishes before streaming out of the parsonage door into the brilliant afternoon sun. Rowland and Frances left for their own home, accompanied by the children. Mac and Sadie were to be blessed with two days of absolute privacy.

Sadie knew that as long as she lived she would remember this day—November 9, 1856—as the sweetest day of her life.

Chapter Nineteen

Muted shades of candlelight cast fanciful shadows on the cabin walls. Sadie stood in the center of room, nervously wondering what to do now that the candles had been lit and a fire built. The little cabin seemed so quiet without the boisterousness of the children.

She smiled at the memory of them waving back at her and Mac as they rode away in the Gardners' buckboard. They would have two whole days to be part of Rowland and Frances's rowdy crew. She was glad for the opportunity that they would have to play with other children. Still . . . Sadie was not sure that she was prepared to be alone with Mac, new husband or not.

What would he expect of her? She pressed her hand to her suddenly queasy stomach and moved to the bed, which dominated the northeast corner of the room. Gingerly, she sat on the edge and bent over, hoping to ease her discomfort.

The door flew open.

"Well, the horse and wagon are put away for the

evening," Mac announced as he entered the cabin. Sadie looked up, blue eyes huge in her pale face. She was not sure if she could go through with this.

Immediately, Mac moved to her. He knelt before her and pulled her small hand into his own. "You okay?"

Sadie nodded miserably.

"Are you sick?"

With her eyes fixed on the pattern of tiny roses in the fabric of her dress, she shook her head.

His big hand cupped Sadie's chin. "Sadie, look at me." He smiled gently as she shyly met his gaze. "You nervous?"

Like tiny shards of glass, tears slipped from her eyes. Her body shook like a leaf in a storm, betraying her every emotion.

Mac's deep voice was both kind and patient. "Sadie, I know that your life with Eldon Pritchard was hell. And I suspect that your intimate experiences with him were less than satisfying. But Sadie, I'm not Eldon Pritchard. I'll do everything in my power to take care of you, to see that you're happy. You know that, don't you?"

Sadie willed her nerves to calm. She concentrated on the handsome lines of Mac's face, on the deep resonance of his voice. Mac repeated his question, "You know that I'd never hurt you, don't you?"

"Yes," she responded timidly.

"There's no hurry, you know," he offered.

Mac's kindness was her undoing. Never had she known a man to be so giving. The thought that he was actually her husband was staggering. Placing her small, callused hands on each side of his handsome face, she peered into his eyes, hoping for a glimpse of his soul. "I trust you, Mac. I trust you completely."

Mac stood and pulled her with him. He left her for a moment to add wood to the fire. Sadie felt totally bereft as she stood alone. When he moved back toward her, there was heat in his gaze. Sadie was surprised to feel heat of her own.

They faced each other. Years of disappointment dared to mingle with silvery threads of hope. A fragile friendship was due to be consummated, eternally sealed.

He reached his big hand to her, felt the thrill of her hand as it joined his, saw the absolute trust that radiated from her blue eyes. Mac silently vowed to make everything right for her. When Sadie remembered tonight, he wanted her to remember that she was cherished.

Still shaking, Sadie removed her hand from his and slowly began to release the tiny buttons that lined the front of her dress. Mac gently brushed her hands away and took over the intimate task. She could feel his breath on her cheek as he worked carefully, intently. She boldly placed her own hand over his, and pressed it to her chest so that he might feel the cadence of her heart.

As they stood shrouded in candlelight, snow began to fall lightly outside the window. He kissed her. His mouth smoothly staked claim on hers, his tongue invading with an unrehearsed orchestration. He pulled her tightly to his hard body and introduced her to his passion. "It's been a long time for me, Sadie. I need you," he whispered, his voice husky.

Her eyes opened wide as he pulled back to observe her face. Mac smiled at her erratic breathing, and accepted her more fully into his heart because of it.

As he led her to the soft bed, her trepidation returned in full. She pulled back, wanting to clear the air. "I'm sorry you're not my first."

His eyes took in her beautiful dishevelment. "I'm not sorry. So what if I'm not your first? I'll be your last, Sadie MacCallister." He pulled her close and added, "I promise to sear your soul so completely that there will never be room for another."

His expression was so unwavering, his words so fierce, that Sadie felt weak. She thrilled with the knowledge that she belonged to this man, and she was suddenly willing to do whatever it took to please him.

They never broke eye contact as they disrobed. Standing unashamedly, they each marveled at the utter beauty of their mate. Sadie pulled back the homey quilts and slid into the large bed, the cold and excitement making her nipples hard. As he climbed in next to her, Mac's eyes glazed with passion.

She gave him total dominance over her body, allowing him access to her throat as he trailed warm kisses down her neck. As he came to her breasts, he held them in the palms of his hands and marveled at their fullness. For the first time in her life, Sadie felt beautiful. She reveled in it, arched her body with feline grace, offered herself in sublime submission to her husband.

He accepted her loving offer, suckling at each breast. It drove him wild with want. Mac trailed kisses down her soft stomach, then teased her femininity. She was unbridled in her yearning, but unsure of what it was that she desired. He gently showed her. With loving caresses he drove her wild. Never had she imagined that this kind of pleasure was possible. She felt as though she was emerging from a fog of inexperience. Sadie clutched at him, her fingers white with the pressure, until she could take no more.

Finally, in a fluid motion, he lifted himself over her; looking deeply into her shocked eyes, he plunged himself into her warmth. She cried out; a pure cry of intense pleasure.

As the pulse of that joy began to mellow, he began to thrust and withdraw from her. Sadie experienced a strange tightening in her loins. It pulled her unexpectedly into uncharted territory. Sadie gasped as the sensation sent shocks through her body. Mac, sensing that her time was at hand, changed the rhythm of his movements. Slow for a moment, then wildly they moved together. When he was sure that she was at the brink, he kissed her deeply, absorbing the screams that erupted from her parched throat.

Sadie felt his seed become part of her, saw him tense and then find his own sweet release. Mac felt her tears on his chest and arms, and knew with a deep satisfaction that this was a first for her.

They lay together as one, and he stroked her curling hair. The miracle of the moment was not lost on either of them. From the seemingly infertile ground of their lonely lives, love had found root and grown.

Chapter Twenty

"Bet you can't catch us! Bet you can't catch us!" Matthew's singsong rang across the brown field. Pulling Grace in a small wagon Mac had made for the children, the boy taunted his older brother. Gamely, Aaron pretended to give chase, which caused Grace to squeal with delight.

Sadie smiled at the baby, who was propped up in the wagon, which wobbled across the uneven ground. "Gracious, Grace is ten months old," she said companionably to the big man walking at her side.

Mac grinned at the children's antics. "Guess we'll be planning a birthday celebration for her soon."

"Matthew, careful with that baby!" Sadie cried as the wagon rolled over a particularly deep rut.

Matthew slowed down, and his older brother steadied the wagon. Aaron bent down to tuck the blankets more securely around his new sister. "She's fine, Ma," he assured his mother.

Sadie watched the children resume their walk at a more reasonable pace, and she counted her blessings.

"Thinking about anything special?" Mac asked.

She released a deep, satisfied sigh. "Just how incredibly lucky I am to have found you, found Grace. I just feel like everything is perfect at this moment. I guess I've never experienced this kind of . . . satisfaction. Even the weather is cooperating. Can you believe that it's warm enough in December for us to be out taking a walk?"

"Well, don't count on it lasting too long." Mac laughed. "This may be the lull before a big white storm!"

Sadie looked up at him, this man who was her husband. She remembered how beautiful she'd thought he was the first time she saw him. Knowing now that his fine appearance couldn't compare with his warm and strong spirit made her appreciate him all the more.

As usual, his hair flirted with his forehead and looked in need of a good trim. She wondered how many times during the past weeks she had run her fingers through that unruly hair, had delighted in the feel and fragrance.

At one time Sadie would have been completely ill at ease with a man like this. But after their wedding Mac continued to treat her with such respect, such reverence, that she was beginning to believe she *was* beautiful. At least, to him.

With unabashed pride she studied his handsome profile, his strong, able body, and thought: *This is my man, my mate for life.* She refused to allow herself to dwell on the ruins from which she and her boys had emerged. All that mattered was the here and now. And right here, right now, she had all she could ever dream of in life.

"Are you staring at me?" Mac teased.

Sadie giggled. "Yep."

Turning to her, Mac pulled his wife to his broad chest. He leaned down and touched his nose to hers. "I can't get enough of you, you know that?" His deep voice sent shivers down her spine.

Without thinking, she blurted a buried truth, "I love you." There, she had said it. The words had rolled around her brain, played mayhem with her heart, and now they were out in the open.

Mac took her upper arms in his grip and pushed her back far enough to examine her face. "You sure?"

Sadie nodded.

He growled, "Good. Because I've kind of grown accustomed to you and those boys, too. I don't want you going anywhere."

They turned to continue their walk. Sadie felt oddly dejected. She wasn't sorry that she had expressed her feeling, but she had hoped . . . hoped for what? That Mac would declare his undying love for her? What had happened to her resolve to appreciate what she had? Mac treated her better than she had ever been treated, provided a home for Aaron and Matthew that once they could only have dreamed of. For now, his kindness was enough. It had to be.

Mac's hand reached down to join Sadie's as they stepped over a fallen tree branch. They walked for several minutes before he spoke. "There is another reason I'm glad you're sure of how you feel," he said quietly.

Suddenly self-conscious, Mac looked down at his

wife. He removed his hand from hers, then ran the back of his rough knuckles over the silky length of hair, which had been hastily tied back that morning. Sadie didn't move, and she stopped breathing altogether.

He slid his hand to her chin and pulled her face toward him. She felt the calluses of his fingers, smelled the wood smoke lingering on his coat sleeve. "I love you, too, Sadie MacCallister. I think I've loved you from the moment I saw you standing in front of my cabin, determined, against all odds, that Matthew was going to get well. I've loved you since I discovered that you are too stubborn to back down from my black moods. I've loved you since the first time I saw you hold Grace and soothe away her tears. I've loved you since that first time you laid in my arms and I realized that your courage, your strength and your gentleness are the rare treasures I've spent my life searching for."

After a lifetime of hurt, his words flooded her with healing warmth. Unbelievably, this fine man saw her as a woman of value. Sadie broke into tears, threw her arms around him, and buried her face in his warm neck.

"Uh . . . this is a good cry, isn't it?" Mac asked gingerly.

She slapped him on the shoulder and laughed. "Yes, you fool! I can't believe how wonderful you make me feel."

"Wonderful? Well, we wouldn't want that."

"Samuel MacCallister, don't you dare ruin this moment by teasing me!"

Mac just stood there, grinning. The fact that he was comfortable enough in his own skin to enjoy making those around him happy was one of the things that Sadie loved most about him. Feeling like a young girl, she couldn't help but return his grin. "By the way, Mac," she baited. "Why are you called Mac? Samuel seems like a perfectly respectable name to me."

"Honestly?" His look became so solemn that Sadie was afraid she'd hit upon a nerve.

She reached out and touched his shoulder. "Do you want to tell me?" she asked gently.

He nodded his head. "It happened at St. Catherine's."

"The orphanage?"

"Yes. I had only been there a few days when it was my turn to take care of the animals. St. Catherine's had all kinds of them. The sisters believed that by taking care of animals, we would take the focus off ourselves and our own losses."

Mac pulled at his collar, then continued, "Well, Jeff Green and Gary Fairlane were assigned to show me around. They introduced me first to a dog or two, and then to a slew of cats. Anyway, they eventually came to the barnyard animals. I met a very friendly pig, a few chickens, and finally, was introduced to the school mascot. It was a huge donkey . . . named Sam. I guess you can imagine how thrilled I was with the prospect of sharing my name with the school jackass."

Sadie detected the grin Mac was trying hard to control, and she punched him once more on the arm. "You're making that up!"

"Yep."

"Mom, Mac!" Matthew cried. The children were practically upon their laughing parents before Mac and Sadie noticed.

Sadie wiped the corner of her eye. "Yes, son?"

"Can we walk down to the lake?"

"Sure, kiddo," Mac replied. He put his arm around Sadie's shoulders and added, "Lead the way."

Sadie's hip bumped her husband's thigh with each step. She still couldn't believe that this was all really happening. Who knew, when she'd been forced to pull out of the wagon train, so fearful for Matthew's life, that so many good things would come of it?

The group quickly reached the shoreline, and Sadie made her usual warnings to the children.

"Really, Mom. We know all the rules by now," Aaron informed her.

Sadie's response was as dry as the sand they were standing upon. "Humor me."

After their long walk, it felt good to pull a blanket from the bottom of the cart and spread it on the shore. Sadie lifted Grace out to join her and Mac on the blanket and was surprised when the boys sat down with them.

In a moment of absolute bliss, Sadie kissed Grace's soft blond hair. She was secretly happy that the baby did not automatically reach for her father. It was nice to know that in Grace's mind Sadie was as much her parent as Mac. As for her own children, the transformation was remarkable. Gone were the fearful glances and worried whispers that had been part of their life when Eldon was alive. The boys were simply able to enjoy being children now. One more thing for which Sadie could thank Mac.

The family enjoyed a peaceful rest. The rhythm of the breaking waves lulled Grace to sleep. Sadie looked out over the crystal blue lake, marveled at the vastness of it. Mac carefully picked small pebbles and threw them into the water. Some he skipped on the water's surface, while others he allowed to drop into the blue depths.

"What are you doing?" Aaron asked.

"Sending wishes," Mac's earnest voice replied. After a moment of quiet he looked at Aaron and arched an eyebrow, daring the boy to ask.

"Sending wishes? How do you do that?"

Mac was clearly pleased that Aaron took the bait. "Can you keep a secret?" he asked. Both boys quickly nodded. Sadie had to admit that her interest was piqued too.

"Long ago, there were two bands of Sioux Indians," Mac began. "The Oglalas lived on this side of the lake, while the Hunkpapas settled on the western shore. The bands rarely mixed, as their leaders jealously guarded their domain. However, a few days a year the tribes would come together to celebrate religious rituals. It was during one of these ceremonies that a young Indian brave from the Oglalas met a shy Hunkpapa maiden. It was clear to each of them after their first few meetings that they were deeply in love. But they knew that their families would never accept a union between them. You see, each had been promised to another—a member of their own band."

Mac picked up a handful of tiny pebbles, shook them in his big hand and continued, "Late in the evening, after the others had gone to their beds, the young brave and sweet young maiden would stand on the opposite shores of Lake Okoboji and dream of one another. One night the brave began thinking of all the things he loved about the Hunkpapa girl. One by one he named her attributes, and with each praise he dropped one tiny pebble into the deep blue waters."

Again, Mac began to toss stones into the lake. "It just so happens, at that precise moment, the maiden was sitting near the bank watching waves race to shore. Lost in her thoughts, it took a moment for her to notice tiny ripples of water, set apart from the larger waves by an unusual silvery color. She cocked her head; it was almost as though she could hear a voice in those silvery ripples. Imagine her surprise when she discovered that it was indeed a voice—the voice of her own true love. The maiden could clearly hear him as he recited all the reasons that he loved her. And as the ripples danced to shore, tiny pebbles coated with that distinctive silver landed at her feet."

"What did she do?" Aaron asked, mouth agape.

"Well, the shy maiden picked up the pebbles and felt a strange warmth in their hard surface. Not sure what prompted her to do so, she tossed the rocks, one by one, back into the water. With each pebble thrown, the maiden sent a private message to her young brave. Each message included something special that she wished for him."

Mac tilted his head to check the reaction of his audience. "As unlikely as it sounds, from that night forward the couple was able to communicate by sending messages across the deep, broad expanse of Lake Okoboji. You see, what they learned was that nothing—not even physical separation—can divide two hearts that have truly united."

His voice was hypnotic, and Sadie found herself disappointed that the story was over.

"That couldn't happen!" Aaron looked doubtful.

Matthew was convinced. His wild red hair stuck out from under a knit cap as he kept his eyes on his stepfather. "So, what happened? Did they ever get married?"

Smiling as though he possessed a delicious secret, Mac said, "Tell you what—I'll save the rest of the story for later. It's bound to be a long winter and you may appreciate it more on a snowy night when we can't get out."

Sadie was surprised when Matthew didn't fuss. It was just another indication of the deep respect he had for Mac.

Mac took the sleeping Grace from Sadie's arms as Aaron threw the blanket in the back of the little wagon Matthew was pulling. Matthew moved up the embankment with his older brother running along beside him.

"So, what did happen?" Sadie asked her husband.

"I'm not telling," Mac teased. "You'll get the rest of story along with everyone else."

Sadie rolled her eyes, but she grinned. She laced her arm through his and leaned her head against his shoulder as they walked.

With the enthusiasm of a fort sentry, Matthew met them at the top of the rise to announce that they had guests.

Sadie was thrilled to see Rowland and Frances Gardner standing near their door. She rushed to give Frances a warm hug. "I take it things are going well," Frances whispered in her ear.

"Very." Sadie nodded.

Taking Grace from Mac's arms, she added, "If you'll excuse us, gentlemen, Frances and I will retire to the house for a cup of coffee." After instructing her boys to stay near, she led her friend into the warm cabin.

Rowland's grin in Mac's direction spoke volumes. Sadie seemed mighty happy, it seemed to say. Mac had no trouble reading the older man's thoughts. "You have no idea," he intoned.

Rowland had the good grace to change the subject. "Come on, let's see this new barn roof you were working on." He smiled again.

As the men discussed repairs outdoors, Sadie entertained her friend. She placed Grace in a little crib, stoked the smoldering fire, then hung Frances's jacket next to her own. To her, even the simple task of preparing coffee while visiting with a friend was a delightful experience.

The two women discussed everything that had happened since they last visited. Sadie was glad to hear that Frances's granddaughter had recovered from whatever ailed her the night of the party. When the hot brew was ready, Sadie served Frances coffee and took a chair across the scarred table.

Frances smiled gently after her first sip. The little lines that fanned her eyes only served to add character to her face. "You seem happy," she observed.

"Oh, Frances, I can't believe how good life is here. And Mac . . ."

"Say no more. Your feelings are clearly written all over your face. You're absolutely radiant."

"Really?" Sadie asked. That had certainly never been a word used to describe her before.

"Think about when I first met you, Sadie. Things were grim. Your husband had just died, your son was

117

desperately ill, and you were so thin I was surprised that a strong gust of wind didn't blow you away. I remember feeling awfully bad for what you were going through."

It seemed so long ago, yet it had been less than six months. "You were so kind to us, Frances. I will never forget how you and Rowland went out of your way to help the boys and me."

Frances put her hand over Sadie's. "That's the way it works out here. And when it comes your time, you'll be in the position to ease the way for someone else. Who knows, if you're as lucky as we've been they may turn out to be dear friends too."

Sadie was touched by her sincerity. She squeezed Frances's hand and wondered how much better things could possibly get. "Thank you."

In her no-nonsense way, Frances pulled back. "Okay, now that we've established how wonderful we are, let's talk business. Everything going okay with the children?"

"Aaron and Matthew are coming along beautifully. They truly admire Mac, and he treats them like his own flesh and blood. And Grace . . . well, I adore her, of course."

For a moment, Frances traced the outer rim of her coffee cup. Her eyes clouded with concern as she seemed to struggle with a decision.

Sadie was alarmed at her change of expression. "What is it, Frances?"

"Something I just remembered, something rather odd."

"Go ahead," Sadie urged.

"Well, Rowland sent Harvey into Granger's Point to

pick up supplies a few days ago, and there was a man in Frank Carpenter's newspaper office asking about you and Mac."

Sadie's eyes widened. "Us? Why would anyone wonder about Mac and me?"

"I don't know. But Harvey had stopped by to pick up back issues of the paper for me. Said he overheard this man asking to see a copy of the announcement concerning your wedding."

A cold chill began at the base of Sadie's spine. For some reason, she didn't want to hear another word.

Frances continued, unaware of Sadie's discomfort. "You know how men are. All Harvey noticed about the man was that he was asking after you. Luckily, Mary was waiting in the wagon when the stranger left the office. She remembered more. Said he was a small fellow, kinda wiry. He had a hat on, so she couldn't tell much about the color of his hair, but she says that when he smiled at her she could feel the hair stand up on her neck. Said there was something shifty about the way he looked at her. You don't suppose it was someone from the wagon train checking on you, do you?"

Sadie felt as though a ghost had walked over her grave. She fought the lightheadedness that overcame her, refusing to allow her mind to consider the horrible possibility of who the stranger might be. She had seen Eldon's body with her own eyes. He was dead!

Later, Sadie was unclear as to how she functioned during the remainder of the Gardners' visit. Blindly, she went through the routine of entertaining, acting as though nothing was bothering her.

She waved as Rowland and Frances departed, smiled as though her heart wasn't beating at twice its normal cadence. She fed the children and put them to bed, without allowing anyone to know how her mind was racing and her pulse was pounding. She made love to Mac with an exuberance that surprised even him, and afterward lay awake listening to the sound of his even breathing. She prayed that she was overreacting. But through the litany of her prayer slid horrible doubts. Hadn't she once heard that nothing good could last forever?

Chapter Twenty-one

Although there was scant distance between the settlers at play and the warriors who watched from the top of a hill, they might as well have been on opposite sides of the earth.

"What are they doing?" Inkapaduta questioned, as he watched the pasty-faced interlopers squeal like children.

Screeching Owl did not attempt to hide his smile. "Playing a game of some sort, like we did when we were young men. Remember, cousin?"

"We never played games together. I was much too old to play with you."

"I watched you play with my older brothers," Screeching Owl answered patiently. "Later, I played those same games with friends of my own."

"That seems a lifetime ago," Inkapaduta said tiredly.

The warriors were quiet for long minutes, content to watch the settlers throw a ball to each other then run in a pattern that made no sense.

"They don't belong here."

"But they're here, cousin. Our people have dealt with their government, have agreed to terms that allow them to call this land their own." Screeching Owl felt as though he had lived through this conversation a hundred times.

"But they don't belong here!" Inkapaduta hissed. "They don't belong here any more than that murdering Henry Lott."

"Henry Lott is gone now, cousin."

"But not before murdering my brother and sister! Not before taking the life of my dear mother!"

Screeching Owl rubbed a hand tiredly over his face. This was well-plowed territory, and he knew how the conversation would end. "I agree that Henry Lott was a bad man, a thief and a murderer. But these people are not all Henry Lott. Perhaps they will be good stewards of the land."

Inkapaduta continued his tirade, as though his words could somehow bring resolution. "Lott stole our horses, then refused to accept responsibility. He ran from his home, then blamed us when his son froze to death trying to warn his cowardly father to stay away. He waited until the men were away from camp to attack our women and children, to murder them."

"These people are not Henry Lott," Screeching Owl repeated.

"We will see," said Inkapaduta. "We will see."

Chapter Twenty-two

Sadie kneaded bread as she listened to Mac's warm voice. Her husband worked with Aaron and Matthew on their lessons each night after chores were done. He taught them the basics: reading and sums. But Mac also introduced the boys to things he had seen, things he had heard about.

"An interesting invention is being marketed by a man named George Bateson," Mac reported. "It consists of an iron bell mounted on the lid of a casket. There's a cord attached to the bell that runs into the casket. You wrap that cord around the dead person's hand, and if for some strange reason the person you buried isn't really dead, he can ring the bell and be freed. Now, as far as I know, the contraption has never actually saved anybody, but Mr. Bateson is sure getting rich."

Aaron's eyes were wide with wonder, while Matthew whooped with glee. "Tell us more!"

Sadie watched as Mac smiled. It was clear that he

was a natural born teacher. "You've heard of baseball, haven't you?"

"No, sir," Matthew answered.

"You haven't heard of baseball? As soon as the snow melts, I'll teach you how to play. It really is a great game, if you can stand a few bruises."

Aaron was intrigued. "How do you get bruised?"

"Well, let me see if I can remember this correctly. I've only played it a time or two myself. First you stand at what is called home plate. With a large stick, you try to hit a ball that is thrown to you from a short distance away. If you're lucky enough to hit the ball, you run like heck! And you'd better be running fast because when a player on the opposing team picks up that ball, he chucks it with all his might right at you."

"Ouch! That sounds like it hurts!" Matthew laughed.

"The idea is not to get hit," Aaron informed his little brother, his tone conveying how dense he thought the boy could be.

"I know that, you bootlicker!"

"Matthew David Pritchard, where in the world did you pick up that vulgar phrase?" Sadie was astounded. Never had she heard one of her children use such language.

"Pa used to say it all the time," Matthew defended.

"Your pa didn't have a mother like me to teach him right from wrong. You are not to call your brother a name like that, do you understand me?"

"Yes, ma'am," Matthew answered begrudgingly.

Mac declared class suspended for the evening. As the boys put away their supplies, he walked to Sadie's side. He leaned down, dropped a kiss on her exposed neck and whispered, "Bootlicker ain't nothing, honey. In my day we called 'em butt kissers!"

Sadie put her hand over her mouth, but it did no good. Gales of laughter erupted, waking the sleeping baby. "See what you've done?" she asked.

Mac smiled unapologetically, and she loved him more deeply for it. She could not lose him. Sadie had spent the last few days convincing herself that she'd been looking for trouble where none existed. Eldon Pritchard had made her life such a living hell that she was having difficulty believing that heaven existed. And it was heaven here. Sadie simply was not accustomed to being happy. Her overactive imagination was trying its best to give her something to worry about.

As she watched Mac help Matthew place his tablet on a high shelf, Sadie resolved to think only good thoughts. She was determined to accept this wonderful life that God had handed her, to resist any temptation to be spooked by the memory of Eldon Pritchard. Eldon had stolen her happiness while he was alive; she was not going to give him that power in death. So what if a man had been asking about her wedding in Granger's Point? Mac had lots of friends; surely one of them was interested in hearing whom he had married.

Peace settled over her as she rocked Grace back to sleep. Mac and the boys stepped outside of the cabin to admire the bright December stars. Mac's rich, deep voice floated back to her as he named first one star, and then another.

Sadie knew that if she could stay in this place, in this exact moment, forever, she would be an utterly content woman.

But if time did have to march on, and bring change

in the process, she was glad that she was with the four people she loved most in the world.

It took only minutes for Grace to fall back to sleep. Sadie savored the opportunity to simply hold the little girl in her arms, to enjoy the peace of the moment. By the time she placed the sleeping baby in her small crib, Sadie was anxious for Mac and the boys to come in from the cold. She longed to revel in the warmth of her husband's big body. Not a moment too soon, the three returned. Sadie's admonishments to get ready for bed quietly worked wonders.

Mac retrieved the boys' pallets from the rafters where they were stored during the day. Within fifteen minutes Aaron and Matthew were snugly tucked in, and Sadie had the exquisite pleasure of climbing into the soft bed she shared with Mac. Mac extinguished the candles, built up the fire, then joined her. Before slipping under the blankets with his wife, Mac pulled the dark curtain that separated their bed from the rest of the small cabin.

He stood next to the bed, his voice low, his smile lazy. "Next year I'm building a bigger place. It'll have six or seven bedrooms on one side, and ours will be all alone on the other."

Sadie's breath caught in her throat as Mac peeled his clothes from his rugged body. Delicious expectation made her restless. Forcing herself to respond to Mac's plans, she asked, "Six or seven bedrooms? Surely we can start with two or three?"

Mac's eyes never wavered from her face as his pants fell to the floor. He eased his big body down next to hers and pulled her to him in one fluid motion. His mouth moved to her ear. For a moment he nibbled its lobe, then sucked lightly. Stopping for a moment, he said, "Don't underestimate me, Mrs. MacCallister. I plan on putting plenty of babies in that sweet belly of yours. I plan on making it my job—loving you and making children with you. Heck, six or seven bedrooms may not be enough!"

Heat pulsed through Sadie's veins. Blood pounded in her ears. The fervor with which she longed for this man shocked and frightened her. She turned to face him and put her hands on either side of his face. With the tip of her tongue she traced his full lips, then boldly pushed her tongue into his warm mouth. While exploring the recesses of his mouth, she wrapped her small hands around his thick wrists. She pushed at him until he rolled onto his back, then pressed her body against him.

As Mac sought to take control, Sadie protested. Beginning at his eyebrows, she kissed him. She left no spot unattended as she moved down his body. Flicking his nipples with her tongue, Sadie was delighted to feel the shock that ran through his long body. Mac's hands roamed her back as she explored his torso. Sadie's mouth pulled gently at his skin, leaving tiny love marks. Finally, she found her prize. Her fingers caressed him as her mouth adored him. Mac's low moans brought her unspeakable pleasure.

Mac took all that he could. Then, pulling at her hair, he begged Sadie to lie on her back. She raised her head, smiled, and surprised her beloved husband by sitting astride him. Mac assisted her as she pressed herself closer. He was hard and ready.

Sadie could see the effort that Mac spent in controlling himself, and it made her feel powerful. Joining their bodies, she dictated the tempo, melding with Mac more closely than she'd ever thought possible, then coyly pulling away. They were covered in sweat, lost in a private Eden. Mac reached between their bodies to gently tease her most sensitive spot. When her fulfillment came, Sadie felt tremors to the tips of her toes. Mac arched wildly back and filled her with his warmth.

At last, Sadie fell to her husband's chest, tiredly placing kisses there. Lovingly Mac stroked her head. Wrapped in each other's love, the two slept peacefully, momentarily shielded from the harsh realities of their world.

Chapter Twenty-three

"Are we done yet?"

Mac looked up from the copy of *A Wonder-Book For Girls and Boys* that he had been reading aloud. "Am I boring you, Matthew?" he asked.

The child shook his head, then swiped an arm across his runny nose. "Uh, uh. I gotta pee real bad."

Mac's eyes widened comically and met Sadie's over Matthew's red head. Sadie smiled at his expression. Love for him washed over her anew. It was these little things that he did, his easy manner and lightheartedness that had once been so hidden, that tugged at her heartstrings.

Mac carefully marked his page. "Well, son, I suggest that you remedy the situation." Only the glint in his green eyes and twitch in his cheek gave evidence of his mirth.

"I've been holding it all day!" Matthew proudly announced.

Sadie momentarily picked up the ball that she had

been rolling to Grace. "Why in the world have you put it off all day, Matthew?"

"It's cold, Ma! Aaron told me that my thing will freeze up and fall off if I pee outside in the snow."

"Did not!" Aaron insisted.

"Did too!"

Mac's deep voice interrupted the boys' squabble. Only Sadie recognized the laughter that laced his words. "Okay, break it up! Matthew, you know perfectly well that you can pull the curtain around the big bed and use the pan. There's no need to go outside in this snow."

Tears shone in the child's eyes. "But Aaron said that men don't use bedpans! He said that only girls use 'em."

"Did not!"

"Did too!"

Mac looked at Sadie and shook his head. "Didn't we just go down this path?"

Sadie shrugged and smiled. She quickly moved to pick up the baby, who had crawled too close to the fireplace.

"You want me to deal with this all alone, don't you?" Mac accused.

Sadie blessed him with her most innocent expression. Mac scowled. "I'll see to you later, Mrs. MacCallister."

Sadie picked Grace up and swung the infant above her head. "Did you hear that, Gracie? Daddy's going to deal with me later. Oooh . . . doesn't that sound scary?" Nothing, in fact, ever sounded better.

Mac forced himself to turn his attention back to the feuding boys. After a deep sigh he announced, "I think what we are suffering from here is a serious case of cabin fever. What would you two say to a day of hunting? We'll leave first thing in the morning. I'll bet Rowland and Harvey would love to go with us."

The argument immediately forgotten, Aaron turned his big blue eyes to Mac. "Really? We can go hunting with you? What about all the snow?"

"The snow isn't that deep yet. We won't go far."

"Did you hear that, Mom?" Matthew asked.

Sadie moved to Mac's side and slipped her arm around his waist. "Yes, Matthew, I heard. Now you go right behind that curtain and take care of business, then get back to your studies."

Nodding in Aaron's direction, she added, "You too, mister."

"Yes, ma'am," both boys replied in unison.

Mac waited until they were busy doing their duty, then turned to his wife. "His thing will freeze up and fall off? That does not sound good."

"Don't you dare laugh, Samuel MacCallister! Matthew believes every word his brother utters. You too, for that matter."

Mac seemed to consider that fact. "If Aaron and I were more sinister sorts we could play terrible games with Matt's young mind." He gave her an evil smile.

Sadie put Grace back down on the floor and wrapped her arms around her husband. "You wouldn't do anything in the world to hurt Matthew, and you know it!" But the miracle was, *Sadie* knew it. With every cell of her body, she trusted Mac. It was a new and wonderful place to be.

Mac smiled, dropped a quick kiss on the tip of her nose, and answered, "You're right. Those boys are priceless. I'd give my life for either of them."

Tears filled Sadie's blue eyes. "They are so lucky to have you," she said. The simple words sounded inadequate.

"We're all lucky to have each other, Sadie." He stared at her for a moment, then asked, "In all the world, what do you suppose the chances were of us finding each other, of making a family that fit so perfectly?"

"One in a million, maybe," Sadie responded.

"If that."

"I love you, Mr. MacCallister."

"Show me," Mac growled.

Locked in a heated embrace, thoroughly pillaging each other's mouths, they didn't notice that Grace had begun to pull herself up Sadie's skirt. From behind the curtain Aaron and Matthew emerged, watching their parents with undisguised disgust.

"Hey, you two! You gonna be doing that all night? We're still hungry," Matthew said impatiently.

"I hear there are bears in the woods. They make pretty good eating," Mac dared the boy.

Sadie laughed. Disentangling herself from her husband's big body, she practically knocked Grace down in the process. Surprised, she quickly scooped the baby up and, with Grace securely in her arms, turned to survey the room. Once again, for just a moment, life was pure bliss. Sadie had to wonder how many moments like this she would experience in her life.

She pulled herself out of her reverie and commanded, "Aaron and Matthew, you get back to studying. Mac, how about getting a little more wood from the pile while I scramble up a snack for the children?"

Mac's eyebrows pulled together. Slipping his arms into his coat, he asked, "You sure you aren't from a military family, Sadie? I could swear you sound like a general sometimes."

"No lip from any of you," Sadie commanded, looking around the room. She pointed her finger at Mac and added, "Especially you!"

"How about later?" Mac grinned indecently. "Can I give you a little lip later?"

Sadie turned away, heat suffusing her skin. She smiled at Mac's laughter, then sighed as she heard him close the door. She propped Grace in the chair Mac had designed for the child, then went about preparing a small snack.

Mac returned with the firewood, then lowered his muscular body into the rocking chair near the boys. Haltingly, Aaron began to read a simple story aloud. Grace cooed happily in her chair as velvety snow drifted past the window. Again, Sadie was assailed with the overwhelming sense that these were the best of times, moments that could never be duplicated. Outside, the world was a dangerous place. But nestled in their cozy cabin, the MacCallisters of Lake Okoboji lived their own version of paradise.

Chapter Twenty-four

Grace cooed contentedly, much to the delight of the smiling Sadie. Sadie leaned over the little girl who waited patiently in the center of the big bed. "Look at you!" Sadie cooed. "You're such a sweet girl."

She slipped mittens over Grace's chubby hands, then stepped back and looked the child over. Covered in several sets of clothing, a coat that was much too large, and a stocking cap that kept trying to slip down to her nose, the baby looked lost in layers of fabric.

"You don't care how much you have to wear, you just want to go outside and play in the snow, don't you?"

Grace bounced on the bed, her movements restricted by Sadie's bundling. Sadie hurriedly donned her own winter attire, then scooped the little girl into her arms. Sparing a moment for a quick kiss on the baby's pink cheek, Sadie promised, "We're going to have lots of fun, Gracie. Daddy and the boys won't be back for a long time, hunting as they are, so we'll have the whole day to ourselves."

Sadie's heart was light as she swung the cabin door open. The snow had stopped falling sometime during the middle of the night, leaving just enough ground cover for a good snowman. Sadie took selfish satisfaction in the fact that she would be the first to introduce Grace to the joys of playing in the snow. They had barely cleared the doorway when Grace began to wriggle in her arms.

Sadie laughed. It was clear that if Grace could speak, she would be saying "I want down, and I want down now!" Obliging the blond-headed imp, Sadie knelt to steady Grace, who reached for her first glove full of snow.

"I'll be damned. She's lookin' awful good for a widow woman."

Sadie's throat fell into her stomach as the voice registered in her mind. Her head snapped up. Slowly, she looked in the direction of that horrifying sound. A man stepped from behind the shelter of a row of pin oaks, still holding the reins of a skinny horse. Instinctively, Sadie pulled Grace close to her breast, then stood to face her worst nightmare. Somewhere within her chest, her heart was shattering; Sadie knew it, and judging from his homely grin, the man knew it too.

"Eldon." Sadie's tone was dead, as dead as her battered dreams.

"Is that any way to greet your husband, woman?"

She'd somehow known. The moment Frances Gardner told her about the stranger in town, Sadie had known it was Eldon. As valiantly as she had tried to convince herself otherwise, she'd known he'd be back for her. As long as the world continued to spin, Eldon Pritchard would be there to make Sadie's life a living hell.

She wasn't sure why she asked, why she would give Eldon the satisfaction of gloating, but she had to know. "How did you manage it, Eldon? I saw you with my own eyes—you were at the bottom of the ravine."

Eldon's smile was as sickening as ever. His beady eyes appeared even smaller in his bloated face. "You must have been real sorry, sweet thing," he sneered nastily.

Sadie would not give him the pleasure of a response. She looked at him blankly, waited for him to spill the entire sordid story. She knew that he would. Eldon always got a kick out of impressing her with his duplicity.

He waited a moment, looked Sadie over, and tried to gauge her reaction. Shrugging, he gave a chilling cackle before launching into his tale. "Good trick, huh? I made you all believe it was me down over them rocks."

Sadie did not say a word. She continued to hold tightly to Grace, who watched the stranger with wide-eyed fascination.

"It was the perfect plan," Eldon bragged. "I was getting pretty sick of my life, ready to move on to something bigger and better. Lucky for me, I stumbled onto a couple of big-mouthed fools who played right into my hand.

"I'd gone to the woods for a little drink and met up with these guys, just sitting near their campfire. They were glad to see a new face and invited me to sit a spell and tell them what was going on in the world." *As if Eldon would know what was going on in the world*, Sadie thought bitterly.

"Like the nice guy I am, I shared my whiskey with

'em. But they were stupid, really stupid. They drank a little, then started bragging about holding up a little bank in Liberty. Well, I knew that they had that money somewhere on them!"

Sadie found herself feeling sorry for the bank robbers. No one deserved to meet his fate at the sorry hand of Eldon Pritchard. She was sure that Eldon had killed them. She didn't have to ask. Sadie had often wondered how easy it would be for Eldon to kill her or one of the boys. She truly believed that if he thought he could get away with it, Eldon would have divested himself of his family long ago.

"Are you listening?" Eldon demanded.

Sadie tiredly nodded her head. She didn't want to do anything to rile him. She had to think of Grace.

"Anyways, like I was saying, those two had more money than they had smarts. I just waited till they fell asleep, then shot the skinny one right through the head." Sadie flinched as Eldon pointed to his own head, gleefully showing her where the bullet had penetrated.

"The fat one woke up, so I had to hit him over the head a couple of times before a bullet put him down. It was just like fighting a bear."

"He was a man, Eldon." Sadie spoke before she thought. Immediately, her spine stiffened as she waited for Eldon's violent response.

He surprised her by simply shrugging his skinny shoulders.

"Well, the long and short of it is that I knew I had found a way out of my life. Sure enough there was a bundle of money in the lining of the fat one's saddlebags. I knew that if I added it to the rest of the money

I had, I could start all over. No whining wife, no snot-nosed kids—I could have the kind of life I shoulda had in the first place.

"I traded clothes with the little guy and pushed him over that cliff. I reckoned that no one would try to get down there to get the body. It was just dumb luck that the little bastard landed on his face. All that was left to do was hide the fat one's body, and I was good to go." Eldon's laugh sent chills down Sadie's spine. She forced herself to look at his face.

From the moment her drunken father had lost Sadie to Eldon in a poker game, then forced her to marry him, Sadie had known that Eldon was evil. But looking at him now, she began to realize that he was crazy as well. An expression of untempered insanity washed over his homely face. It twisted his features into a nightmarish mask.

Suddenly the man sobered, cocked his head, and fixed his eyes on Sadie. "Guess you found some money in my trunk by now, huh?"

Sadie was confused. "Surely after staging your death you wouldn't risk being seen alive. How did you get the money back to the wagon? And why?"

Eldon grinned. "Ah, Sadie girl. I stuck them bank robbers' money right in my pocket and took off with their horses. I got me that money in my trunk off of that old man I did odd jobs for in Saint Louie. And if you're wondering why we skedaddled out of Missoura so quick, there's your answer."

"Tell me you didn't kill Mr. Mayfield, Eldon." Sadie shuddered at the thought of the old man who had been so kind to her family.

"Had a hell of a time finding ya," Eldon said, ignoring her question. "Everyone in that damned Granger's Point was real tight-lipped about your whereabouts. Seems folks like that new man of yours." As though a thought had just occurred to him, Eldon added, "You know, I'm kinda surprised that you took up with another man so quick. You never seemed to be a woman who enjoyed men much."

Sadie wanted to scream. Of course she had never had the opportunity to enjoy a man. All her life she had been surrounded by louts. First her drunk of a father, then Eldon. Her nerves were frayed. "What do you want, Eldon?"

"Whose brat?" Eldon's shifty eyes trained on Grace.

Sadie desperately wanted to divert his attention. "The money is in the barn. I left it in your old trunk." Without waiting for him, she turned and walked toward it.

In the barn, Sadie knelt next to the trunk while keeping her hold on Mac's baby. She lifted the heavy lid with one hand and managed to pull the burlap sack containing Eldon's ill-gotten gains from the interior of the chest.

She stood and thrust the bag at Eldon, who had followed her. "Take it. Take it and leave, Eldon. You wanted your freedom. You have it now." With tears in her eyes, she implored, "You have what you want. Please just take it and go."

"Why, thank you. Right kind of you."

Sadie trailed after Eldon out of the barn and saw him mount his scrawny horse. In silence she watched him, wishing that someone would shake her and wake her from this horrible dream.

"Just one question, Sadie girl," Eldon added conversationally. "You gonna tell that new husband of yours about my miraculous return?" He laughed at the pall that washed over her face. "I didn't think so. Wouldn't want him to know that the woman he's bedding is another man's wife. He'd throw you out like a sack of snakes.

"I'll make you a little deal," he offered after a moment, his eyes roaming her form. Revulsion buzzed up Sadie's spine as he scratched his sparsely bearded chin with a dirty finger. She waited to hear his terms. "You keep all this a secret for a while longer, and I'll lie low."

"What do you want from us?" Sadie asked, her voice hoarse with loathing.

Eldon smiled. His thin lips parted to reveal stained teeth. "It has occurred to me that you marrying this MacCallister fella could work to our favor."

Cold rage boiled through Sadie's belly. Stiffly, she asked, "How?"

"Now, Sadie girl, I haven't worked out all the peculiars yet. Maybe he'll just pay us to leave without telling all his neighbors that he's a bigamist. Or"—Eldon's beady eyes examined the property—"this is a mighty fine setup . . ." He pierced Sadie with his stare, then stated matter-of-factly, "Maybe I'll just decide to take it all."

She shook violently. Clutching Grace more closely, Sadie knew that she was looking at a killer. Eldon Pritchard could easily decide that killing Mac would be the cleanest way to take all that Mac had worked for. She would not let that happen. "I'll tell him, Eldon. I'll tell him you were here!"

Eldon only chuckled. "Now, don't get all riled up, Sadie. It was just a thought. I doubt that even I could get away with killin' MacCallister. The law would be on my ass for the rest of my born days. Nope, a smart man sticks to killin' vagabonds. Ain't no one around to miss 'em."

Sadie felt sick. She swayed slightly and asked, "What do you want? What can I do?"

"Why, that's right kind of you, Mrs. Pritchard." Scratching his chin again, he added, "But not right now. There's a payday in this, I just know it!"

Eldon relaxed upon his horse. Gathering her courage, Sadie warned, "I won't let anything happen to Mac, Eldon. I will tell him, no matter what you say."

Eldon's voice sliced through the air, pinning her with its venomous strength. "You do, and I'll see to it that one of those brats of yours disappears."

"What do you mean?"

"Oh, I think you know. You do anything—and I mean anything—to mess up my plans, and I promise you one of them boys is dust."

"They are your sons, Eldon!"

The man shrugged dismissively. "You know I could never stand 'em. They were always underfoot, always screaming about something." His muddy eyes dared her. "Don't try me, woman. I could take one of them boys out as easy as I did the bums in the woods. I ain't quite sure how I'm gonna use any of this yet, but I do know that you ain't gonna stand in my way."

Sadie was desperate. "But why involve us?" she cried. "Eldon, listen to me. You were miserable when we were together. You faked your own death just to get away from me! Why in the world don't you just get as far as you can from here, forget you ever knew us?"

"And miss the chance to get my hands on all of

this? Don't be a fool, Sadie. All I gotta do is come up with a good plan."

She didn't know that she was crying, couldn't feel the tears that ran down her face. "Ah shucks, honey," Eldon said, "you don't need to cry about me leaving. I'm sure we'll be seeing each other again." He gave a quick nod and added, "You can count on it."

His horse kicked up snow as Eldon rode back toward town. Grace's mittened hand stroked Sadie's cheek. Sadie realized that the baby was probably freezing.

This cannot be happening, she thought as she walked numbly back to the cabin. Sick to her soul, she wondered how she would get through the day. If Eldon had put a bullet through her heart, he could not have exacted a more painful revenge.

With every fiber of her being Sadie wished that she could turn the clock back twenty-four hours. Was it only a day ago that she marveled at the tranquility in her life? Was it only yesterday when she'd believed that happiness was an attainable goal for a mere mortal?

Chapter Twenty-five

Tension filled the tiny cabin. Sadie thought she would go mad with it. The snow that had seemed so charming only weeks earlier now drifted in mounds around the perimeter of the dwelling, making it perpetually dark.

Aaron and Matthew, who had always gotten along remarkably well, were at each other's throats. They disagreed about which game to play, then argued about the outcome. Grace was teething and, at eleven months old, attempting to walk. If she wasn't crying about the pain in her mouth she was wailing out of frustration. Sadie loved her children but she thought that if she had to be cooped up with them much longer she might go stark raving mad.

Mac spent as much time as possible out of the cabin. He dug a tunnel to the barn where he could be away from the lunacy in the house. Sadie resented his getaway, yet needed distance from him too.

Since the day Eldon had returned from the fires of Hell, Sadie felt as though she had been consigned there. She could no longer look at Mac without wondering if he saw her for what she was: a bigamist. She certainly had not set out to be, but the fact of the matter was Sadie had two living husbands. Although she attempted to act as though nothing had happened, Sadie knew that Eldon's return would change the course of her life. And it could only be for the worse.

She sometimes wished that she had gone into the house the day Eldon appeared, pulled Mac's gun down from the rafters, loaded it, and blown Eldon Pritchard right back to Hell. But in her heart Sadie knew that she could not do it. As much as she hated him, she would not stoop to killing Eldon. Yet.

If the January weather had been more cooperative, she would have found an excuse to travel to Granger's Point and talk with an attorney about the possibility of having the first marriage dissolved on grounds of abandonment. But how would she tell Mac? "Oh Mac, guess what? Remember the bastard of a husband who died on our journey here . . ."

Besides, Eldon would surely carry out his threat to harm one of the boys if she crossed him. She could not risk her children.

Even if she could tell Mac without fear for her family, how would he react? Did he love her enough to stay with her through this? How could he? Sadie knew that despite Mac's protestations to the contrary, she was a plain woman. Mac was the kind of man who turned every woman's head, eight to eighty. Throughout their entire relationship Sadie had been elated, but curious as to why he would choose to be with her. Besides being a caretaker for Grace, what else did she provide him? Three more mouths to feed? A tortured background to recover from? Sadie knew that she was no prize. Eldon's return just drove that fact home.

It hurt to acknowledge it, but she had been lucky to land Samuel MacCallister—a lot luckier than he had been to find her. Why would he choose to stay with her when he had already gotten what he needed: a body to keep him warm in bed through the winter and someone to be with Grace until she was a little more independent? By spring Grace would be old enough to toddle in the yard while her father worked. Frances would be happy to look after her when Mac was in the fields or hunting. Mac could even hire Eliza or Abbie Gardner to watch Grace when he needed extra help. Why did he need Sadie, anyway?

She wished with all her being that she had the courage to confront Mac with the truth, to trust that their love would see them through. But how could it? How could he possibly love her enough to stay by her side through this nightmare? Whenever she looked at his handsome face or watched his easy manner, Sadie was assaulted by doubts. In Sadie's mind, a man like Samuel MacCallister could not possibly want to be with a woman such as herself. He deserved a refined woman, a woman he could be proud of. Though she fought it, profound self-doubt caused Sadie to wonder how she could have ever imagined herself to be that woman.

And yet, she knew with a gut-wrenching certainty that Mac would have to be told. She could not hide Eldon's existence forever. *But you're happy!* her mind cried. *Just give yourself a little more time, a moment longer to know joy.*

Sadie made a deal with herself. She would hold on

to Mac and the picture-perfect family until spring. And though it wasn't nearly long enough, for a few more months Sadie would have all that she had ever dreamed of. Then, though it would be the hardest thing she had ever done, she would present him with the facts.

In her mind's eye Sadie could already see what his reaction would be, could visualize the light leaving his eyes, the smile disappearing from his face, see him becoming a virtual stranger. She could picture giving Grace one final kiss before turning back to see Mac's features for the last time. To memorize them.

The knowledge that the end was near only made her feelings for Mac more intense, more exquisite. If she recoiled from his touch as night, it wasn't because she didn't want him. She simply knew that she could not disconnect her emotions from her body. The more she made love to Mac, the more difficult it was going to be to leave him.

There was also the concern of pregnancy. Only weeks earlier Sadie had dreamed of suckling Mac's child. But now she had more than she could handle worrying about the children she had. She had no clear plan of where she would take the boys once the truth was out.

How would Aaron and Matthew cope with learning that their father had staged his own death only to escape his family? How would they survive losing Mac? They loved him, respected him, wanted to be just like him. For Sadie, it hurt to think.

Chapter Twenty-six

Despite the fact that the weather outside the barn was frigid, Mac was covered in perspiration. He found that working his body to utter exhaustion helped to numb his mind. There was not a cobweb to be found in the barn, not a tool out of place.

He was tired of thinking, tired of wondering how he could be such a gullible fool yet again. First his mother, then Cynthia. Had he ever actually expected Sadie to stay with him?

Mac collapsed on a sack of feed. Head in hands, he determined that women the world over were the same: self-serving, conniving . . . But Mac could not bring himself to call Sadie a name—any name. And that was the crux of the problem. Although he knew that she had another man, he still loved her. Even though he suspected that she was only waiting for spring thaw to leave, he wanted her.

He had known for weeks. He'd seen the tracks left in the snow the day he took Aaron and Matthew hunting. Sadie had tried to brush them away, but to Mac's eyes they were clear and telling. She had tried to pretend that nothing had changed between them, but they both knew better.

His gut still clenched when he thought about her behavior since that day. At first it was subtle; she was simply a bit quieter than usual. But then she'd begun to pull away from him at night. If he went to bed after her, Sadie would pretend to be asleep. The one night she did succumb to his stroking, she'd made love with a burning intensity then cried into the night.

Mac pounded the sack of feed until his hands hurt. What was he going to do? Why Sadie? He had actually begun to believe that this was a woman who would love him, who would stay with him. The idea of losing someone he had trusted so completely left him feeling adrift—and angry. Angrier than he had ever been in his life. Was she laughing at him? Did she and her lover consider him a fool?

For the sake of the three innocent children, they pretended that life was fine. They celebrated Aaron's eleventh birthday and Grace's first. They treated one another with benign politeness, but Mac knew the truth.

In a way, Mac couldn't blame her. When he'd proposed to Sadie, she was alone in the world with two growing boys to feed. He'd offered her a roof over their heads and food in their stomachs. Mac didn't doubt that Sadie loved those boys. He didn't even doubt that she loved Grace. Sadie would have married anyone to protect those children.

He promised himself that he wouldn't think about the other man, but it was no use. He couldn't help but wonder if it was one of the men from the bachelors' quarters. They lived close by, and Mac remembered well their reaction to Sadie the night of the Gardners' party. Was it someone from Granger's Point? Someone she knew previously?

Finally, he decided that all the brooding was senseless. He was no closer to knowing anything definitive than when he set out to clean the barn.

Questions, all questions. It was high time he begin to look for some answers.

Chapter Twenty-seven

The weather was actually cooperating. Although her nerves were raw, Sadie was grateful for the opportunity the children had to play outdoors. The sun had shone for days, melting the snow enough to allow them access to the yard.

She smiled as she watched Aaron and Matthew frolic. She placed Grace on the ground and allowed the baby to pick up handfuls of the feathery snow. Grace's laughter was a sweet sound to her ears.

She attempted to ignore Mac, who stood negligently against the doorframe of the barn, his black mood marring the perfection of his features. He watched the proceedings emotionlessly, like a vulture waiting for the kill. Sadie wondered who this stranger was who had taken over the face and form of the man she loved so deeply.

Finally, the children decided that they'd had enough. Sadie ushered them to the cabin door. Mac's deep voice followed her. "I want to talk to you."

Sadie was tired of his surliness. "So, talk," she said.

When he didn't respond, she could not resist looking at him. Mac's eyes penetrated her across the yard, his voice low and menacing. "I don't think you want the children to hear about your visitor."

She froze. Her heart slowed, her breathing stopped. Forcing herself to move, Sadie stuck her head in the door of the cabin and asked Aaron to help his brother and sister get out of their winter gear. When Aaron assured her that he would, she shut the door and walked woodenly to the barn.

By the time she walked through the barn door, Mac had disappeared into the dark interior. Sadie was momentarily blind. Not wanting him to believe that he had the advantage, she walked to the center of the building. Showing a bravado she did not feel, she asked, "So, what do you want to talk about?"

Mac thrust a burlap sack into Sadie's hand. As though she had been handed a ball of fire, it fell from her scorched fingers. "What the hell is this?" he demanded.

"Where did you get that?" Sadie recognized the bag as the one that had contained Eldon's stolen cash.

"Hanging on a branch near the cabin," Mac answered. "This note was attached."

With shaking hands she accepted the written missive.

Sadie,
Thank you for taking care of the contents of this
bag for me. I surely enjoyed our time together. See
you soon.
Love, E.

She was shaken but not surprised. Sadie knew that Eldon would use any opportunity to torment her. She did wonder whom he'd gotten to write the note for him. Eldon could neither read nor write a word.

"How touching, Sadie. A note from your lover."

"He's not . . ." Sadie began.

Mac tightly gripped her upper arms. Even through the thickness of her coat Sadie could feel how tightly he held her. "Not what, Sadie? Don't lie to me. Don't you dare lie to me. For months I have believed every word your sweet lips uttered. Tell me, are you capable of telling me the truth?"

Sadie could not bear the look of disgust on his face. Even as she considered telling Mac the truth about Eldon, she could hear the death knell ringing on their marriage.

"And don't you turn away from me!" Mac demanded. "I was fool enough to believe you for months. The least you can do is level with me now."

She turned to him, allowed herself to look him in the face. Tears swam in her eyes. "I love you, Mac. That is the truth. For all of my life I will love only you."

"So, show me," Mac commanded.

"What?"

"Take that coat off and show me how much you love me." Venom dripped like honey from Mac's smooth voice. Hurt and anger made his body taut.

Slowly Sadie removed her heavy overcoat. It fell from her nerveless fingers to the floor of the barn. Mac studied her face, then moved his gaze down to examine her body. Although she was fully clothed, Sadie felt exposed. Mac's mossy green eyes did not miss a detail as they ran back up her worn dress.

NAME: _____

ADDRESS: _____

_____

_____

TELEPHONE: _____

E-MAIL: _____

_____ I want to pay by credit card.

__ Visa   __ MasterCard   __ Discover

Account Number: _____

Expiration date: _____

SIGNATURE: _____

*Send this form, along with $2.00 shipping
and handling for your FREE books, to:*

Historical Romance Book Club
20 Academy Street
Norwalk, CT 06850-4032

*Or fax (must include credit card
information!) to:* 610.995.9274.
*You can also sign up on the Web
at* www.dorchesterpub.com.

Offer open to residents of the U.S. and
Canada only. Canadian residents, please
call 1.800.481.9191 for pricing information.

If under 18, a parent or guardian must sign. Terms, prices and conditions
subject to change. Subscription subject to acceptance. Dorchester
Publishing reserves the right to reject any order or cancel any subscription.

"Take your hair down," he commanded.

She didn't want to rile him—not because she was afraid that he would hurt her, but because she could see the terrible pain he was in and was afraid that denying him would cause him more. One by one, Sadie removed the pins that held her hair. When she was done, her light locks hung in loose curls halfway down her back.

Mac sneered, hating how beautiful she was to him, hating himself for wanting her.

Sadie was unsure of what he wanted. All she wanted to do was to make him happy, to somehow erase the terrible truth of Eldon's visit from their lives. She looked down at the floor, wondering how their life together could have taken such a terrible turn.

His hands were on her shoulders. Sadie sucked in her breath at his closeness. Suddenly, Mac tore the weak fabric from her shoulders. The rip sounded obscenely loud in the little barn. The horses began to whinny in their stalls.

Mac's mouth followed the path of the rent material. He kissed the tender skin that lay beneath. When both shoulders were exposed, Mac looked down at his wife. In that moment he knew that there was nothing she could do to make him quit loving her, and it made him furious. He felt like a prisoner to this overwhelming emotion, with Sadie as his captor.

Cursing himself for a thousand kinds of fool, he pushed her to the feed bags on the floor. He grabbed her hand and pressed it to his hardness. "Feel this, Sadie. Do you do this to the other man? Are you a poison in his blood, like you are in mine?"

He didn't give her time to answer, instead kissing

153

her deeply. His mouth pressed a little too hard, his hands moved over her body a little too roughly, but he didn't care.

He went wild as he felt her return his kiss. Mac realized that she was arching her narrow hips toward him, and he lost all conscious thought. Working on primitive instinct, he pushed up the skirt of her battered dress. The material bunched under her hips, allowing him greater access. Mac removed her undergarment and threw it over his shoulder. He pushed his pants down, releasing his hard shaft.

Sadie could not, would not, take her eyes off her husband. She knew that he was not in control, but that was fine with her. She wanted him, needed him, at least one more time. As he lifted his big body above hers, Sadie spread her legs, giving him full passage. She was startled by the ferocity of his entrance, but welcomed it. She met his every thrust, and when he bent down to kiss her, she took control of his tongue.

Their rhythm grew to a fevered pitch, and Sadie wrapped her legs around Mac's broad back to ride with him to the sweet heights of release. She opened herself to him, physically and emotionally, as she accepted his seed. Crying out in pleasure, they became one.

For long minutes, they attempted to catch their breath. Sadie was aware of the stickiness on her legs but was loath to get up and do anything about it. After his breathing returned to a more reasonable rate, Mac was the first to stand.

He avoided looking at her as he pulled his pants back up his long legs. Somehow, during the height of their mindless passion, he had made a decision of sorts. When he spoke he sounded tired, yet determined. "I don't know where that note came from, Sadie. I don't know who made the tracks in the snow, and I guess I don't really expect you to tell me the truth. But I do know that I'm not a man to be toyed with. Make a decision. I expect you to decide exactly what you plan on doing. If you don't want to be here, leave."

Time seemed to come to a standstill as he walked out of the barn. Sadie knew that this was the time to call him back, to tell him the whole story.

She started to call his name, but the word stuck in her throat. For a flash of a moment Sadie heard her father's voice, convincing her what a burden she was. Eldon's voice followed, bragging about the ingenious way he had escaped his life of drudgery as her husband. It was all painfully clear in Sadie's mind. If a man as repulsive as Eldon Pritchard found her repugnant, how could Mac possibly love her enough to stay by her side?

He'd told her to make up her mind, and she did. Sadie's life was bound to be lonely. Right now she had her children, but soon they would be grown and gone. What then? For the short time given her, Sadie was determined to indulge in the joy of being near Mac and Grace and the boys. She would absorb each moment into her battered spirit. Then, when the time came to leave, she would know that she'd had in her life this one special season—this winter when she first tasted bliss.

Chapter Twenty-eight

In his camp, Inkapaduta rolled to his side, gently cradling the head of his sleeping wife. With his free hand he stroked her face, marveling that she had become even more beautiful through their many years of marriage.

Like a knife in his gut, her labored breathing cut him. The rattle in Crying Star's sunken chest haunted his sleep. Inkapaduta had fought many enemies in his life. He had killed more men, Indian and white, than he could count. He had bravely dealt with any challenge that reared its head.

Only two foes had proved elusive: Henry Lott and the health of his woman. With a sense of grim fatality, Inkapaduta realized that his wife would soon die, the battle would be lost. Somehow, as he struggled through the night, he gained comfort in knowing that his life still had purpose. For as long as he drew breath,

Inkapaduta's hate for Henry Lott would sustain him. If it was the final act of his mortal being, he would avenge the horrible deeds visited upon him by the white man.

Chapter Twenty-nine

Sadie squeezed her eyes tight in an attempt to control the hot tears that threatened to escape. Her back pressed against Mac's nude chest as his warm breath kissed the top of her head.

They'd shared few conversations since that January morning in the barn. Sadie was wracked by guilt for not just telling Mac the entire story, but also paralyzed by the knowledge that she might never see him again.

She had to wonder how Mac had known about the tracks. She could clearly remember the day when Eldon reappeared from the dead, the day her own dreams died. Eldon had barely ridden out of the yard before Sadie rushed into the house to put Grace in her crib. With the intensity of a madwoman she'd run back outside, broken a low-hanging limb from a tree and wildly attempted to brush away the tracks Eldon's sorry horse had left.

Apparently, her efforts had been for naught. Mac had noticed them.

Although her heart pounded in her ears and her mind was barely able to produce a rational thought, Sadie knew that she could not let Mac know about Eldon's sudden return from the depths of Hell. Not yet. Just a little more time. And the boys . . . the effect it would all have on Aaron and Matthew was too horrible to contemplate.

How could Mac believe that she would take a lover? If she hadn't been so wrapped up in her own guilt, Sadie would have been angry that he could think so little of her.

Outwardly she was calm, but inside her gut clenched. She wondered how she was going to get through this day and every day after until Eldon showed his ugly face again. And he would. As sure as she knew that the sun would rise in the morning, Sadie knew that Eldon Pritchard was not done with her.

Only at night, long after the children found the release of sleep, did Mac and Sadie communicate. They rarely said a word, but their bodies spoke volumes. The intensity of their coupling expressed the fear and anguish that had become the hallmarks of their marriage. It mocked the optimism with which they had entered their life together. Each was convinced that it was only a transitory relationship, and each became obsessed with squeezing the life from every moment of intimacy, creating memories to carry with them.

As Sadie spooned against Mac, her body replete in their lovemaking, she felt his warm hand cup her breast, his thumb gently rub across the crest. She fought back the tears and wondered if it might have not been better to have never known Mac's love. The greatest threat from Eldon Pritchard was not the physical harm he could do her, but the happiness he could snatch away with no more than a snap of his fingers. Sadie hated him.

Even though it had been eight weeks since Eldon had shown up on her doorstep, Sadie was sure that the children were unaware of the turmoil swirling around them. Mac continued to teach the boys, but more importantly, he was still a good example for them. Sadie continued to care for the family, savoring each moment of domestic normalcy.

Even as she lay in his arms, she fought for the strength to confide in him. Why, she wondered, was she so able to share her body, but still unable to trust him with her darkest secret? Why couldn't she shake that feeling of inadequacy? When Mac told her that he loved her, why couldn't she just take him at his word?

It was like walking into quicksand. The harder she worked to get out, the more deeply she became caught. Mac's hard length pushed against her, and she turned to the man who meant the world to her, wishing that she had the courage to trust him with her secret. Sadie was tired—tired of worrying, tired of waiting for the other shoe to drop. For just a few moments she longed to leave it all behind, to completely immerse herself in Mac, to indelibly imprint her love upon his heart.

God, she prayed, as she turned and kissed her husband's neck, *help me figure a way out. But first, let me lose myself in this wonderful man.*

And she did.

Chapter Thirty

In the wee hours of the morning, as the rest of the county slept, the band of bedraggled Sioux Indian warriors approached the intimidating gates of the fort. Knee-high snows and bitter cold temperatures impeded their travel. Weak from hunger, their first concern was not for themselves, but for the women and children left at camp. With the hollow-eyed look of their women seared in their memories, and the piteous cries of their starving children ringing in their ears, the warriors considered the officers at Fort Peterson their last hope. As difficult as it was to beg food from these interlopers, it would be unbearable to watch their loved ones perish slowly and needlessly.

It was said that the spirits, in an attempt to chase away the whites by making game scarce this long winter, had become lost in the blizzards. In their confusion, the spirits had also frightened away the game that would sustain the Sioux people.

Staggering toward the front gate, their leader hoarsely requested admittance. One of the guards spat rudely over the side of the tall compound wall and told him to wait. Aware of the slight, the Sioux leader straightened his back and lifted his chin. His coarse red hair fell gracefully down his back, and his black eyes focused on the remaining guards. To a man, they all backed up, if ever so slightly.

There was something about this Indian that struck them as odd. It was more than his stature, although he was taller than those he led. It was more than the fierce expression on his pockmarked face or the oddity of his red hair. There was a resolve in his eyes that declared he would not go down without a fight, a look that indicated that even though his pride had been battered his will remained strong.

Power radiated from this leader, and for a time all the Sioux seemed to bask in it, to absorb some of that strength. Each of them stood a little taller.

It wasn't long before the first guard came back. With a sneer, he told the Indians that they would have to leave. The officer in charge had announced that the U.S. Army was not in the practice of providing handouts. It was a difficult winter, and the Army had their own men to look out for.

The braves turned as one to walk away, too proud to express disbelief. The officer's pronouncement was as good as a death sentence for their women and children.

Inkapaduta pretended not to hear the taunting jeers of the white men as he walked away. Like a shroud, he wrapped his dignity around him. In no way would he stoop to let these trespassers know how desperate his people were.

But his hate grew with each step. Even with all he had suffered at the hand of Henry Lott, Inkapaduta had never believed that his enmity could be so deep, encompass him so completely. Within the belly of the hopeless man grew the seeds of revenge.

Chapter Thirty-one

"But why now, Mac? Why can't you wait until the weather is more cooperative?" Sadie attempted to control the anxiety in her voice.

Exasperation flitted across Mac's face. He closed his eyes and took a deep breath before attempting an explanation for the third time. "Because there is absolutely no game out there, Sadie. Nothing. No rabbits, no squirrels, no deer, nothing. Our supplies are dangerously low. If it hadn't been for all the snow this winter I would have attempted this trip weeks ago. As long as Joe and Asa are going to make the trip down to Fort Dodge, I'm going with them."

"Why can't you just go to Granger's Point?"

"The winter has been tough on everyone. It's March, and Granger's Point has few supplies left. We need to head for a bigger town."

How could Sadie explain what she was experiencing? It was as if she _knew_ that Mac's leaving would change the course of their lives. "But . . ."

"No buts, Sadie. Look, we've got to get some food. You've done a great job of making do, but these kids are going to start going hungry soon. You don't want that, do you?"

Sadie shook her head miserably. She missed him already. The emotional distance that had separated them for weeks only added to the pain of actually watching him walk out the door. A sense of foreboding choked her. Sadie feared that something enormous was about to happen, something that would impact them all forever.

Mac walked to the table and mussed Matthew's hair. "You two help your mother around here while I'm gone, you hear?"

"Yes, sir," Aaron and Matthew answered.

Mac looked down with surprise at Sadie's hand on his sleeve. It had been weeks since she had spontaneously touched him outside of bed. "How long do you think you'll be?"

"At worst, a few weeks."

"Weeks!"

"I know it seems like a long time, but the roads are bound to be a mess. I'm counting on you, Sadie. If you're careful, you've got enough here to get you by for that long. I'll push like crazy to get home. I know Joe Thatcher isn't going to like leaving Elizabeth and their baby alone for long either."

"At least Elizabeth has Lydia Noble to talk to!" Sadie lamented. She couldn't believe that the whine in her voice was her own. Her time had run out. She had to tell him the truth about Eldon, had to make sure he understood why she had changed.

She was ashamed to look up into Mac's serious face.

The first thing she noticed when she finally braved a peek was how very tired he looked. "Mac, I am so sorry."

He studied her intently, knowing he loved her. God knew how much. For weeks he had attempted to close himself off to Sadie, but his heart wasn't cooperating. His greatest fear was watching her walk out of his life.

When had fear begun to control his actions? Resolutely, he grabbed her hand and pulled her to the door. His eyes never left her face as he donned his big coat. "I don't know what's going on with you, but I do know a couple of things. Damn it, Sadie, you're part of me. No matter where you go in this world I'm there with you. Can't you see that?" His eyes were twin shards of intensity. "Nobody and nothing is going to come between us."

Sadie couldn't take her eyes off of him. As he spoke, her heart soared. All this time she had been remembering the words her father, and then Eldon, had battered her with. She couldn't see how this man standing right in front of her, this wonderful man, saw something inside of her that was beautiful and worthwhile. But he did.

They heard the unmistakable sound of a wagon pulling into the yard. Mac grimaced. "I gotta go." He reminded the children to be on their best behavior as he pulled the door open.

"Wait!" Sadie cried. "You can't leave yet. I have something I should have told you a long time ago."

Mac knew that if Sadie was about to confess to infidelity, now was not the time. He could not accept that kind of information then ride away for weeks. "Not now, Sadie."

"But . . ."

"No, we'll take care of everything when I get home."

He walked out the door. "Mac!" Sadie grabbed his coat sleeve. "Please, look at me," she implored.

He turned, and Sadie realized that for the first time Mac looked vulnerable. It struck her then that she had the potential to hurt this man. To destroy him. She'd had it all along. She wanted to clear the air, men waiting or not.

Mac moved a step closer and spoke, his voice low. "What do you want from me, Sadie? What can I say to make things right between us?"

"It's all a mess, Mac. I've made a mess of everything."

Mac looked down at his wife and ached for her. "Have a little faith in me, Sadie."

"Hey, MacCallister, daylight's burning," Joe Thatcher yelled good-naturedly.

"Morning, Joe. Morning, Asa." Mac nodded out at them.

"Your wagon ready?" Joe asked.

"Yep, took care of it this morning."

Joe's brother-in-law, Asa Burtch, jumped down from the wagon bench. "I'm riding with Mac," he announced. Then, smiling at Sadie in the doorway, he added, "I've been with Joey here all winter. Frankly, I'd pay to hear the sound of someone else's voice."

"Well, good, 'cause frankly I'd pay to get away from your stench for a few hours!" Joe shot back. His words caused Asa to laugh sharply. It was clear that the two men had an easy relationship.

Asa joked, "You know Joe Thatcher *acts* like a real tough man, but in about a week he'll be bawling like a baby 'cause he misses my sister and little niece. There won't be a thing we can do to shut him up!"

Joe leveled a look of disgust at his young tormentor. "It would only be fair. There's not a thing we can do to shut you up any day of the week."

Mac laughed. "Enough, guys. Enough. If we didn't need supplies so darn bad, I wouldn't be leaving my wife either."

Sadie's heart swelled. She walked out into the yard. It was the first lighthearted comment she had heard from Mac in weeks. Their easy banter was one of the things she missed most. In a few steps she was in Mac's arms, her face pressed against his thick coat. "I'm going to miss you more than you know," she said simply.

With one big finger Mac tilted her chin up toward him. He had only one word for her. "Faith."

"Okay, you two. Shouldn't you have taken care of all this last night?" Asa called.

"Shut up, Asa," Mac and Joe answered in unison.

It was bitterly cold, but Mac's tender smile warmed Sadie to the bone. "Get in the cabin; it's freezing out here." When she hesitated, he added, "I'll see you soon. I promise."

Sadie luxuriated in one last look at him before nodding a quick goodbye to both Joe and Asa. She rushed back through the cabin door, shut it behind her, and leaned her body against its solid frame. She wondered if she had made the right decision. What had Mac meant by "faith"? Was faith going to be enough to save their family, to erase the danger of Eldon Pritchard?

Chapter Thirty-two

Sadie was stirred from her daydreaming by a loud, persistent banging. It sounded as though it was coming from the direction of the barn. Sadie hoped so. She would hate to lose part of the cabin roof on a night like this. With a tired sigh, she rose from the rocking chair, pulled her coat off the peg next to the door and slipped it on.

She took a quick look at the children, made sure that they still slept soundly, then removed the bar that rested across the door. The force of the wind practically knocked her over as the door flew in against her body. The heavy door hit her foot, sending a shaft of pain up her right leg.

A need to cry overwhelmed Sadie. She missed Mac, missed his strength and his protection. She did not want to go out into the night alone. What she wanted to do was push the door shut, crawl into bed and weep until Mac returned. What she forced herself to do was check the children one more time, limp out of the cabin and pull the door tightly closed behind her.

For a moment the wind subsided. When Sadie was relatively sure that the door was going to stay closed she looked around the dark yard for the source of the sound. She shuddered at the moonless night, glad that she was so familiar with the property. Only able to see a foot or two ahead of herself, she carefully made her way around the side of the house.

The wind picked up again. The skirt of her nightdress tangled wildly around her ankles. Her hair, which she had taken down hours earlier, whipped at Sadie's face, stinging her skin. Undeterred, she continued to seek the source of the sound. There it was again . . . *thump, thump, thump*. Following the noise, Sadie walked toward the barn.

The heavy door swung back and forth like an American flag. It hit the side of the building with each swing. Relief flooded her. True, she wasn't usually afraid of the dark, but something about this night was giving her the willies.

One of the boys had probably forgotten to latch the barn door after exiting it earlier. Sadie took hold of the door and slowly began to push it back into place. The wind fought her for control. She wanted to push her long hair out of her eyes but couldn't spare the hand.

So intent was she on struggling with the big door, it took a moment for Sadie to realize that she was being held against a human chest. As soon as her brain registered the fact, she opened her mouth to release a terrified scream. A hand clapped over her mouth and a threatening voice whispered in her ear. She recognized that voice.

Eldon pulled her into the dark interior of the barn and with some effort, drew the door closed behind him. Sadie was livid. Had he set the entire thing up, or was the barn door a lucky coincidence?

"Don't move," Eldon commanded. Out of habit Sadie obeyed. She wouldn't put it past him to have a loaded weapon.

Two lanterns were lit in quick succession, sending light to bounce off the walls in a crazy pattern. The wind managed to eke its way into the drafty barn, giving supernatural life to the flames.

"What are you doing here, Eldon?"

"Is that any way for a woman to greet her husband?"

Sadie's response was tight. "I am not your wife."

"I'm afraid you're a mite confused, Sadie girl. I distinctly remember winning you off your pa in a card game years ago. Trouble is, I can't decide whether I got the best end of that deal."

"What do you want?"

The look in Eldon's eyes was chilling. "You, darlin'. All I ever wanted was you. From the first time I laid my eyes on your sweet little body, I've wanted you."

Sadie stood, unwavering. She would not let him see the fear or revulsion she felt. He would not see her cower.

Eldon moved closer, touching her only with his words. "It's too bad those brats came along, Sadie girl. Since we've been apart I've had a lot of time to think. I've been thinking about how happy we were before they were born. Remember, Sadie?"

"I remember thinking that you were the most despicable, disgusting creature ever sent to crawl the earth." Sadie didn't know where the courage came from, but she knew that she'd had enough. This thing with Eldon had to come to a head. She couldn't live with him hovering over her shoulder for the rest of her life.

"Ah, Sadie, you don't mean that," Eldon crooned as he ran a dirty hand up her arm.

Sadie pulled away as though burned by fire. "I *do* mean that, Eldon Pritchard. The only good thing you've ever done in your entire sorry life was to give me those boys. How dare you say that our life would have been better without them!"

Eldon didn't hit her. In fact, he seemed pleased by her show of spirit. "You're even prettier when you're all riled up, Sadie girl." Sadie stood her ground as he moved closer. "I'll bet that new man of yours has taught you some fancy tricks, hasn't he?"

She tried not to gag at the putrid smell of Eldon's breath, at the nauseating odor of his unwashed body. Eldon waited for what to him must have seemed an eternity, then wrapped his wiry arms around her. Burying his head in her neck, he pressed sloppy kisses there.

Sadie struggled, but she was held by his lustful strength. She tried not to call out as he fell with her to the hard ground. Above all, she could not wake the children. They could not know that their father was alive.

She had to think, to be smarter than Eldon. Sadie forced her body to relax, to lie still. "Is that a new horse, Eldon?" she asked, fighting to keep her voice casual.

Surprised, he followed her gaze to the horse he had taken the liberty of stabling in a stall. The animal was a beauty: reddish brown with a black mane and tail.

"Yep. He's mine," Eldon answered proudly. "I got all

kinds of new gear, Sadie. You should see all the things I've bought."

This was a ridiculous conversation to be having. Eldon's weight still rested on her, his smell still permeated the close confines of the barn. But Sadie needed to buy time, and if appealing to his vanity did the trick, so be it. He prattled on about all his new belongings while Sadie pushed herself to think of an escape.

Even as her mind spun with possibilities, Eldon lifted his weight from her and stood. He walked to his horse, lifted the flap on the saddlebag, and extracted a gun. Sadie was terrified until it occurred to her that he was simply bragging about a new possession.

"Yep, it's called a Colt .45, or sometimes, a Peacemaker. A real pretty baby, isn't it?" Eldon stroked the shiny weapon. "Got it off a man in Granger's Point. He was just traveling through, but seemed willing to part with this beauty for the right price."

Sadie's plan suddenly fell into place. "It's really nice, Eldon," she said, standing slowly. Then, swallowing her bile, she asked, "But can you come back here? I kinda liked the feel of your hard body pressed to mine."

Eldon grinned, pushed the weapon back into the saddlebag, and joined her in the center of the barn. "Guess that man of yours can't do for you what old Eldon could do, huh?"

Shivers of revulsion ran down her spine, but Sadie forced herself to smile timidly. "No, Eldon. He's just so big and raw. You know I've always preferred my man to be a little more polished."

Eldon's skinny chest puffed out as he seemed to readily believe her lies. "See, Sadie? See what I mean about us getting on real good? When I heard tell that your new man was leaving town with those other fellas, I just knew that I ought to give you one more chance."

Sadie mentally commended herself on her restraint. Out of curiosity, she asked, "How did you know that they were leaving?"

"Oh, that was easy. That Burtch man came into the general store in Granger's Point while I was there a week or so ago. I was standing behind some dry goods so that he couldn't see me. He was asking for flour and such. When the owner told him how low they were on supplies, the Burtch fellow said it was okay, 'cause him and his brother-in-law and MacCallister was thinking of heading down to Fort Dodge this week.

"It was easy from there. I snuck on the property tonight, just like I did when I tied that bag to the tree. I seen that MacCallister's wagon and horse were gone, so I knew I'd have you to myself."

"Oh, Eldon, you are so clever. I'd forgotten that about you." Privately, Sadie thought how lucky she was that Eldon was such a thickheaded dolt. What man in his right mind would fall for her act?

As it was, he never even raised an eyebrow. The thought of her children sleeping peacefully in the cabin gave Sadie the courage to do what she must. "You've changed, Eldon," she observed.

"I have?" His big Adam's apple bobbed as he moved closer.

"Yes. You're much more sophisticated than you were when . . . well, before you left."

"Well, I have been living in the hotel right in

Granger's Point. When we were in Saint Louie we were way out in the woods. Maybe that's changed me."

"I don't know," Sadie mused. "It seems like more than that. I mean, you just seem so much more in control." She sidled close to him, chest to chest, and forced herself to touch his bony arms. "I've thought a lot lately, too, Eldon. I know that we had a rough marriage sometimes, but the fact of the matter is, you were my first . . . you know. Lover. And a woman just never forgets the man who teaches her everything."

"I knew you'd see it my way!" Eldon crowed.

As though struck by a sudden inspiration, Sadie cried, "Let's go! Right now, Eldon. Let's just saddle my horse and ride out of here."

For the first time Eldon looked doubtful. "What about the brats?" he asked.

"What about them?" Sadie shrugged. "Mac should be home in a day or two. Aaron can take care of things around here for that long. I'll write a quick note and tell them I'm leaving."

"You'd leave your boys with this MacCallister character?"

It was essential that Eldon believe her. "Sure, Eldon. They like him. Don't know why, but they do. And Mac likes kids. It'd be perfect. I could go with you and not have to ever worry about Aaron and Matthew."

"But . . ." Eldon suddenly seemed hesitant. This was too easy, even to his simple mind.

Sadie closed her eyes and forced her hand to Eldon's crotch. Laying it softly there, she murmured, "I could be good, Eldon. Real good."

"Okay. You go write the note and I'll saddle your horse. You learned to ride horseback?" he asked.

"Yes, Mac taught us all," Sadie lied. Figuring out how to stay on the horse was the least of her problems at the moment.

The first thing that she noticed as she left the barn was that the wind had settled some. She quickly darted into the house, changed from her nightdress into a sturdy dress, kissed each of the children, and packed a small bag. She reached under the bed, pulled out a small box, opened it, and found it empty. She hurried to the fireplace and ran her hand over the mantel. Nothing!

Sadie had to hurry. She didn't want to give Eldon time to saddle the horse then search for her. She didn't want him anywhere near her children. Aaron rolled over on his pallet, a little snore escaping his throat. She had to hurry.

Eldon was just leading the horses out of the barn as she left the cabin. "There you are," he called. "For a minute there I was afraid that you changed your mind."

"Don't be silly." Sadie laughed nervously. "I'm ready anytime you are."

She walked to the dappled horse that Eldon had saddled for her and slung her small pack over its neck. The startled animal nervously danced away. By sheer will Sadie pulled the horse back, speaking gently to soothe it. She'd seen Mac do that. And like she'd seen Mac do a hundred times, Sadie placed her foot in the stirrup and attempted to swing her free leg over. Her skirt became tangled around her leg, nearly causing her to lose her balance. Feeling lucky that she hadn't fallen on her face, Sadie stood beside the horse and tried again.

"Ain't it gonna be kinda hard to ride all the way to town in that skirt?"

Darn. She hadn't considered that. "No," Sadie answered smoothly. "I ride in skirts all the time. Mac doesn't believe in a woman wearing anything other than a skirt."

"Well, I know one thing I'd rather have my woman wearing than a darned old skirt. . . . Nothin' at all."

Eldon's quiet laughter made Sadie want to throw up. The man was truly vile. This time, luck was with her as she attempted to mount the horse. With the ease of a pro she landed smoothly on the saddle. Now, if she could just hold on while the animal began to move.

Eldon was atop his own mount. "C'mon, I'll lead the way."

Sadie held on for dear life. She had never much liked horses, and this one was scarier than she would like to admit. It felt like she was sitting twenty feet in the air. It didn't take long to figure out that the horse responded to tiny tugs on the reins, which gave her some sense of relief.

Her determination grew as she watched Eldon's back bob up and down. She could worry about Eldon Pritchard for the rest of her life, or she could take care of him tonight. Sadie knew as sure as she breathed that Eldon would haunt her forever if she didn't take action. She meant to give him a scare that he would never forget—but first she had to get far enough away from the cabin to protect the children.

They had ridden for about an hour when Sadie let out a cry. The clouds that had gathered so quickly earlier had blown away, leaving a clear sky and bright moon.

"What is it?" Eldon asked, clearly irritated at being detained.

"I don't know. I think my horse just slipped in the snow. And I'm cold, Eldon. Do you think we could rest for just a moment? Please?"

Eldon looked at her, long and hard. He finally acquiesced. After all, tonight was going better than he dared believe.

"Could you help me down? I'm so tired."

Eldon dismounted and helped Sadie do the same. "About how much farther?" She asked.

"To Granger's Point?"

Sadie seriously wondered how the man got through the day. Where did he think she was asking about? "Yes." She nodded.

"I don't know. Another hour in this slush, I guess."

Sadie casually walked to Eldon's horse. "What is this?" she asked, running her hand over the saddlebag.

"A saddlebag, Sadie girl. You know that."

"This bag looks kind of special. Not like the ones I've seen."

"I gotta piss," Eldon announced, bored with the conversation. "You stay right here."

He turned, walked two feet, and noisily went about his business. When he turned back to Sadie, his eyes widened, then narrowed. Sadie thought that he looked a bit like a deranged frog. She pointed his Colt .45 right at his skinny chest, surprised by the weight of the weapon on her arms.

"Don't move an inch, Eldon. I would like nothing better than to end your miserable life."

"What the hell are you doing with that thing?"

"What does it look like? I'm negotiating. You know what negotiating is, don't you, Eldon? It's when one person makes a demand and the other person gets something in return. Now, my deal is this: You stay away from me, you stay away from Mac and my children, and I'll spare your worthless life."

"But . . ." Eldon looked confused. Everything had been going so well.

"But, nothing. You get on your horse and ride to Granger's Point. As soon as you get there you get your things together and ride out of town. I don't care where you go, as long as it's far from here." Sadie trembled as years of abuse fogged her thoughts. Her voice was cold and deadly serious. "If I ever see your face again, I will kill you. And don't doubt me, Eldon. If you come within a thousand miles of my children I will feed your brains to the buzzards.

"There won't be a moment of my life when I let my guard down," she continued. "I'm going to expect to see you around every corner, and if I do, I'll be ready for you. Now, get on your horse."

Eldon swallowed hard, then swallowed again before mounting his horse. "My gun . . ." he began.

"Don't be a fool, Eldon. It's mine now. A little gift for all the years of hell I put up with. Now, go!" Sadie stood on the wet ground, looking up at the man she had hated for so many years.

Eldon was angry, but he eyed her warily. Then, without warning, he charged. His big horse ran straight for her—Sadie knew with every intention of killing her. She saw it in his muddy eyes. She stepped to her left, closed her eyes and squeezed the Colt's trigger. Her arms were practically torn from their sockets, but she squeezed it again.

When she dared open her eyes, Eldon was slumped over his horse. Blood trickled from his head and poured from his upper chest. His horse had stopped dead in its tracks, nervously waiting for some sign from its master.

Acting on pure instinct, Sadie grabbed the loose reins of Eldon's horse and pulled the animal in the general direction of Granger's Point. Yelling loudly, she smacked the horse on the rump and watched the startled beast ride away, carrying Eldon with it.

Sadie would later wonder how she managed to ride her own horse back home. Her mind flitted wildly during the entire trip. She wondered where the bullets had entered Eldon, and she wondered what the folks of Granger's Point would say when his horse returned with him dead on its saddle. Or would Eldon just fall off the animal, left to rot on the frozen prairie?

She wasn't sorry. It was kill or be killed. Sadie rode into her yard and returned the tired mount to the stable. The entire time she spent lighting the lanterns in the barn, relieving the horse of its saddle and brushing the poor animal down, Sadie reminded herself that she had done the right thing. It was not only for herself that she had acted, but also for her family. For Mac, and their life.

That thought made her feel a little better as she finally extinguished the lamps, left the barn and walked down the hill to the big lake. By moonlight she looked for the small hole in the ice the boys used for fishing. A quick stomp of her heel was enough to break the thin layer that covered the fishing hole. Sadie took one last look at the weapon that lay so heavily in her hand. Then she threw the Colt .45 with all her might into the deep waters of Lake Okoboji.

Peacemaker, indeed.

Chapter Thirty-three

Stoically, Inkapaduta watched as the scaffold was erected. His belly burned and eyes smarted from unshed tears. His woman was gone. No amount of anticipating her death could have prepared him for the terrible reality. Already he missed her sweet smiles, her gentle soothing. No one had ever truly known or cared for him as his wife had.

Feeling old, the proud warrior entered the teepee they had shared. Her life was gone. All that had given him joy, all that had stilled his heart and calmed his anger, had died. It would have shocked Inkapaduta to know that the keening wail he heard came from his own parched throat.

The big man fell to his knees, brought down by his own breaking heart. Shock numbed him, but not enough. Not nearly enough.

The winter had brought with it wicked snows, thick and blinding blizzards that blanketed their little camp for months. All food had disappeared. Children cried in hunger. It humiliated Inkapaduta that he failed to provide for his family, his people. His wife's stomach had rested upon her spine as she'd taken her last labored breath and her eyes had been darkly shadowed. They were *all* dying a slow, undignified death.

Warriors like Screeching Owl insisted that there was no one to blame for the difficult winter, no one to blame for the lack of game. He counseled patience. "Warm weather will bring us game and a renewed spirit. You will see, my friend," he had promised.

But promises weren't enough. Sorrow choked Inkapaduta. For years he had controlled his desire for retribution, out of respect for his woman. Now she was gone and his soul was gone with her.

Chapter Thirty-four

Sadie could almost understand now why people turned to drink. She had always considered the use of alcohol to be a weakling's way out, but Lord, how she wished she had some whiskey. Something to help with the terrible anxiety that threatened to rip her stomach apart. She would give anything to feel numb for a little while.

It had been two days since Eldon surprised her in the barn, two days since she'd put two bullets into his miserable hide. What had become of him? Had he been found and buried in an unmarked grave? Or had he survived and was he, even now, plotting his revenge?

For a brief time that afternoon Sadie was able to escape the torture of wondering. The sun had warmed the earth sufficiently to melt most of the snow. Sadie walked with the children down to the shore where they planned to share their noonday meal. She knew that she could not let the business with Eldon touch her children. She would do whatever it took to protect them.

At mealtime, Sadie spread a tarpaulin over the slightly slushy ground. After gathering the children together on the cover, she served them rehydrated apples, fresh bread and a jar of peaches Frances Gardner had given them for Christmas. It was simple but filling fare.

Sadie thought that she could sit at the water's edge forever. It was one of the few places in the world where she found absolute peace. As she watched fresh water fight for dominance over melting slabs of ice, she tried to wipe all unpleasant thoughts from her mind.

She was not going to allow herself to think about Eldon or the terror in the barn, or all the blood pouring from his fresh wounds. . . .

"Ma, look!" Aaron was smiling down at Grace, who had evidently had enough of the fresh air. The baby was collapsed on the tarp, sound asleep. Her little pink mouth was slack, and she released a gentle snore with each breath. Her fine blond hair stuck out where her hat had slipped up on her head.

Sadie stroked the babe's pink cheek. "She's tuckered."

"She sure sleeps a lot," Matthew observed.

"She's a baby, Matthew. You slept a lot when you were her age too."

"It seems boring, doesn't it, Aaron?"

Aaron rolled his eyes. "She's just resting up so that she can outrun you when she gets older."

Matthew was outraged. "She's a girl! She'll never be able to run faster than me!"

"Right, Matt. If we had a grandma, I'd bet *she* could run faster than you."

The glove had been thrown, the challenge presented. Matthew could not back down. "C'mon, let's race. First one around the tree with our names carved in it is the winner!"

Matthew had played right into Aaron's hand. Without giving his younger brother time to react, Aaron jumped from his spot and yelled, "Go!"

Sadie wasn't sure how Matthew could run with all the screaming he was doing. Sure enough, Aaron hit the tree first and returned to the blanket, winded, but pleased with himself. Matthew felt that he had been gravely mistreated and it showed on his red face. "That wasn't fair, Aaron. You didn't give me a chance!"

Aaron was totally unconcerned with his younger brother's assessment. "I won, fair and square. Just admit it, Matt."

Sadie watched in mute surprise as, for the first time in their lives, Matthew marched over to his older brother and hit him in the back of the head. "Matthew David" she admonished, still not believing her eyes. "What in the world possessed you to hit him? It was just a race."

The red in Matthew's face and hair were a remarkable match. Tears welled up in his green eyes as he faced his mother. "I'm mad enough to swallow a horned toad backwards. Madder than a peeled rattler. I'm madder . . ."

"I get the idea, Matthew. But where did you get the notion that hitting Aaron would solve anything? You could have given me the opportunity to talk to him about teasing you. Better yet, you could have told him how it makes you feel to be teased. But we never, ever, turn on someone in our own family in anger."

"Pa hit you all the time. Aaron and me saw him. Sometimes he even hit us."

Sadie's head dropped. The curse of Eldon Pritchard would not die. What he had done to his children was unforgivable. "Were you proud of your pa when he hit us, Matthew? Did you think that he had a good way of dealing with his anger?"

Matthew's head dropped. "No, ma'am. I don't want to be like Pa. I mean, I know he was our kin and all, but I'd rather be like Mac any day."

Sadie patted the spot next to her and waited for Matthew to sit. She put her arm around her son and pulled him close. "Your father had a pretty rough life. Maybe he just turned out like his own father, I don't know. But Matthew, you are like Mac. You've got a good heart, just like Mac does. You just have to learn to make decisions based upon what you know is right and wrong, not whatever will make you feel better for the moment."

Matthew turned his face up to his mother and smiled timidly. "Okay, Ma. Do I gotta tell Aaron I'm sorry?" At Sadie's nod, he groaned, "I thought so."

He looked at Aaron and tried very hard to do the right thing. "I'm sorry you cheated on that race, Aaron. I'm sorry that I got so mad, and I'm sorry that I called you that really bad name that you and Ma didn't hear 'cause I was running too fast."

Sadie didn't have the heart to make him rephrase his apology. It was enough that he had actually offered one. Scowling at her oldest son, she scolded, "Aaron, you know better than to tease Matthew. I want you to stop thinking of ways to frustrate him."

Aaron blessed her with his most guileless expression. "What am I gonna do with all my time?" Laughing at the look on his mother's face, he held his hand out to his brother. "C'mon, runt, let's go get our fishing poles. I'll bet we can catch some supper."

Long after dark, as the children slept peacefully, Sadie contemplated a terrible question. Had she done it for them? Had she shot Eldon Pritchard to ensure their safety? Or had she followed him halfway to Granger's Point knowing that she was going to shoot him? Had she wanted him to force her hand?

As Sadie stood alone in the dark of the cabin, she could admit to herself that she'd wanted to put a bullet directly into his evil heart. Why else had she searched the cabin for Mac's gun? She'd known as they rode off the property that she was going to do her best to end Eldon's life that night. Eldon charging his horse at her had only given her the excuse.

Sadie paced the cabin, longing for exhaustion and the escape of slumber. As she walked past the shelves that held their diminishing food supply, Sadie noticed something shiny among the goods. Mac's gun.

She picked the gun up, wondering how it came to be on the shelf. Aaron's voice drifted from his pallet on the floor. "I put it there, Ma. I'm sorry."

Sadie moved to her son's side and knelt next to him. "Why, Aaron?"

Her boy blinked, then looked away. Sadie gently turned his face toward her. "Can you tell me?" she asked.

"I've been having bad dreams, dreams about Pa. I keep dreaming that he's not dead." Tears filled Aaron's blue eyes. "I hated him, Ma. I know that's not right, but he was always bad to us and I hated him!"

Aaron swallowed hard and attempted to finish his thoughts. "A few weeks ago, while everyone was sleeping, I thought I saw him looking in the window. I was so scared, Ma! It looked just like him. I covered my eyes, and when I looked again he was gone. It was just a bad dream."

The boy shook his head. "The other night when it was windy and you went outside—"

"You were awake?" Sadie interrupted. "Aaron, I just went out to close the barn door."

"Yeah, I know. But you were gone a long time, so I got the gun out from under your bed and kept it with me. I wanted to have it just in case."

Sadie carefully asked the next question. "Were you awake when I came back in?"

"No. I was real tired. I must have fallen back to sleep."

Her shoulders relaxed. "And you slept with the gun all night? Aaron, do you know how dangerous that is?"

"I'm sorry, Ma. I knew you would be mad. I haven't had the time to put it back in the box, so I just put it on the shelf. I didn't know what else to do."

Sadie wanted to shake him and kiss him all at once. "Don't you ever pick that gun up without my permission—do you hear me, Aaron?"

"Yes, ma'am."

She stroked her son's blond hair. The poor child had been terrified by the thought of seeing his own father. Sadie knew that he probably *had* seen Eldon. Eldon must have peeked in the window the night he'd left the note and burlap bag on the branch. The thought sent chills up her spine. "You know what? I don't blame you for hating your father. He was very bad to us. But he's gone, Aaron. He's dead and can never hurt us again. Okay?"

Aaron nodded tiredly. "Okay. I'm sorry about the gun, Ma. I promise I won't do it again."

"And I'm sorry about the bad dreams. You go to sleep, son. I'll watch over you."

Sadie watched her oldest child nod off to sleep and hoped to the depths of her soul that Eldon *was* dead.

Chapter Thirty-five

"Ma, it really hurts!"

Sadie turned a worried gaze to Aaron, who had been complaining of a toothache all morning. The fact that Aaron complained at all was evidence of how painful the tooth must be. "Ma," he cried again.

Sadie wrapped a scrap of fabric around several small pieces of ice, and moved to her son's side. Placing the ice on his swollen cheek, she tried to comfort him. "Mrs. Gardner once told me about a remedy she used when Abbie had a toothache. I'll bet she'd be happy to share it with us. Do you think you'll be okay here without me for a little while?"

Aaron nodded his head tearfully. "I'll take care of Grace, Ma," Matthew offered, his eyes full of worry for his big brother. "I'll even take care of Aaron."

Sadie smiled at her little boy. He would be nine years old tomorrow, but was trying hard to act like a man. "Thank you, Matt. I won't be gone long. If you're very quiet, Grace may even sleep until I return."

Dana George

She kissed both boys on the forehead, savoring the feel of their smooth skin beneath her lips. How she loved these children of hers. Sadie would do anything for them, and that included going out in the snow for a toothache remedy.

As she slipped her coat on, Sadie felt oddly reluctant to leave. Her anxiety was ridiculous, she told herself. She could get to the Gardners' and back in less than an hour. After taking a deep breath, she smiled at her children, said goodbye, and opened the door.

The sky threatened. Rain or snow, Sadie couldn't tell, and the moody gray clouds gave no clue. It had warmed enough to begin melting the long icicles that hung from tree branches, sending tiny shards of crystal dropping to the soggy earth.

She moved quickly to the barn, then hitched a horse to the wagon she and the boys had been stranded in seven short months earlier. She didn't think that she could deal with another horseback ride; otherwise she would have left the bulky contraption at home.

Sadie drove the old wagon out of the wide barn door, and she smiled at Matthew's face pressed to the cabin window. With the frost that remained on the windowpane, it was difficult to clearly make out his features. Matthew wiped the window the best he could, smiled brightly and waved. Sadie returned his wave, fighting the urge to simply unhitch the horse and return to the warmth of the cabin.

By the time she had traveled halfway to the Gardners' place, Sadie had convinced herself that her earlier fears were due to her recent experience with Eldon. She wondered if the day would come when she no longer worried about her dead husband.

Finally, the Gardner cabin came into view. Frances was returning to the house from the barn when Sadie drove up.

Clutching Frances's hand was her four-year-old grandson, Albert. Sadie couldn't help but smile at little Albert's resemblance to his father.

"Hello there!" Frances called.

"Hello, Frances. I come seeking your expertise."

"Well, I can see this is going to be a short conversation," the woman responded with a grin.

Sadie accepted Frances's assistance as she stepped down from the wagon. "You two been out playing in the snow?" she asked.

"Heavens, no! Little Albert here had a bee in his bonnet today, and I thought I'd take him out to the barn to run off a little stink. You darn near drove the whole family crazy, didn't you, Albert?"

"Yep!" the boy answered proudly.

"He reminds me of Matthew," Sadie observed.

Frances laughed. "Oh dear, that gives us something to look forward to!"

"It's clear that you know my boy."

Two things struck Sadie as they walked into the neat little cabin. The first was how many people occupied the small structure. In addition to Rowland and Frances were three of the pair's four children, their son-in-law, two grandchildren, *and* a guest visiting from Waterloo.

"Don't take your coat off just yet," Frances whispered before introducing Sadie to their visitor, Robert Clark.

Her second observation was the absolute warmth with which she was welcomed. She wondered what they would think of her if they knew that she had shot a man two nights earlier, that she had pumped two bullets into his sorry body. Forcing the thought from her mind, she smiled at those who welcomed her. She would worry about the Gardners' reaction when and if the truth ever came out.

Frances encouraged Rowland Jr. to play with little Albert, then threw a sympathetic look in Sadie's direction. "C'mon, she said as she grabbed Sadie's arm. "I forgot to show you the bed Rowland is building for me. It's back in the barn."

Cold air filled Sadie's lungs the moment they left the snug little cabin. The morning sunlight caressed her face.

"It's a little busy in there, isn't it?" Frances said as they walked toward the barn. "I find myself coming up with the most imaginative excuses to be by myself."

"You have a wonderful family, Frances—a family most people can only dream of."

"Oh, I know that. Believe me, I appreciate every moment with my brood. In fact, you may think I'm crazy, but as crowded as we are in there, I actually miss Eliza."

"She's in Minnesota?"

Frances nodded. "Visiting friends in Springfield. The move here was really tough on her. The solitude is a bit daunting for a sixteen-year-old girl."

"Solitude? In your home?" Sadie laughed.

"Well, you got me there. Eliza actually never has a moment to herself. But she does miss the company of other people her age." The light in Frances's face dimmed and her brow furrowed. "It seemed especially important to Eliza to visit this winter. Sadie, it was so hard for me to say goodbye to her."

Sadie smiled. "Of course it was. You're her mother. I once heard a woman say that having a child is like allowing your heart to walk outside of your body."

Frances looked into Sadie's earnest face. "You're right. Eliza is sixteen. It won't be long until she's a wife and mother herself. I jealously wanted to guard every moment with my daughter. I was lucky that Mary and Harvey wanted to settle here near us, but I doubt that I'll be so lucky with Eliza. She likes the excitement of a big city." Frances touched the side of Sadie's head. "You are one smart girl, Sadie MacCallister."

Sadie wanted to harrumph. How smart could she be? She had believed that her louse of a husband had fallen to his death. She had foolishly fallen in love with another man, knowing full well that fate would exact a steep price.

Determined to keep her problems to herself, Sadie encouraged Frances to show her the bed Rowland was making. Frances led her to the rear of the small barn and stopped in front of a work area the man had fashioned. Even in the filtered light of the barn, it was clear to see that Rowland did wonderful work. Gorgeous oak had been expertly crafted to form the main frame of the bed, and intricate carving accented the headboard. "It's breathtaking!" Sadie enthused. "Really, Frances, Rowland does beautiful work. He could go into business and make a fortune."

"Don't you dare tell him that. I want him to finish mine before he even starts thinking about working for someone else!"

Sadie wondered how in the world the Gardners were going to fit that huge bed into their little cabin. Curiosity must have shown on her face because Frances laughed before answering her unasked question. "It's a mite big for our place. But in the spring Rowland will start on a new house for us, and Harvey and Mary can have this one. He's promised to build us a real bedroom."

Realizing how long she had already been away from her children, Sadie placed her hand on Frances's arm. "Goodness, Frances—I nearly forgot! Aaron has a terrible toothache. Do you suppose you could share your remedy?"

"Absolutely. It'll only take me a minute to get it together."

The two women walked out of the barn, discussing the inconvenience of being so far away from a doctor. Sadie slowed as she saw a group of fierce-looking Indians nearing the cabin from the north.

"Keep walking," Frances directed, her voice taut. "They sometimes show up. I let Rowland deal with them."

"They visit you?"

"They're probably just hungry. They'll get what they need and leave."

"But aren't you low on supplies?" Sadie asked. She wondered what the Indians would do if the Gardners refused to give them what they wanted.

Rowland smiled at Frances as his wife walked through the door, but his expression immediately sobered at the look on her face. "What is it?" he asked.

"We've got company. Sioux." Frances's words were spare, her back stiff. "They look hungry."

Sweat broke out on Sadie's upper lip as she watched the braves file into the tiny Gardner cabin. Some carried guns, others knives. Uninvited, the warriors began to fill up the small room. Sadie's eyes widened at the fearsome sight the Indians presented. Some of the younger braves were covered in a sticky substance. It took long moments for Sadie to recognize the substance as blood. Her eyes darted to Frances, wondering if the older woman had noticed. Frances met her gaze and shook her head imperceptibly, as if to remind Sadie to keep calm.

Sadie fought to control a bubbling hysteria. She turned her attention to the apparent leader of the group. Well over six feet, he towered over the other men. His skin was weathered and tough, like an old deer hide. His red hair added to his dramatic appearance. The old man squinted as he looked around the cabin, as though he could barely see. Sadie's breath stopped as his eyes settled on her, rested there for a moment, then moved on.

Sadie felt a hand on her arm, and looked over her shoulder to see Mary Luce gently tugging her away from the center of the room. Along with Mary, Sadie stood against the wall, watching the proceedings with a sense of dread. She just wanted to be home. Sadie desperately needed to put her arms around her children.

"It will be fine, Sadie," Mary whispered. "They come by from time to time. There's never any harm done."

"Why are they covered in blood?" Sadie sought to keep the panic out of her voice.

"Maybe they've been hunting," Mary said. "Don't try to read anything into it, Sadie. They'll leave soon."

Baby Amanda began to whimper in her bassinet. Mary hurried to her daughter's side but was stopped by the beefy hand of the old Indian leader. The big man walked to the crib himself, lifted the crying child out and turned to his companions. For long minutes he spoke, his passionate words commanding the attention of every soul in the room. Although the settlers did not understand his language, they were mesmerized by his fervor. A shaft of fear shot through Sadie.

When he was done speaking, the leader roughly placed the baby back in her bed. He did nothing to impede Mary, who ran to pick Amanda up.

The Indians demanded to be fed. Sadie stood stock-still. Her heart pounded dreadfully in her chest. Her eyes sought Rowland, who was busy showing one of the braves the workings of the mantel clock. It was clear from Rowland's posture that he was attempting to keep things relaxed. If he was anxious, he was certainly hiding it well. Harvey Luce caught Sadie's attention. His tremulous smile was meant to encourage her, but somehow only added to her anxiety. Sadie quickly moved to assist Frances in meal preparation.

Food was as scarce in the Gardner household as it was at the MacCallisters'. Frances and Sadie did what they could to provide a meal for the intruders. The best they could offer was dry biscuits and beans. Hoping that would be sufficient, they served the Indians. Sadie tried not to stare at the splattered blood dried on the cheek of one young brave. He seemed oblivious to the impact his frightening appearance was having on his hosts.

The leader appeared disgusted by the fare. He stalked to the small cabinets near the fireplace and rifled through the scant reserves stored there. Angrily, he marched back to the table; then, after a word to his companions, tore into the food provided.

Frances and Sadie retired to the far side of the cabin, standing near Frances's children. Despite her determination to be strong, Sadie's eyes teared. "I need to get home, Frances!" Her voice was a hoarse whisper.

"And you will," Frances assured her. "Just as soon as they're gone."

For two terrifying hours the Indians sullenly invaded the Gardner homestead. They barely spared a glance at the adults, but seemed very interested in the children. Mary kept Amanda clutched to her breast, and Sadie held a subdued Albert on her lap. Abbie held tightly to six-year-old Rowland Jr.'s hand.

Abruptly, the Indians left the cabin. Before leaving the property, they detoured to the small penned area where Rowland kept his few head of cattle. With loud whoops they drove the valuable cattle down the beach. As Rowland began to protest, Harvey Luce's arm stayed him. "No, Rowland. A few cows aren't worth dying for."

Still in eyesight of the Gardner cabin, the Sioux began to shoot the bawling animals. Curiously, the hungry braves left the fallen cattle where they lay. "I'll be damned," Rowland muttered.

"They're gone. That's all that matters," Frances said, her voice shaking.

"Something's up." Rowland looked his wife in the eyes, wanting her to understand the severity of the situation without alarming the children. "They'll be back. You can bet they aren't going to leave perfectly good meat to rot on the shore. They're toying with us, Frances."

Sadie was amazed by the control in Frances's face and by the depth of her own alarm. "I've got to get home. Now."

"I'll go with you, Sadie," Harvey Luce offered.

Rowland looked at his son-in-law. "Get the kids and bring 'em back here, Harvey."

Now that the gravity of the situation had been spelled out, Sadie felt numb with fear. She felt like she was in the middle of a bad dream. Nothing was worse than being away from her children when they needed her.

Sadie realized that Harvey was trying to comfort her. She caught only the end of his sentence, "—went south, so we shouldn't run into them on the way."

Unable to do more than nod at the Gardners as she left, Sadie was grateful for Harvey's presence on her wagon. She looked at his solemn profile, saw the worried expression that flitted across his plain face, and drew comfort from the fact that he was with her. Harvey Luce was the sturdy type that it took to settle on these dangerous frontiers.

"They took the cattle, but none of the horses. Why?" Sadie wondered aloud.

"There's no figuring the Indians today," Harvey answered. "Nothing about the way they're behaving feels right."

With each clip of the horse's hooves, with each turn of the wheels, Sadie's heart rose to her throat. In just a few minutes she would be home with her arms around her three children.

"Are you a praying woman, Mrs. MacCallister?" Harvey asked.

"Yes," Sadie answered, wanting to add that she had done little more than pray for the past year.

"Good. 'Cause I think we're all going need to do a lot of praying today."

Sadie had the urge to cry, but she knew that it would serve no purpose. Taking Harvey's advice, she stared sightlessly at the passing scenery and prayed with all her might. "Please, God," she implored, "take care of my babies. Just take care of my babies."

Chapter Thirty-six

"How long do we gotta stay here, Aaron?" Matthew's
voice squeaked with fear.

"Shh! Just a little while longer." Aaron looked
around the cramped interior of the hollowed log that
had once served as their fort. He hoped that he done
the right thing in dragging Matthew and Grace out
across the snow-covered field and into the woods
where they'd crawled into this narrow hiding spot.

"Were they bad Indians?" Matthew asked.

Aaron pulled his skinny arm more tightly around
Grace, who was bundled inside his coat. He quickly
gave thanks that his sister was such a happy baby.
Grace viewed the entire experience as though it was a
wonderful adventure. Patting her head, Aaron wished
that he could avoid Matthew's question.

"How come you think they were bad Indians?"
Matthew persisted.

"I don't know, Matt. I just went outside to pee and

could hear them coming down the shore. They were whooping and hollering, and I just got scared."

"Maybe they were celebrating something. Mac says that the Sioux sometimes come by here to trade. Maybe that's all they were doing."

Aaron did not want to worry his brother, but something about the entire scene bothered him. When he'd heard the Indians along the shore, Aaron had crept as far as he dared through the dense woods, hoping to catch sight of them. The group was heavily armed. The sight of several young braves who swung dead chickens over their heads mesmerized Aaron. The blood that had spurted from the freshly killed poultry rained in a sickening shower around the laughing men. The sand and snow on the banks of Lake Okoboji were littered with the mangled carcasses where the Sioux had moved up the shore.

Aaron's legs had pumped faster than he ever thought possible as he'd run back to the cabin. "Grab Grace," he'd called as he barged through the door.

"Why? What's going on?" The freckles on Matthew's fair face had stood out like red ants on pale sand.

But Aaron had snatched the blankets from his mother's bed and stuffed them in the center of a big quilt, the corners of which he tied together to form a sack. "Now, Matt! Don't ask any questions. Just grab the baby and let's get out of here!"

The look of panic on Aaron's young face had galvanized Matthew, who'd hurried to pick Grace up out of her crib. On Aaron's command he'd pulled their coats off of the pegs that hung in a row near the door. He'd precariously balanced Grace in one arm and the coats in the other.

"C'mon," Aaron had pleaded. Noticing Matthew's difficulty, he'd swung the quilt over his shoulder and taken the baby from his brother's arms.

It wasn't until now, when they were safely settled inside of the hollow log, that Aaron gave Matthew a sketch of the situation. Again, Matthew repeated his question. "But what made you think we had to run from them, Aaron? Maybe they just wanted to visit."

Aaron knew that it would serve no purpose to worry Matthew, so he invented a simple answer. "They didn't have any women with them, Matt. I just figured that if they were going to come visit, they would have brought their wives with them. You're probably right and I'm just worried about nothing."

"That's okay. This is the most fun we've had all winter!" Matthew snuggled closer to his brother. "But this coat sure isn't keeping me very warm."

"Open that quilt up and let's put those blankets over us."

The boys sat quietly while Aaron fed Grace tiny pieces of dried apples. Finally, Matthew's low voice asked, "Were they going toward the Gardners' cabin?"

"No," Aaron lied.

"What if Ma comes back home while we're out here?"

Aaron wanted to scream, wanted to cry, but instead he kept his voice calm and tried to sound sure of himself. "She won't. She hasn't been gone long, so we should beat her back with no problem."

"But what if she does get back and doesn't know where to find us?"

Any fool could find us, Aaron thought wildly. *We left tracks in the snow that a blind man could follow.* Aaron knew that if the Indians wanted to find them, they would have no trouble. Maybe leaving the cabin hadn't been such a good idea. It was just that Aaron had been so shocked to see them, and so afraid.

In answer to Matthew's question, Aaron said, "It'll be okay, Matt. I won't let anything happen to you. I promise we'll get back before Ma gets home. Look— Grace thinks this is a lot of fun!"

Grace was indeed smiling at her two big brothers, a mushy piece of apple dangling from her pink lips. Matthew settled in quietly, pushing his body close to his sibling's under the warmth of the blankets. Grace would occasionally reach her hand over to touch Matthew's red hair. She seemed to marvel at its bold color, and at the way it stuck out every which way.

Matthew rested his head on Aaron's shoulder, glad to allow Grace to entertain herself with his red locks. "You know," he said softly, "I wouldn't let anything happen to you either, Aaron."

Aaron willed himself not to cry. He prayed for a dozen things at once. He beseeched God to keep his mother safe at the Gardners'. He pleaded that the Indians would not be interested in the tracks leading to the woods. But most of all, he prayed that he hadn't done the wrong thing in bringing his little brother and sister to this hiding spot.

As fat drops of cold rain began to pelt the little hideaway, Aaron knew that God had heard him. The faster and harder the raindrops fell, the more hope

Aaron allowed himself to feel. It wouldn't take long for their footprints to be wiped away in the melting snow by this rain. Wordlessly, he said thank you and scooted closer to his brother.

Chapter Thirty-seven

"Don't fight me, Sadie. We're going back! We can't do anything here."

Sadie sat on the wagon bench next to Harvey, shaking from fear and cold. She could not believe that they were headed back to the Gardners' without her children. The clouds had opened up, visiting upon them a miserable, pelting rain. "Where could they be, Harvey?" Sadie cried. "Where are my children?"

Harvey's brown hair was plastered down by the rain, his round, passive face etched with concern. "Let's think about this sensibly. The Indians came down the shore from the north, right?" Sadie nodded her head. "That means that they came by here first. We would have known if they'd had the children with them."

"But the blood!" Sadie shook violently as she remembered the sight of the young braves covered in splattered blood. "They had blood all over them!"

Harvey turned his attention back to driving the horse and wagon. He'd love to stop and comfort Sadie but knew that he didn't dare. As much as he assured her that the Indians were gone, he doubted the truth of his own tale. He did believe that there was an explanation for the blood. "Remember the dead chickens we saw on the way here? There was blood all over the beach. Maybe the Indians were practicing some kind of ritual."

He twisted the reins in his weather-reddened hands, wishing he knew the words that would bring comfort. "My suspicion is that since the Howes are north of you, they saw the Indians first. Joel knew that Mac was down in Fort Dodge, so he came by to check on you and the children. When he found out that you were gone he probably just took the kids home with him."

"You think so?" Sadie asked hopefully. She knew that Mac would do the same if Joel were gone.

"Yeah. It sure makes sense. Think about the items that were missing from the cabin. They probably took the blankets for the children to cover up with in the back of Joel's wagon. Their coats are gone, Sadie. Do you honestly think that the Indians would have stopped to get their coats if they took them?"

Harvey's quiet logic made her feel a little better, although every nerve in her body screamed for her to stay home and wait for the children. Harvey would not think of leaving her alone. Determined to do as Rowland instructed, he was going to get back to their cabin right away. The soft-spoken man had actually threatened to return Sadie to the Gardners by bodily force if necessary.

Frances and Rowland met them at the cabin door. "Where are the little ones?" Frances asked before they had even rolled to a stop.

Harvey spoke up, "They weren't there. I suspect that Joel Howe went by to check on them, and finding them alone, took them back to his place."

Rowland shot Harvey a questioning glance, while Frances hurried Sadie down from the wagon. Frances put her arm around the shaken woman and led her into the cabin.

"You take the chair at the table, Sadie. I've got a little coffee left. We can really go wild."

Sadie appreciated Frances's attempt at levity, but was choked with worry for Aaron, Matthew and Grace. She reminded herself that the cabin had shown no sign of struggle. The children's shoes and coats were gone. Surely, Harvey's theory was correct; they were probably having the time of their lives playing with the Howe children. She drummed her fingers on the oak table and wondered when Rowland would think it was safe for her to ride to the Howes' for the children.

Harvey had done his best to convince Sadie that it was pure foolishness to make the trip until they were sure that the Indians were completely out of the area. He implored her to think with her head and not with her heart. The Sioux were probably no threat at all, but just to stay on the safe side, they should all stay put behind closed doors.

Frances had just placed a cup of hot coffee in front of her when the door burst open. "They're back!" Rowland called. The tension in his voice chilled the room.

Harvey shot through the door behind him and headed for a trunk in the corner. Pulling open the heavy lid, he began to pull out weapons: long, mean-looking shotguns and several pistols. "What's the plan, Rowland?" Harvey asked over his shoulder.

"Bar the door!" Rowland replied.

"No!" Frances placed her body between her husband and door.

"They're up to no good, Fran. We gotta protect ourselves this time."

"I think we're all overreacting. How many times have these Indians come to our home, taken what they wanted, and left us unharmed? To bar our door to them now would be the greatest of insults. Do you want to start a war over our misplaced suspicions?"

"Listen, Frances, there is something different about this. They've been hanging around this area all day. They killed our cattle and Harvey says that there are dead chickens all along the shore. These are hungry men. Why aren't they just taking the meat back to their families?" Rowland grabbed his wife by the upper arms, hoping that she would listen to reason. "I know it's too terrible to believe, but we're in trouble here."

Frances would not be moved. Her voice was low and trembling. "Look around this room, Rowland Gardner. These are our children, the reason we moved to this godforsaken frontier in the first place. Do you want to risk their lives by insulting those savages?"

Rowland Jr. was standing on his tiptoes next to the south window. "They're here, Pa!"

"What do you want me to do, Rowland?" Harvey asked, still busy loading weapons. Young Robert Clark nervously assisted.

Rowland's voice was full of exhaustion. "Put 'em up, Harvey. We'll ride this one out and hope they're friendly."

Frances and Rowland's eyes met in silent understanding. There was nothing more precious to either of them than their children. While it was a risk to trust these Indians, it was a risk they were going to take.

Sadie picked up her coffee cup, placed it on the sideboard, and moved to Mary Luce's side. She spoke gently to little Albert, whose blue eyes were wide with fear. "Why don't you come let me hold you, Albert?" Trustingly, the four-year-old held his chubby arms up to her.

His mother Mary, who sat in the rocking chair with baby Amanda, mouthed the words "Thank you," and tried her best to smile. It was difficult under the circumstances.

In all, nine braves filed into the cabin. There was nothing friendly about their demeanor, although Rowland attempted to engage them in conversation. Finally, the big one, the pock-faced leader, demanded flour.

"We don't have much left, but you're welcome to what we have," Rowland offered amiably.

Something was wrong. Frances felt it first. She suddenly knew that she had been terribly wrong to allow the Indians into her home. She looked around the cramped cabin. In this room were gathered the people she loved most, and she knew with a shattering certainty that she had just gambled away their lives.

It was the dream. Frances's recurrent nightmare had looked precisely like this. Mary was holding Amanda close, just like in her dream. Rowland Jr. and Abbie held tightly to one another, and Harvey stood in tense silence, just like in her dream. Poor Robert had just come for a visit. Frances looked at his handsome face, his waving hair, and felt a keen sorrow for him. As her eyes settled on Sadie MacCallister, Frances finally knew who the faceless woman in her visions had been.

Wildly, she wondered how to stop the inevitable. In agonizing detail, Frances Gardner sought to memorize for eternity these beloved faces. She longed to gain Rowland's attention, to warn him that his instincts had been correct. Rowland would know what to do.

Sadie watched as Frances looked slowly around the room. Her friend's gaze passed over the Sioux as though they were not present and settled one by one on each member of her family. Her eyes were huge, her features tight with concern. Sadie longed to put her arms around the older woman, to offer comfort.

And then Frances looked at her. As long as she lived, Sadie would remember the expression on Frances's frightened face. For a long, meaningful moment Frances simply looked at Sadie, and with an almost imperceptible nod, smiled tremulously. She attempted to mouth words, to convey some urgent message, but was interrupted by the violent report of gunfire.

All eyes turned to Rowland who was bent over the flour barrel. Frances's husband stiffened as a neat circle of blood spread across the center of his back. It was if that single gunshot flung wide the gates of Hell. Sadie couldn't breathe, couldn't think, above the sudden sound of screaming and crying.

From somewhere behind her Sadie heard Harvey Luce curse sharply then scramble for his weapon. He was gunned down mid-stride. Robert Clark was caught in a crossfire and died immediately.

In that split second, Sadie looked for Frances. Frances ran toward the children, horror written on her face. She died quickly, cut down by a bullet to the chest. Mary's cries, the baby's wailing and Sadie's own labored breathing played in horrible concert in her mind. Methodically, the Indians were obliterating all life from the cabin.

Mary thrust her baby into fourteen-year-old Abbie's arms and moved to the aid of her husband. In her mind, Harvey was not dead, could not possibly be dead. After a vicious blow to the head and bullet in the back, Mary fell atop the man she had sought to protect. Albert cried out for his fallen mother.

All the while, Abbie stood in mute shock. Rowland Jr. clung piteously to her skirt. For several tense minutes the Indians stopped their slaughter. The wails of the baby seemed to delight some of them. Sadie stood four-year-old Albert on the floor next to her, and reached for the baby. Perhaps if she could stop the crying, the warriors would turn their attention to something else. Already, a few of them were busy rifling through the Gardners' possessions.

Amanda was snatched from midair by a pair of strong brown hands as Abbie attempted to pass the baby to Sadie. In the blink of an eye another brave was upon them, pulling at Albert. Sadie screamed and fought like a madwoman to keep hold of the little boy. Likewise, Abbie battled for the life of her young brother.

A cruel blow to Sadie's head knocked her to the floor. Albert, stunned and limp, was dragged from the cabin. Rowland Jr. was pulled by two braves out of Abbie's thin arms. The girl cried pitifully as she helped Sadie sit up. The two survivors clung together in the corner of the bloody cabin. Sadie jerked as she heard the tortured cries of the children, the dull thuds that accompanied their pain, and then the merciful quiet. "Oh, God," she cried. "Oh, God."

Sadie looked at Abbie. Fear and shock painted the girl's skin white as snow. The Indians were outside the cabin destroying everything that lived, even peeling the bark from the trees. It was at that moment that Sadie decided to do whatever it took to protect Abbie from what she was sure would follow. She stood and, on wobbly legs, moved to the bodies of Harvey and Mary Luce. Without looking at either of them too closely, she pushed Harvey's heavy body aside enough to see the butt of his pistol. She pulled the surprisingly heavy weapon from beneath his still-warm form and walked toward Abbie.

"Father, forgive me," she muttered, hoping that she would have the strength to do what needed to be done. She could not allow Abbie or herself to be tortured by those outside.

She had to step over Frances's body to get to Abbie. The look of terror in her friend's eyes assured Sadie that she was doing the right thing. Those deep green eyes looked up as Sadie neared. Not a flicker of emotion registered as Abbie recognized the weapon in Sadie's hands. With a look of utter resignation the girl bowed her head, ready for the inevitable, inviting it perhaps. Sadie's arms shook as she attempted to aim the gun. Tears flowed freely down her face. She pressed her finger to the trigger, trying to see through the veil of tears that blinded her.

Suddenly, Sadie felt as though she had been hit with an anvil. Her arm went numb and fell uselessly to her side. The red-haired leader of the Sioux stood next to her, his chest heaving furiously. He put his massive arm around her and dragged her out the door. After a shout to one of his men, he handed Sadie to another warrior. Abbie was carried outside as well.

Sadie refused to look at the bodies of the others, but Abbie could not seem to pull her eyes from the grisly scene. Sadie realized, with a mixture of dread and relief, that she and Abbie had been spared. For some inexplicable reason, they had not shared the others' fate. Her head ached and her arm felt as though it had been broken—but they were alive.

Ahead of them warriors were on horses; behind them a brave prodded them with a stick. Their shoes were soaked through with slush and mud. Walking next to her Abbie began to cry as the reality of the situation began to sink in. With her good hand, Sadie took hold of Abbie. As a tribute to Frances, she was determined to see that the girl got through this terrible experience. It would be her final gift to her friend.

Chapter Thirty-eight

Six hellish days. The Sioux, at the command of their leader Inkapaduta, moved up the banks of Lake Okoboji, systematically ridding themselves of the whites who had settled there. Not a man was spared.

As the rampage continued, the ranks of hostages grew. Best friends Elizabeth Thatcher and Lydia Noble were dragged, cold and numb with terror, into the Sioux camp. Elizabeth cried ceaselessly, grieving the loss of her baby, Dora. Lydia, who had watched her husband shot down and her young son killed, stared into space. She would communicate with no one. When Sadie reached out to the young woman, Lydia recoiled.

Several days into their forced march, the Indians met up with their own families. The group of bloodied warriors was greeted warmly by their tribe. The hostages were essentially ignored, treated more like dogs than humans.

Through the long night, the women held on to the

hope of survival. They sat together on the cold ground, their wrists tied together, then to a tree. Sadie tested the rope, hoping to loosen its purchase. Hopelessness coursed through her as she realized how well they had been bound. Even if she did manage to work her hands free, what then? She was surrounded by Indians. Escape was impossible.

Late in the evening, snow began to swirl around the hastily erected camp. Sadie's immediate concern was freezing to death. She looked at young Abbie, who was tied next to her. Abbie's lips were blue with cold and her teeth chattered uncontrollably. Sadie had to do something.

"We need a fire!" she called out. No one heard. After a few minutes a young maiden walked by. "Hey!" Sadie cried.

A beautiful brown face turned her way. Black eyes, fringed with long, black lashes, watched the captives passively. Sadie licked her lips, then wished she hadn't—they would probably freeze together. "I have no idea if you can understand me, but we're freezing to death. We're too far outside the camp to feel any heat from your fires."

The lovely woman continued to stare, not a flicker of recognition on her face. Sadie was surprised when she heard Lydia speak, then wished the younger woman hadn't. If she wasn't careful, the girl was going to get them all killed. "Who cares about getting warm?" Lydia said. "I hear that freezing to death isn't such a bad way to go. Just let the little squaw get back to whatever dirty bastard she was servicing."

Sadie quickly looked to the pretty maiden and hoped she didn't understand. She implored, "All we need is to be a little closer to one of the fires. Do you think we can do that?" When the woman didn't react, Sadie became more desperate. "There must be some reason we were chosen to survive. A ransom, perhaps. We are worth nothing dead. But if you don't find some way for us to warm up, that's exactly what we'll be. We're going to freeze to death out here."

Sadie wanted to cry when the maiden stalked off. A few minutes later though, she returned. At her side was one of the braves who had been in the Gardner cabin. His silky brown hair looked like it had been cut with a dull knife. As the woman spoke in her native language, his jaw thrust out stubbornly. Judging from his inflexible stance, Sadie was about to give up hope. This was not a man to show mercy.

The conversation between the two became heated. The young woman spoke excitedly, pointing sharply to punctuate her words. Finally, with a sharp finish, she threw her braided hair over her shoulder, thrust her chest out and marched away. The warrior's dark eyes followed her. He watched as she slipped back into the activity of the camp. Indecision was marked clearly on his face.

Sadie saw this as her opportunity. "If you'll only . . ."

The man's sparkling eyes snapped to her. "If you are very wise you will not say a word," he warned. Sadie was surprised by his use of English, but she managed to keep from gaping.

The Indian stood with his hands on his hips and slowly examined the group sitting huddled on the ground. He bent and, with a quick, jerky action, cut the rope that bound them. "Come," he commanded, turning his back to the captives. Sadie stood first, then gave Abbie a hand up. Elizabeth rose slowly, pain evident on her pretty face. Lydia followed, wearing a mutinous expression.

They came to a teepee situated on the edge of the camp. From its interior stepped the pretty young maiden. A beauteous smile lit her face as she saw the brave leading the captives to the warm enclosure. The brave muttered an oath, then scowled at the young woman's tinkling laughter. He looked at Sadie, whom he seemed to consider leader of the group. "Stay in the warmth, white woman. If any of you attempt to leave, I will kill you." He looked back at the maiden, shot her his most vicious expression and added, "You, I will kill with pleasure."

The maiden chuckled as she led the captives into the teepee. The moment she left them alone, the white women gathered around the warmth of the small fire in the center of the structure. "Filthy savages!" Lydia spat.

Sadie turned to her, trying to remember how pretty she'd been the night of the Gardners' party. Now the girl's dark brown hair was matted, her clothes in tatters, and her face twisted in bitterness. Sadie knew that the woman was going to be a problem. All it would take was one angry word from her to rile the Indians.

"Lydia, you have got to watch what you say! I know that you're upset, but if we're going to survive this we're going to have to use all of our cunning. That means that you can't say whatever comes to mind!"

Lydia's eyes flashed dangerously. "Don't you dare tell me how to behave, Sadie MacCallister! How many family members have you watched die this week? How many children have you heard crying for you while you stood by helplessly?"

Elizabeth attempted to put her arm around her friend but was viciously pushed away. Lydia stepped toward Sadie, tiny bubbles of spittle forming in the corners of her mouth. "Just who are you, anyway?" Looking to the other women, she added, "Don't any of you find it odd that our new neighbor managed to be away from her cabin when the Indians struck? That she sent her husband away just in time? Why, she probably hid her children away, knowing what the savages were up to!"

Sadie backed away from the ranting woman. Her accusations were ridiculous, and there was madness in her eyes.

Lydia pointed to the dark red spatters staining the front of her dress. "This is what happens when you're standing too close to your family as they die, Mrs. MacCallister. Until you can show me the blood of *your* family, don't you dare tell me how to behave. Don't you dare."

She sat down heavily by the fire and stared into its bright flames. Sadie knew that there was no way she could comfort the woman. She only hoped that Lydia would somehow find her way back to sanity. While Sadie's heart broke for her, she knew that Lydia had no chance of surviving this captivity without a measure of restraint.

Sadie turned her attention to Abbie and Elizabeth, who had drawn away from the spectacle. "C'mon, you two, get over here by the fire. *Now*, Abbie," she commanded when the young girl hesitated. Abbie was Frances's child, and Sadie would protect her with her life.

They sat around the small fire, holding each other

for comfort and warmth, and Sadie allowed her thoughts to drift to her precious children. While she was confused about where the three might be, Sadie dared to feel some hope.

"Sadie?"

"What is it, Abbie?" she whispered softly to the young girl by her side.

Abbie seemed to have read her thoughts. "Where *do* you think Aaron, Matt and Grace are? When the Indians made us stop back at your cabin, I thought they were going to hurt them for sure. But no one was even there."

"I don't know. I keep turning it over in my mind, but I can't come up with an answer."

"We know they weren't in the barn, 'cause the barn was searched. And we know that they weren't . . . with the Mattocks, because we saw them." Abbie shuddered.

Sadie closed her eyes to the thought of how they'd been forced to step over the bodies of the Mattocks. Mary and the children had died clutching each other. James Mattock and another young man, whose name Sadie could not recall, died together, away from the rest of the family.

"Why do you suppose they weren't all together? Why do you think they left their cabin?"

Sadie's first instinct was to demand that Abbie stop asking these questions. It hurt to remember. But the girl was young and seemed to need answers. It was as though she believed that if she knew every detail of the slaughter, she could somehow make sense of it.

She focused on Abbie's last question. "The Mattocks?"

"Yeah. Why do you think they were all spread out like that?"

"My guess would be that the Indians visited the Mattocks in the morning, just like they did . . . your family." Sadie's breath caught in her throat, and her chest burned at the thought of the Gardners. She forced herself to continue. "Maybe after that first visit, the Mattocks got scared. They appeared to be heading toward your cabin. It's possible that they intended to stop at our place first, gather the children and me, and then go on to your cabin where we could all stick together. Mary appeared to be trying to protect her children when they died. James and the young man who was visiting must have been attempting to guard their retreat."

"But your children weren't with them," Abbie stated.

"No, they weren't."

"They weren't with the Mattocks or with Lydia's parents, and we know that they weren't at your cabin." Abbie seemed determined to keep her mind on something other than the atrocities she had witnessed. Suddenly, her eyes lit up and she grabbed Sadie's hand. "The woods!" Abbie exclaimed. "What if they had time to run to the woods?"

Sadie's mind swam at the thought. It would be so like Aaron to find a place to hide if he felt Matthew or Grace was in jeopardy.

"I'll bet they saw the Indians and ran for the woods! That's what I would do, if I had time."

Sadie prayed that the girl was right. It made sense. The only things that they had found missing after the first scare with the Sioux were blankets, the children's boots and coats. She wrapped her arm around Abbie's thin shoulders, hope filling her. "It's possible, Abbie. It's just possible."

The night wore on, and with it, the celebratory war dances. Sadie sat in the snug teepee and listened to the chants of the elated Indians. She wondered how they could possibly find joy in the heartache they had inflicted. Abbie lay next to her, gently snoring, escaping for a short time the ruins that her young life had become. Howling wind wrapped itself around their shelter, threatening to usher in a full-blown blizzard.

Sadie tried not to look at Lydia, whose bitter countenance portended tragedy. It was clear that Elizabeth was trying hard to be strong. After all, she needed to survive if she was ever going to see Joseph or her brother Asa again. Sadie smiled at the dainty blonde and wished that she could somehow ease her anguish.

Thank God that Mac, Joseph and Asa had gone to Fort Dodge. Sadie wasn't sure how she would have coped with losing Mac to the rampage. Perhaps he might find her, save her. . . .

She looked again at Lydia, and realized that if she were in the woman's place she might be reacting in the same way. This woman had no reason for hope.

Suddenly, Lydia looked up and met Sadie's gaze across the fire. Although light bounced off the woman's dark eyes, Sadie could see no life there. She shivered, then wrapped her arms around herself. Sadie was struck with a premonition that chilled her. Lydia's time was running out. Although she was still walking this earth, Lydia was as dead as her husband and child.

Chapter Thirty-nine

Tranquil portraits of good times flashed through Sadie's mind as she searched for a measure of peace: Aaron's first word, Matthew suckling at her breast, quiet moments sitting by the lake. Then new pictures would take their place: Grace's head on her shoulder, Frances Gardner handing her a warm coffee mug, Rowland's gentle teasing.

And Mac—Sadie's head swam with images of Mac. The memory of his touch was enough to transport her away from the beating of drums, the incessant war dances. In the darkest hours, Sadie found comfort in the sweet memories of her time spent with Mac. Every kind word he'd said to her, every compliment he'd paid, each time his eyes had lit at the sight of her, these were the thoughts that sustained her. After twenty-six years of believing that she was worth nothing, Sadie suddenly wondered if she'd been wrong. Mac thought she was strong and beautiful. He really did. Her children thought she could do no wrong.

Frances and Rowland Gardner, two of the finest people she'd ever known, had trusted her to do the right thing. Maybe it was time for Sadie to see herself in a different light, one filtered through the eyes of those who loved her rather than through the eyes of controlling, abusive men like her father or Eldon.

Day after day the Sioux pillaged, then celebrated late into the night. While her weight dropped and her body weakened, Sadie felt her spirit grow. She would survive. She would see Abbie through this horrible captivity, regardless of what the cost might be.

Sadie could not determine how many captors there were. Some days the band consisted of fifty, some days three times that. Vagabonds, they came and left at will. Early one morning a small group of warriors left, only to return with one final captive. Margaret Ann Marble.

Sadie's heart went out to the sad-eyed woman. She had met William and Margaret Ann at the Gardners' party, where she'd been struck by the obvious closeness the couple shared. Though she had believed that she was inured to the tragic stories, Sadie wanted to weep when she heard William had been shot down.

In fact, Sadie came to realize, as she attempted to block the chants from her mind, no one's life was immune to heartache. She herself came from the harshness of backwoods life, Lydia was raised in a warm and loving home, and Margaret Ann had more money than she could possibly spend in one lifetime, yet life had handed them all the same terrible situation. It was how they persevered that was going to determine the outcome.

Sadie looked up as the woman moved to sit next to her. She asked, "How are you, Margaret Ann?"

Dana George

"It doesn't seem real, does it?"

Margaret Ann's brown eyes were sad, so very sad. Just looking at her made Sadie want to cry. "One minute William was alive, setting up a target in the yard for the Indians to shoot at, and the next . . ."

Sadie reached for the woman's hand. "You know what I've been thinking about these past six days? I've been wondering how in the world I ever imagined my life to be without joy. For years, while I was married to Eldon, I spent every waking moment thinking about how miserable I was with him. And to be sure, Eldon was a horrible man. But, Margaret Ann, why didn't I spend more time thinking about the really wonderful things in my life? Why didn't I appreciate the special time with my children more? I would give anything to spend just a little more time with the people I love."

Margaret Ann pushed her heavy, dark hair from her face and seemed to strengthen. "You can, Sadie. You can spent time with them right here"—she pointed to Sadie's head, then to her chest—"and right here. No matter what happens to us we can be with the people we love, in our hearts and in our minds. Even the angriest Indians can't take that away from us."

For the first time in nearly a week, Sadie cried. She laid her head on Margaret Ann Marble's shoulder and sobbed. Through the night, as snow began to pile around the teepee, the two women sat together. They would sleep for a short spell, then quietly share their sweetest memories.

Somehow, Sadie and Margaret Ann, so deeply immersed in grief, found strength in each other and in themselves.

Chapter Forty

Inkapaduta sat in his teepee, listening to the war dance. As snow continued to blanket the earth, the celebration continued.

The warrior was old enough to be honest with himself. For more than twenty years he had dreamed of avenging the deaths of his mother and sisters, of eradicating the whites from the shores of the sacred blue waters. Now it was done, and he was left to wonder where the joy was.

The White Man's blood soaked the ground surrounding Okoboji, yet his mother was still dead, his sisters still no more than a memory. What had these killings accomplished?

Inkapaduta would go to bed tonight with his arms just as empty, his heart just as scarred, as the night before. He had only memories to warm him.

He moved to the thick furs that served as his bed and laid his tired body down. A single hot tear scalded his leathery cheek.

Chapter Forty-one

Palo Alto County, Iowa

"Asa, if you weren't my brother-in-law I'd shoot you just to put me out of my misery!"

Asa Burtch laughed. Annoying Joe Thatcher had become one of his favorite pastimes. "Admit it, Joe. You'll miss me when I'm gone."

"Gone? That's a laugh. You're building a cabin less than a mile away from Elizabeth and me. You're gonna be a thorn in my side for the rest of my natural life."

"Did you hear that, Mac? Why, I think he hurt my feelings!"

"I couldn't help but hear," Mac answered drolly. "You two are talking loud enough to wake the dead."

"I can't help that Joe won't let me ride in the same wagon with him." Asa raised his voice. "I have to yell to be heard over the creaky old bones of that nag Joe insists pull his wagon. Good thing he's got two horses, 'cause that old thing doesn't even have the energy to swat flies with her dried-up tail."

"Oh, you've stepped in it now," Joe roared. "Jennybelle has plenty of good years left in her."

Asa's roar of laughter rang across the open prairie. "Jennybelle? You named your horse Jennybelle? Lord have mercy—Pa was right about you! He kept warning Elizabeth that there was something wrong with that Thatcher boy."

Mac chuckled. The two men were definitely entertaining. For two weeks they had needled one another with no indication that either was ready to give up. Their banter was almost enough to keep his mind off how cold he was. Almost.

Asa finally got tired of yelling over the swirling roar of the wind and spoke quietly to Mac. "You sick of this snow yet?"

"Yep. I can't believe we actually made this trip in two weeks, considering the weather we've put up with."

"It wasn't so bad on the way down, but I thought we were in trouble for sure when the fresh batch hit."

"Let's just be grateful that we were able to push through. My family needs these supplies something awful."

Asa elbowed Mac in the ribs. "You missing that pretty wife of yours?"

Mac turned to the man and grinned. "More than you can imagine." And it was true.

"That bad, huh?"

"Asa, there were nights out on the range when I would've traded my right ball to put my arms around that lady."

Asa nodded. "Yep. But don't you think she would

have been kinda put out with you for making a trade like that?"

"Hey, what are you two laughing about?" Joe called from the wagon ahead of them.

Mac began to answer, then noticed several riders bearing down on them from the north. "We've got company, Joe!"

Within minutes they were met by three men, their faces flushed with cold. Mac pulled his wagon even with Joe's. "Whoa! Those horses aren't going to go far in this weather with you pushing them like that," he warned the strangers.

"Gotta get to Fort Dodge!" one of the young men responded, his words coming out in smoky puffs. "We need to inform the Army."

Joe voiced their question; "What happened?"

Another of the young men spoke up. "It was terrible! Injuns killed nearly everybody in the Spirit Lake area. Just wiped 'em out!"

Mac's heart nearly burst. His voice was hard as steel, his eyes boring into the excited man. "Exactly where did this occur?"

The man couldn't seem to recall the name of the place. Mac's heart continued to pound, and despite the cold, he broke into a sweat. "Where was it, man?"

"Lake Oko . . . Lake something."

"Okoboji?" Mac provided.

"Yeah, that's it! All up and down the lake, the dirty Injuns just broke into their cabins. Killed everyone in sight."

Mac swallowed back the urge to cry out. With remarkable restraint, he asked, "Everybody? Are you sure that *everyone* is dead?"

"Hey, you three aren't from there, are you?"

"Just answer my question!"

The first man spoke again. "No, sir. We heard that a fella by the name of Markham—"

Joe interrupted, "Morris Markham? He lives in our cabin."

The young man attempted to hide his sympathy. The devastation he had witnessed at Morris Markham's cabin was staggering. "Mr. Markham was out rounding up stray cattle at the time of the, uh, attack. He's been real helpful because he's been able to identify bodies."

Joe's face crumpled. "My wife, Elizabeth, was in that cabin. And my little girl—my little girl was there."

"I don't know about the little girl, sir. But I do know that Markham says there's no sight of the two women who lived there. There's talk that some of the women were taken captive."

"I'll kill those sons of bitches!" Asa Burtch snarled. "If they lay one hand on my sister, I will personally see to all their executions."

Mac didn't want to know, but he forced himself to ask. "Farther down the lake, did you go farther down the lake? My wife and three kids were there."

The man's face conveyed his sympathy. "Tell you the truth, Mister, from what we hear it's the same all the way down the lake. But don't take our word for it. We just hightailed it out of there to inform the Army in Fort Dodge."

Mac's eyes met Joe Thatcher's. Understanding flashed between them. "C'mon, Asa," Joe commanded, "let's get home."

For once, the genial expression on Asa Burtch's

bronzed face was absent. He jumped from Mac's wagon and moved to Joe's. "We'll see you tomorrow, Mac. Don't do anything on your own, you hear? We're in this together. Just get to your place and take account. We'll decide on our next step tomorrow."

Mac gave a quick nod of agreement, then startled the horses into pushing across the snow-covered prairie. He didn't have time to argue with Asa or Joe, but there was no way he was sitting on his hands, waiting for a committee decision when there was action to be taken. He could hear the men calling to him as the horses kicked up snow, but couldn't make out their words over the pounding of his heart.

He rode like the demons of Hell were after him, and hoped that his animals were up to the rigors of the trip home. Already, they were breathing heavily, sucking in great gulps of air to combat the strain on their tired bodies. "C'mon, you can do it," Mac coaxed, praying he was right.

Gray smoke billowed from the chimney as his cabin came into view. Was it possible that his family was safe at home? He didn't stop to wonder how the cabin might have been spared, but jumped down from the wagon and barged through the front door.

Five sets of startled eyes met him. "Reverend Long, what are you doing here?" Mac asked.

The minister who had married Mac and Sadie only months earlier stood slowly and laid aside the book he'd been reading. "Mac . . . ."

With profound relief Mac looked into the faces of Aaron and Matthew, saw that Grace was sleeping quietly in Mrs. Long's arms. "Where's my wife?" Mac fought to keep his voice level. "Where's Sadie?"

The reverend put a comforting hand on Mac's taut upper arm. "Why don't we go outside for a moment?"

"Where is my wife?" Mac asked again, his voice tight with fear.

"Mac, we will discuss this out of the hearing of your children."

The look of anguish on Aaron's face brought Mac to his senses. He walked past Reverend Long and flung open the door. The preacher followed him out, closing the door softly behind them.

"What happened here? Where's Sadie?"

Reverend Long sensed what Mac's reaction would be. Hoping to prevent a scene that the children would hear, he answered, "We'll speak in the barn."

"No, we will not! I want to know where my wife is and I want to know now!" Mac had been wound tighter than a spring since hearing news of the massacre, and he didn't want to wait a moment longer.

At the age of sixty, Reverend David Long was a man who knew how to handle himself. Standing straight, he stood eye to eye with Mac. Although he was much thinner than the younger man, the reverend had a look of authority about him that would brook no argument. "I am not telling you a thing within earshot of your children. If you are too worked up to think about them, so be it, but they are still my primary concern."

Shamed, Mac followed the man into the barn, wondering how horrible the news must be. The preacher finally spoke. "One week ago, Indians began a rampage along the lake. One by one they ransacked the homes, killing and looting. They shot cattle in the head, killed livestock, even stripped the bark from the trees.

They wanted to eradicate all signs of life, to wipe away the existence of the settlers here."

Mac swallowed hard. "My wife . . ."

"Will need a great deal of strength to survive the ordeal she is faced with."

"She's alive?" Tears lit Mac's green eyes. He had been so sure that Sadie had died in the attack, so terribly afraid.

Reverend Long nodded his gray head. "She was in the home of Rowland and Frances Gardner when the attack began. She was there to find a remedy for Aaron's toothache. The Gardners were cut down in one brutal sweep."

"Dear God! Rowland, Frances, the children . . . ?"

"Eliza was away visiting friends, so she no doubt has yet to hear of the tragedy. For reasons we do not understand your wife and young Abbie were taken captive. They are being held along with Mrs. Marble, Elizabeth Thatcher and Lydia Noble."

"I'll kill them!" Mac snarled. "I'll leave today—hunt them down and kill them like dogs!"

Reverend Long's hands around Mac's upper arms were like steel bands. Standing nose to nose with the furious man, he insisted, "You will do no such thing. You will thank God that your wife survived that bloody day, then you will wait for the Army to organize a rescue party. I know that you're distressed, but I don't think I need to remind you that your children have been through a terrible trauma. They need you, Mr. MacCallister."

Relief that Sadie was alive mingled with terror over what she must be going through. While every instinct urged him to run to her rescue, Mac knew that he would need a plan to be successful. He also knew that the preacher was right. The children needed him. "The Sioux left our home untouched. Why?"

From behind them Aaron's voice answered, "The Indians came here, Mac, but I hid with Matt and Grace in the hollowed-out fort in the woods." Aaron walked into the barn, his coat unbuttoned, his hands pushed deep into his pockets.

Mac's voice was thick with emotion. "How did you know to do that, son?"

"The Indians were acting crazy. They were hollering and slinging dead chicken blood all over everything down on the beach. I just got scared and took off with Matt and Grace. We took some blankets and stuff."

"They didn't follow you?" Mac hoped Aaron couldn't see the terror he felt at the thought of his children so close to danger.

"I guess they couldn't see our footprints after it started to rain. It was almost dark when I figured it was safe to come home. I kept feeding Grace so she wasn't hungry, but she was getting awful cold. We all were."

Mac walked to the boy and wrapped his arms around his shoulders. Aaron laid his head on his stepfather's chest before allowing tears and exhaustion to overtake him. "Ma never came home though. They told us that she was with the women who were taken away."

Mac fought to control his own tears. "That's right, Aaron. Your mother was taken. But you know what that gives us? That gives us a chance to get her back. Things are a whole lot better than they could have been." Mac bent down to look into the boy's face. "I am so proud of you. You used your head and you protected our family."

Reverend Long joined the pair. "We came as soon as we heard the news. The missus and I thought it would be best to stay here with the children until you got back."

Mac slapped the preacher on the back. "Thank you, Reverend Long. Forgive me for snapping at you. I do appreciate you looking after my family."

"You'll be going with the rescue team then?" Mac's nod confirmed the man's suspicion. "You can count on us to take care of things while you're gone."

Mac was overwhelmed. In the blink of an eye life had changed irrevocably. Nearly all of his neighbors were gone, wiped away as though they had never filled his life with companionship. Yet Sadie and his children survived. The miracle of the moment shared space with raw sorrow.

He suddenly wondered what might have happened if Sadie had not gone to the Gardners for a toothache remedy. Looking at Aaron, he asked, "How is your tooth doing?"

"Gone." Aaron smiled weakly. "Matthew tied a string to it and yanked it out a couple of days ago."

"That's my boy," Mac responded, not knowing how those words made Aaron feel, not noticing how he stood a little straighter at the sound of them.

Asa Burtch visited later that evening, bearing a solemn tale of death and destruction. They were to meet the following day to discuss their rescue options. Mac thanked Asa for the news, then wondered how he was going to get through the night without Sadie.

Did she know how much he loved her? The weeks prior to leaving for Fort Dodge had been difficult, as though some invisible wall had been erected. Why hadn't he cleared the air before riding off with Joe and Asa? Why hadn't he told her that he didn't give a damn about her secrets, that the joy of being with her outweighed any insecurities he had? Why hadn't he told her that she was the woman he'd been searching for all of his life, that her presence was like oxygen to him?

His helplessness was like a living thing, choking him. Mac knew that he would do whatever it took to have Sadie back. He rubbed his tired eyes and wondered again how he was going to make it through the night.

Chapter Forty-two

Lydia Noble's eyes flashed dangerously at the fat Indian who stood over her. Knocked to her knees after repeated refusals to carry his pack, she glared up at him. As were all the captives, Lydia was now dressed in the garb of the Sioux.

The Indian dropped the heavy pack next to Lydia, smiling in satisfaction as it hit her shoulder on the way down. The pack landed with a thud on the snow-covered ground. It was the only sound that could be heard as curious Sioux and nervous captives surrounded the two combatants. All were anxious to see the particular outcome of this battle. For days Lydia had refused the young brave's orders and now, it seemed, the moment of truth had arrived.

Once again, the Indian ordered her to pick up the wet pack. His exaggerated gestures gave meaning to his unintelligible words.

"Get it yourself, you fat, sweating pig!"

Sadie heard a sharp intake of breath from the spectators. No one defied Roaring Cloud. Not only was he the son of Inkapaduta, but he was also known for his vicious nature. Remarkably, Roaring Cloud did not react. He stepped closer to Lydia and repeated his order.

Lydia's sharp laugh surprised them all. She raised her head defiantly, piercing her persecutor with her stare. Even her dark hair shook with repressed rage as she answered, "Not on your life, you baby-killing son of a rattlesnake!"

Roaring Cloud's meaty fist struck Lydia's upturned face with lightning speed. Lydia flew to her back in the snow and lay there unmoving for long, tense seconds. She pushed herself to her elbows, then back to her knees, finally standing before her nemesis. The crowd grew restless, wondering when the captive would submit. Lydia moved to within a foot of Roaring Cloud and, glaring at him, spat in his face.

Before the brave had the opportunity to knock her senseless, a commanding voice broke through the crowd. Inkapaduta strode into the clearing. His deep voice called to his son. With a disgusted look at the scarlet imprint of Roaring Cloud's fist on the captive's cheek, Inkapaduta pulled his son away from the sight. The rest of the Sioux quickly disbanded, returning to the task of setting up camp.

Sadie waited with the other captives for Lydia to join them. Lydia gave the pack, which still lay on the cold ground, one final kick before she walked defiantly back to the other women.

"She's going to get killed for sure," Margaret Ann whispered to Sadie.

"I'm afraid you're right," Sadie agreed.

Lydia joined the group, her face bright with rage.

Sadie attempted to keep her voice neutral as she warned the young woman, "Lydia, surely you know that you can't continue to defy them. Roaring Cloud seems intent on humbling you. You'll only end up getting hurt."

"Hurt? That's a laugh! What else can they do to me? The filthy animals have already taken my husband and son."

Sadie resisted the urge to back away from Lydia's intense stare. "I know how you feel. We've all suffered through this ordeal, but you . . ."

"Have we all suffered, Sadie? Have you suffered as I have? Did you watch them put a bullet in your husband's back? Did you feel them rip your son from your arms, hear the pitiful cries of your only child while they bashed his brains?"

Lydia moved so close, Sadie could feel the warmth of her breath. "Did you know that when they took us to my parents' cabin, they were kind enough to allow Elizabeth and me to carry our babies with us? Dora was already dead, but my little John moaned all the way there. Can you even begin to imagine how that felt?"

Sadie could not bear to hear more. "I'm sorry, Lydia. You're right. Please . . ."

"Please what? Please don't tell you about how I found my thirteen-year-old brother beaten, but alive, leaning against a tree? About how when I tried to bring him comfort the Indians finished him off right before my eyes? Did you have the blood of your baby brother on you when you were kidnapped, Sadie? Did you?"

Margaret Ann wisely pulled Sadie away from the raging woman. "We need to get our shelter built," she stated calmly as she led Sadie to a spot where Sioux women were busy erecting teepees.

Sadie began to shake. Margaret Ann held tightly to her hand. "Are you all right?"

"I'm afraid she's gone mad. She's seen too much, felt too much. Isn't it unbelievable? Just a few months ago we were all together; happy, healthy and celebrating the fall season. The entire world has turned upside down." It seemed too much to bear.

Margaret Ann stopped and turned to Sadie. She pushed her brown hair from her forehead with work-roughened hands. Her intelligent brown eyes, the most captivating feature in an otherwise plain face, sparkled with intensity. "It has occurred to me, Sadie, that we have a chance to survive this captivity. If they wanted to kill us they would have done it by now. We need to keep each other strong. We need to remember the things about our loved ones that we admired. For instance, I loved the way my William laughed at his own jokes. I loved the way he called me Mrs. Marble."

Margaret Ann shook her head and continued, "We cannot spend our time thinking about those last awful moments. We'll all go mad with those thoughts. We will survive, but it will take all the strength we possess to do so."

Sadie nodded, glad for Margaret Ann's company. She'd forgotten herself for a moment.

She followed as Margaret Ann joined the Sioux in building the teepees. She was expected to perform menial tasks, but Sadie was glad for the opportunity to keep busy. She was afraid that if she spent her time wondering where her children were, she would become as unhinged as poor Lydia.

One of the Indian maidens indicated that the captives were all to occupy the same teepee. The five women had only been in the structure for a moment when young Abbie voiced the question, "Why do you think they're allowing us to be together tonight? They usually keep us separated."

"Who knows? Who cares?" Lydia stated dully from a spot she had claimed on the floor. "Everybody be quiet; I'm going to sleep."

Moments later another Indian woman entered the structure, carrying bowls of unidentifiable gruel. The thought of food, unappetizing as it was, was enough to rouse Lydia. "I'll be, I thought the savages had decided to starve us to death!" she said.

No one bothered to say that, at some point, they had all believed that. As hostages, they often went for days without food. But in all fairness, Sadie could not help but notice the swollen stomachs of most of the Indian children, or the hungry look of the adults. It was clear that the Sioux themselves were subsisting on little.

Elizabeth Thatcher looked up weakly from where she sat on the floor. "Someone else eat this," she urged. "I'm not hungry."

Sadie wondered why she had not noticed the flush on Elizabeth's face earlier. Kneeling next to the woman, she pushed a long blond lock of Elizabeth's hair from her wet cheek. "Elizabeth, you're burning up! Why didn't you tell us you were ill?"

"I'll be fine," Elizabeth insisted. "I just need a little rest."

"Yeah. Did you notice how that filthy son of the chief has been following her around? Working her like a dog!" Lydia spat.

Sadie had indeed noticed the extreme dislike Inkapaduta's younger son, Soaring Eagle, directed toward Elizabeth. In all her childish innocence, Abbie asked, "Why is he so mean to you, Elizabeth? You do everything he asks."

"I don't know, Abbie," Elizabeth answered tiredly.

"Oh, yes she does," Lydia interrupted. "My sweet, innocent friend Elizabeth knows exactly why Soaring Eagle is out to get her."

"Stop, Lydia."

"Oh no, Elizabeth! Let's tell the others how brave you are. Let's tell them about how the first time Roaring Cloud hit me you tried to stop him. How you tripped him to stop him from coming after me. How all the other young braves laughed at the sight—all but Roaring Cloud and Soaring Eagle.

"So you see," Lydia continued. "Elizabeth's attempt to be a hero earned her an enemy. What a fool."

Elizabeth turned to her lifelong best friend. "What's happened to you, Lydia? Of course I tried to protect you. You would have done the same for me."

"Don't count on it," Lydia snapped.

"Lydia, that's enough!" Shock was evident in Margaret Ann's voice. "Elizabeth is your cousin, and your friend. She has suffered as much as you have."

Lydia turned calmly to Margaret Ann. Tilting her head, she asked, "Tell me, has my friend Elizabeth lost her child *and* husband?"

Margaret Ann put her hands on her hips. "So that's what this is about? You're angry because Joe Thatcher didn't die? You are—"

"Stop!" Elizabeth cried, her hands over her ears. "I don't want to hear any more." Her shoulders heaved as she sobbed, "I can take anything the Indians do, but I can't take the bitterness between us."

"Abbie, see if you can get us some water," Sadie directed. "Elizabeth, you lie back and let me see if I can figure out what's wrong with you."

Elizabeth did as she was asked. Her cornflower blue eyes wet with tears, she looked up at Sadie. "It's my breasts, Mrs. MacCallister. They hurt something terrible."

"You were nursing Dora?" Sadie asked gently as she pulled the soft leather top down from Elizabeth's shoulders. Elizabeth nodded and closed her eyes tightly. Tears ran down her cheeks.

"It's all right," Sadie soothed. "We'll see what we can do."

With a remarkable measure of self-control, Sadie remained passive as she examined the blackened cracked mass that Elizabeth's breasts had become. Wordlessly, she signaled for Margaret Ann to join her. "Oh my," was Margaret Ann's only reaction.

The two women knelt on either side of Elizabeth. Sadie spoke softly as Margaret Ann soothed the young woman's brow. "You have an infection, Elizabeth. I had one while I was nursing Matthew. I know how terrible you feel, but we'll do everything we can to help you recover quickly."

Elizabeth nodded. "Thank you. I'm sure I'll feel better in a few days."

Cold air ushered Abbie through the flap of the teepee. "Sadie," the girl cried. "The Indian who's been bothering Elizabeth wants her, now! I tried to tell him that she's sick, but he doesn't seem to care. What should I do?"

"It's fine," Elizabeth said, pushing herself up. "It's best that I do whatever he asks."

"I'll talk to him," Sadie insisted.

"No, Sadie. Thank you, but we all know that it would do no good. I'll just see what he wants."

The other women watched helplessly as Elizabeth pulled her top back over her infected breasts and walked weakly out of the teepee. "She's a goner, for sure!" Lydia declared sullenly.

Sadie'd had enough. "Will you kindly keep your thoughts to yourself? Elizabeth does not need your ugliness to make things more difficult for her!"

"Yes, ma'am," Lydia said nastily, then curled into a ball at the far end of the shelter.

"Do you think she'll survive it?" Margaret Ann asked, a worried furrow running between her dark eyes.

Sadie looked at her, surprised at how much weight the woman had lost, how much they all had lost, and answered honestly, "I don't see how, Margaret Ann. Soaring Eagle has been working her like a pack mule, and I have never seen a breast infection as severe as hers. I wish she'd told us days ago. Perhaps we could have done something for her then."

She smiled then, kindly. "You look tired, Margaret Ann. Why don't you go ahead and try to get some sleep."

"I'm fine. I'll stay up to help with Elizabeth."

Abbie Gardner spoke. She seemed to have aged years. Gone was the little girl who had begged to play with Grace. "They've been working you awful hard too, Mrs. Marble. Please, get some rest and I'll help Sadie."

"Nonsense, I've worked no harder than the two of you," Margaret Ann insisted.

"We haven't had to march mile after mile through the snow with an Indian toddler on our hip," Sadie responded.

"Yeah, you've carried him every day. Why? Is his mother sick?"

"I don't know why they chose me for that particular job, Abbie. Perhaps because they know that I lost no children of my own and would be less inclined to harm theirs."

The three women continued to talk in the cold, dark teepee, none of them bold enough to ask for the materials to build a fire. Snow piled up outside.

An hour later, Elizabeth stumbled in. Sadie rushed to assist her. Elizabeth's extremities felt like ice; her teeth chattered. "He made me carry wood. Back and forth I carried it. First to one pile, then he would change his mind and I would carry it to another."

They got Elizabeth out of her wet clothes, then under one of the meager blankets the Indians had assigned them. Having heard about the smallpox infection the government introduced to some Indian tribes via blankets, Sadie was concerned when the only covers the Sioux offered their captives were stamped U.S. ARMY. But regardless of the risk, Sadie believed there was no choice: use the blankets or freeze to death.

Elizabeth continued to shiver beneath the rough covering. "We've got to get her warmed up," Margaret Ann said.

Abbie's eyes lit and, before either woman could stop her, she slipped out of the teepee. Minutes later she returned. In one arm she carried a few pieces of wood, and in the other hand a small, blazing twig. "Look!"

she whispered excitedly. "There was still a small fire burning near the center of camp!"

"Abbie, you're a wonder," Sadie enthused.

"Did anyone see you?" Margaret Ann asked.

"Just the old man with the marks on his face. My heart practically stopped when he looked at me, but then he just looked away like I was invisible."

"I don't think he sees very well," Margaret Ann remarked.

Sadie was thoughtful for a moment. "That, or he didn't want to see her. Haven't you noticed that he gets the most pained expression on his face when he sees one of us? And he was the one who stopped Roaring Cloud from beating Lydia senseless today. It's almost as though . . ."

"What, Sadie?" Abbie asked.

"I don't know." Sadie shook her head, dismissing the question. She knew that it would sound crazy to tell them that the old man seemed grieved by their presence. There was an air of sadness about him that touched even her. Despite the cruelties he had inflicted, the rampage he had directed, the man appeared to be suffocating in his own sorrow.

Instead of sharing those thoughts with the others though, Sadie suggested that they all get some rest. Abbie built a small fire in the center of the circular room. Sadie lay close to Elizabeth, hoping that the warmth of her body would bring a measure of comfort.

"Sadie," Elizabeth said softly.

Sadie touched the young woman's shoulder. "What is it?"

Elizabeth's voice cracked as she asked, "Are you scared?"

Sadie contemplated her answer. She could hear the chatter of Elizabeth's teeth. She knew that it would be cruel to tell her the truth. "The worst is over, Elizabeth. All we have to do now is get you well and figure out a way to get you back to Joe."

A single tear ran down the woman's feverish face. "Joseph," she whispered. "I want to see my Joseph."

"You will," Sadie assured her as she patted her thin shoulder. She could only hope that she was right.

Chapter Forty-three

"I know you're anxious to find your wife, but use your head, Mac! Wait a day or two more, and the Army will be here for sure."

Mac stared obstinately at Asa Burtch, his eyes fired with impatience. "I'm done waiting, Asa. First we heard the Army was right behind us; now we're hearing just a day or two more. Which is it? Are we certain they even organized a search party down in Fort Dodge?"

"They'll be here, Mac," Asa answered, his voice heavy with his own frustration.

Mac looked around the Thatcher cabin, knowing that all the scrubbing in the world couldn't wipe away memory of the crimes that had been committed here. "Damn!" he muttered as he rose to pace the room.

"I know it's hard for you to sit on your hands, but you gotta think about your kids."

"Why didn't we just get a group together from Granger's Point and head out when this first happened?" Mac slapped his thigh in frustration.

"Because the Army has experience in dealing with these situations. They have people who can negotiate."

"Negotiate nothing. I want Sadie back, now. And I *was* the Army for twelve years, Asa. I know what I'm doing when it comes to Indians."

Asa rubbed his hand tiredly over his face. "We want Elizabeth back too, you know."

The pain in Asa's response caused Mac a moment's pause. He sometimes felt as though he was the only one in the world caught in this web. It was easy to forget that there were other families, just as worried.

He released a deep breath. "I'm sorry. I can't imagine what it was like for you, Joe and Morris, having to bury Alvin, the babies *and* the Howes. I can only thank God that Aaron got his brother and sister out of the cabin when he did."

Asa smiled weakly. "That's a bright boy you got there. You were real lucky."

"Yeah. I'm not sure what I would have done if—"

"But it didn't. They're fine."

"I know, I know. But you know what really bothers me?" Mac asked. "It drives me crazy to think that Sadie has no way of knowing that her children are okay. She loves them so deeply, it must be tearing her apart."

"Then you will have the pleasure of telling her the truth when she's released."

"Or rescued," Mac insisted.

Asa laughed. "Oh, you are going to be great fun. I can just see how well you're going to get along with whoever is commanding the Army unit."

"Just so long as he knows that I don't want my wife in the hands of the Sioux any longer than necessary.

I'll let them attempt negotiations, but I promise you, if for one moment I believe it's not working, I'm going in there on my own." He had too much he needed Sadie to know.

Mac pulled his coat from the back of a chair and shrugged into it. "Aren't you going to wait for Joe and Morris to get back?" Asa asked.

"Just tell them I was here, will you? Ask 'em to bring word if they heard anything in Granger's Point. I gotta get back to the kids."

"Aren't the Longs still with them?"

"Yeah. But I'd like to spend as much time with them as I can before we leave." Mac opened the door, allowing a surge of fresh snow to sweep in.

"You be careful out there," Asa warned.

Mac turned back to the big man. "Thanks, Asa. I know none of this has been easy for you. You've been a good friend."

"It'll be over soon."

Mac nodded, but silently he wondered if he believed it.

251

Chapter Forty-four

Sadie struggled to put one foot in front of the other. Exhaustion had become a constant companion, a friend who numbed the mind. She could feel the blisters on her feet that had broken open and knew, by looking at the other captives, that her skin was burned the color of red clay. But she didn't care. Step after mind-numbing step, they followed the Sioux northward. Fear for her children's well-being had become a deep ache. She vowed to deal with it when she had the energy.

The sun beat down mercilessly, making a mushy mess of the landscape. Indians and captives trudged across the plains, focusing on each next step. In the distance she could see a swelling river and wondered how they all planned to cross it.

Sadie turned tired eyes to Elizabeth Thatcher, marveling again at the young woman's recovery. Elizabeth had been in her third day of a raging fever when one of the few old women in the tribe surprised the captives with a late-night visit. Wordlessly, she crouched next to the ill Elizabeth, pulled the blanket back to reveal her infected breasts, and placed some kind of foul-smelling poultice on them. The woman had then forced Elizabeth to drink a dark liquid, murmuring encouragement to her when she seemed too weak to swallow. Night after night the old woman slipped into the teepee to tend to Elizabeth. Only after she was satisfied the young hostage would live did the woman disappear, like a mist, back into her tribe.

Margaret Ann walked next to Sadie and noticed the direction of her gaze. "It's amazing, isn't it?" she asked softly. "I thought she would die of the fever for sure."

Sadie looked around carefully before saying, "Soaring Eagle still seems determined to punish her. He was particularly vindictive when he figured out how ill she was."

"Worked her like a mule."

"I can't believe she survived." Sadie agreed.

Margaret Ann was thoughtful. "Do you ever wonder why some of us live, while others die? I mean, why did they shoot Will but spare me? Out of the Gardner household only you and Abbie were left. It doesn't make any sense."

"I don't try to make sense of anything, Margaret Ann. It's enough to simply get through the day. If I start thinking about Frances, or Rowland, or the children . . . Sometimes I think if I allow myself the luxury of thinking of my own children or Mac, I'll lose my ability to survive."

Margaret Ann reached her hand out. "If we have to be in this predicament, I'm glad we're together."

Sadie laughed, her voice raw. "What a pathetic thing to say. Look at us."

Margaret Ann took in Sadie's sunburned face, her dirty, braided hair and the way the Sioux dress hung like a sack on her thin body. "We're alive," she said solemnly. They'd said it before, and it was more true than ever: they had to be each other's strengths.

Sadie nodded and began to ask where the little boy was who Margaret Ann was normally assigned to carry. She was stopped short by the bark of a command. The voice was loud and angry. She shaded her eyes with her hand, and looked to its source. Soaring Eagle was up on his huge horse, glaring down at Elizabeth. He shouted again, his words a jumble of indistinguishable grunts. "He's on a rampage again," Margaret Ann observed.

Sadie took a deep breath and shifted the load of furs she carried to her left hip. "I'll go see what I can do."

Allowing herself no time to think about the consequences, Sadie wove her way up the line. She passed Lydia, who seemed unconcerned with the predicament her best friend was in. She tried to smile reassuringly at Abbie, whose eyes were wide and brimming with tears. Finally, she reached Elizabeth.

Gathering her courage, Sadie looked up at the angry man. Rays of brilliant sunshine brought out the bluish highlights in his black hair. The scowl on his face seemed incongruous on one so young and handsome. It was difficult to believe that he was brother to the fat, homely Indian who loved to torment Lydia.

Soaring Eagle's horse pranced nervously as its master shouted down at the women. From the corner of her eye, Sadie could see the Indian who had spoken with them the first night of their captivity. He spoke English! Turning to him now she implored, "What is he saying? What does he want?"

"He wants the white haired woman to cross the river before the rest."

Sadie could feel the hair on the back of her neck bristle. "Why?" she asked the Sioux.

"I do not know," he answered honestly. "But I think your friend should do as Soaring Eagle commands."

Sadie studied the Indian's serious brown eyes and noted the change in his attitude toward her and the other hostages. He had been cold and cruel that first night; wouldn't have helped them at all if it hadn't been for the intervention of the pretty young maiden. He now seemed almost sympathetic to their plight.

"I'll do it, Sadie," Elizabeth said quietly. "I'll go across the river first."

Their translator spoke for a moment with Soaring Eagle, then turned back to the women. "He is satisfied." Soaring Eagle looked anything but satisfied as he rode off. Sadie couldn't miss the long look their translator gave Elizabeth before he, too, rode away. She knew that the knot in her stomach would not disappear until they were safely across the river.

They were soon on the bank of the Big Sioux. April thaw was in full swing. Like children racing to the finish line, the current sped to the mouth of the river. Sadie eyed the logs that bridged the swift water, hoping that the makeshift bridge would hold until they crossed.

As the Indians milled about, she lined up behind Elizabeth, anxious to get across and back on solid ground. The air of tension was suffocating. She spoke conversationally to ease the strain. "The band seems to have grown. There must be at least a hundred and fifty Sioux here today. A week ago there weren't more than fifty or sixty."

Sadie didn't realize that Lydia had taken the spot behind her in line until the other woman spoke. "They multiply, like rabbits."

Lydia's voice was so loud, Sadie was sure that she could be heard by the entire tribe. "Lydia!" she warned, turning quickly. "You have *got* to watch what you say!"

There was no life in Lydia Noble's eyes as she blandly surveyed Sadie. "You're a real follow-the-rules type of girl, aren't you, Mrs. MacCallister? Your life must be pretty darn boring."

For a moment Eldon's face flashed through Sadie's mind. She wondered what Lydia would think of the fact that she'd been married to two men. And that she'd shot one. People began to press toward the bridge.

Sadie was glad to have an excuse to look away from Lydia. "Come on, Elizabeth," she said. "Let's hurry and get across. I don't like the look of that water."

Elizabeth looked down at the swirling currents of the Big Sioux and shuddered. Squaring her shoulders, she stepped onto the logs that spanned the river.

Sadie followed closely behind. Sweat popped out on her forehead and lip. She laughed nervously. "I don't know what I'm so scared of. This crossing has probably been used a hundred times."

"Just don't look down," Elizabeth advised. "I think it will be easier if we don't look at the water."

Sadie took Elizabeth's advice and kept her eyes

trained on the distant shore. She hadn't realized that so many of the Sioux had already crossed. Squinting into the sun, she could see that Soaring Eagle was striding toward them on the narrow bridge. That could only mean trouble.

Without realizing it, Sadie began to pray. The anxiety that had plagued her all day came back with a vengeance. Instinctively, she moved as far to one side as she could, pulling Elizabeth with her. Maybe Soaring Eagle would just pass them without comment.

Her heart slowed to a dull patter as Soaring Eagle stopped before Elizabeth, a grin on his good-looking face. He took the heavy pack from Elizabeth's arms then motioned for Sadie to take it. Slowly Sadie accepted the burden, curiosity and fear in her wide blue eyes.

Elizabeth Thatcher turned to her. Tears streamed down her cheeks and a gentle smile graced her full lips. With a voice completely devoid of self-pity, she said to Sadie, "Tell Joe and my parents that I survived only to see them once again. I would gladly suffer all that I have suffered again, if only to see them one more time."

Without warning, Soaring Eagle savagely pushed Elizabeth into the swift current of the river. With a splash she landed and after a moment of pushing her long hair from her face, she began to swim for shore.

Like a boy with a new game Soaring Eagle ran past those on the bridge and bounded to shore. Meanwhile, Elizabeth valiantly fought the strong pull of the cold water. After long minutes of struggle she crawled up on shore.

Soaring Eagle rushed to her. Sadie cried out as he cruelly hit Elizabeth with a club. Again and again, the brave struck Elizabeth, who was attempting to gain her footing. Still, she would not concede defeat. Her will to live was too strong.

Elizabeth fell back and drifted downstream a few more feet, then tiredly pulled herself to the sandy bank. Soaring Eagle raced along with her. Each effort to pull herself out of the cold currents was rewarded with another blow to the head.

Forgotten were the furs and heavy pack in her arms; Sadie left them on the bridge and ran to shore, screaming in terror at the sight. "Stop!" she cried. "That's enough, that's enough!"

The sight of Elizabeth Thatcher fighting wildly for her young life was branded on Sadie's mind. She would never forget the vision of Elizabeth clawing her way up the bank only to be pushed back in the water by Soaring Eagle. She would never forget Soaring Eagle's cruelty, or the fact that of all those milling about, watching the hideous sight, no one tried to stop him.

She would never forget the scream that tore from her throat as Soaring Eagle tired of the game and shot Elizabeth Thatcher in the head. Sadie would always recall the feel of the strong arms that wrapped around her as she attempted to reach the young woman.

Finally the strong arms wrapped around her chest loosened, and Sadie was able to numbly walk down the riverbank. Long after Elizabeth's battered body had floated away, Sadie stood at the water's edge and stared into the murky depths.

Chapter Forty-five

The soft earth gave way with each step Mac took down the steep incline. Eyes fixed on the little boys sitting on the sandy beach, he prayed he would say the right thing. Aaron looked over his shoulder at the sound of his approach. Pain emanated from his blue eyes.

"Hi," the boy offered.

Mac forced his lips into a smile. How he'd grown to love these children. He would do anything to protect them, to ease their suffering. "Hello, boys." As was his habit, he reached down and ruffled Matthew's red hair. "Wanna scoot over?" he asked.

Matthew made way for the big man to ease down next to him. For a few minutes the three sat quietly, taking in the beauty of Lake Okoboji. "I've got to leave for a while."

"We know," Aaron responded.

"The rescue team from Fort Dodge finally got here. They've got scouts who believe they know the direction the Sioux would have taken your mother."

Neither boy said a word. The silence pulled at Mac's heart. "I know that it will be hard for you to have both your mother and me gone, but I have to do whatever I can to get her back. You know that, don't you?"

Aaron answered for both boys, "Yes, sir."

"Reverend and Mrs. Long will stay here with you until I get back. You two will need to help out. Aaron, you make sure you keep the horses fed and the cow milked. Both of you help with Grace. Mrs. Long is crazy about her, but Grace still responds best to her own family."

Aaron stared into the water. "I wish we were a real family."

"What do you mean, Aaron? We *are* a real family," Mac said, surprise in his voice.

"No, I mean I wish you were my real pa."

Mac swallowed back the lump that threatened to render him speechless. "In a way, what we've got is better. When a man puts a baby in a woman's body, he has no choice but to accept whoever's born as his child. When I asked your mother to marry me, I knew that by marrying her I was taking on the job of being your father. I chose you as my children as surely as I chose her for my wife."

Aaron's eyes lit with the possibility. "Really?"

"Absolutely." Mac smiled down at him.

"Then as soon as you bring Ma back we can be a whole family again."

The faith he had in Mac brought with it staggering responsibility. Mac hoped he could live up to it. He knew he would die trying.

Matthew was uncharacteristically quiet. Mac put his arm around the littler boy's shoulders. "You okay?"

"Remember the story you told us?" Matthew asked. "The one about the Indians who could send thoughts to each other across the water? Do you think we could do that for Ma?"

Mac remembered how enthralled Matthew had been with that story. How he'd hung on every word, wanted to hear more. He looked at Aaron, hoping the older boy wouldn't laugh at his brother's request.

Aaron stood. "I think that's a good idea, Matt. I'll go first." Picking up a smooth tan stone, Aaron walked to the water's edge. For just a moment he stood perfectly still, his blond head bowed. Then, with perfect precision, he sent the rock skipping across the surface of the clear lake.

Mac picked up a handful of tiny pebbles and waited for Matthew to do the same. Side by side, the three men who loved Sadie stood on the shore and tossed wishes into water.

Although he knew it was only a childish story, Mac prayed that Sadie would somehow feel the love they were sending. That it would keep her alive and safe.

Chapter Forty-six

Activity bustled around her, but Sadie was shrouded in her own dark silence. Sightlessly, she stared into the dangerous depths of the Big Sioux. She tried to forget the sight of Elizabeth Thatcher's courageous struggle to live. She refused to give way to the scream that worked its way from her soul.

When would it end for her? Were they all going to die as Elizabeth had? Sadie wondered if it would be better to get it over with now. Surely they were all going to perish at the hands of the Sioux.

Light filtered through the trees on the opposite bank, creating silvery ripples in the swift water. It was enough to distract her. Sadie could swear that, despite the fact the current was rushing downstream, tiny ripples pushed toward her. She lifted her head, intent upon further study of the strange phenomenon. Then she saw him.

A toddler, unsteady on chubby legs, teetered on the edge of the river. Sadie quickly looked around, expecting to see the boy's parents rush to snatch him from danger. No one seemed to notice his peril.

As if in slow motion, Sadie watched the child bend to retrieve a stick, then tumble headfirst into the swirling water.

Her first instinct was to let him go. A life for a life. Soaring Eagle robbed Elizabeth of her life; now the Big Sioux would exact her revenge.

But she knew, even as she ran toward the boy, that she could not allow it to happen. There had been too much senseless death. She slipped down the wet bank, landing hard on her rear. Pain radiated up her arms from where she tried to break her fall.

Sadie would not be stopped. Suddenly this was not some nameless Indian boy, but he was Aaron, Matthew, and Grace. She was determined he would survive. Unlike the Gardner children, unlike Elizabeth and Lydia's children, this child was not going to die.

Mud and grass clung to her dress; her hair curled wildly about her face. What was left of her braid hung down her back. Her blue eyes were fixed on one thing: the little boy soundlessly screaming, tossed by the vengeful water.

She chased him down the riverbank, unaware that others were just now noticing the boy's plight. It never occurred to her that the river might be victorious. Sadie was intent upon rescue.

The child's limp body was thrown about like a rag doll, the river's plaything. Sadie knew that if he were thrown against one of the many boulders that dotted this stretch of water, his life would be snuffed. But that would not happen.

She knew that she had only moments. Running like

she had never run before, Sadie tore down the river-bank, ignoring the low-hanging tree branches that scratched her face and chest. Finally, she judged the distance to be sufficient.

She stopped in front of an old willow tree. Grabbing hold of the longest branch she could find, she waded into the icy cold of the Big Sioux. She refused to panic as the swift current pulled at her. She held tightly to the tree branch, praying that it was long enough to meet her purpose.

The boy rushed toward her. Just a foot more and she would have him. Her hand slipped down the willowy branch until she held the very tip. Her arm stretched until she thought it would be torn from its socket.

He was still too far! In a moment of utter panic Sadie lifted her leg to block the child's passage. For a split second the tired boy held tight to her calf. It was just enough for Sadie to pull him to her, and to grab his chubby body with her free arm.

The boy clung to Sadie's chest and neck. She turned back to the riverbank and, using the willow branch, worked her way to shore. She and the child competed for great gulps of air.

By the time her soaking foot pressed into the soft, sandy bank, a hundred pairs of eyes followed her progress. Out of the group emerged a man. Sadie knew from the terrified expression on his face that he was the boy's father.

Sadie was too exhausted to speak, too drained to cry. The frightened child reached for his father. Word-lessly, the man took his son into his strong arms. His black eyes searched Sadie's. In that space of time, the world was still. The Indian and the hostage were simply two parents, each with a fresh appreciation for the fragility of life.

The Big Sioux River was forded and the march continued. Sadie wanted to recall every moment of that day. If she did manage to survive, she wanted to tell Joe Thatcher not about his wife's terrible death but about her tremendous will to live. About her love.

The sun set as usual, the birds sang their evening praise as though the tragedy of the day had never occurred, and Sadie knew that the earth's rivers would continue to flow when her own end came. Life would go on. But she was surprised to realize that, despite the pain exacted by living, she longed to remain part of the flow.

Chapter Forty-seven

"I don't care if the trail's as cold as a witch's tit; that's my sister out there and I want her back!"

The red-faced lieutenant sputtered nervously. "I-I'm sorry, Mr. Burtch. We've followed the Sioux as far as we can. Their trail completely vanished near Heron Lake."

Asa moved his burly body menacingly toward the anxious young officer. Frustration over weeks of delay had finally taken their toll. First a blizzard had hit and several officers froze to death. Then the infantry was thirty hours late arriving in Springfield, where the Sioux had massacred more settlers. "Look, you little weasel—if you don't figure out a way to find my sister, I'm gonna cut you into pieces so small your own momma won't recognize you."

The lieutenant's eyes bulged. Only a strong hand on Asa's arm could pull him away. A deep voice reasoned, "C'mon, Asa, this is accomplishing nothing."

Asa allowed himself to be led away, then shook his

arm out of the man's grip. He looked at his companion. "Tell me something, Mac. How in the hell did they manage to lose the tracks of over a hundred Sioux?" He shook his head in disgust, his sandy brown hair the exact pale color of his normally tan face.

"We'll figure something out," Mac promised.

"Yeah? What makes you think so? This entire rescue effort has been a catastrophe. What makes you think our luck is going to improve?"

Mac studied Asa's flushed face, knowing the kind of gut-twisting anxiety the man was experiencing. Calmly, he responded, "Because we have to succeed. Anything less is unthinkable."

Asa seemed to deflate a bit and looked more like what he was: a brother worried about his sister. "I'm sorry, Mac. I know that I've been a horse's ass, but when I think about what's happening to our women I get crazy."

The sun began to set as Mac and Asa moved to the cookfire, the congregation point for many of the rescue group. Most were Army regulars, but there were also a few civilians anxious to help. Mac and Asa helped themselves to a cup of coffee before finding a couple of large rocks outside the radius of the fire.

Silently they sat, each searching for the next logical move. They were joined by Joe Thatcher, who seemed bent by the experience. "Any ideas?" Joe asked tiredly.

"Yeah. I'm going on, alone." Mac looked steadily at the two men. "I spent more than a decade chasing Indians in Kansas. I probably have more experience than all these regulars put together."

"Not a chance!"

"Look, Asa, I know that it's gonna be hard for you to

stay with the Army, but use your head. We all know the reason this expedition's been such a mess. It's rescue by committee. It takes forty men to decide when to belch. No wonder they lost the Sioux's trail. I'll have more luck alone following the trail and getting close to the Sioux camp. I've experience and—"

"I'm not sitting on my hands," Asa began.

"No one expects you to. You and Joe need to keep a fire lit under this group. It wouldn't take much persuasion to get them to turn back. You two have to keep reminding them of why they're out here. And, on the off-chance they stumble on the Sioux camp, you need to be with them to make sure our women are protected."

"He makes sense, Asa," Joe conceded. "They're spinning their wheels, waiting for someone to make a decision. Let Mac see what he can do. And if he thinks he can do better alone . . . It won't be hard for him to find us when he knows something. If he needs us."

"You fellas mind if I join ya?" called a voice from out of the darkness.

Mac waited for the man to walk into view, then looked him over. He stared hard, wishing he knew what it was about the stranger that struck him the wrong way.

He watched as the man lowered himself to a boulder. "Hey, these do make pretty good chairs!"

"Something happen to your shoulder?" Asa asked, his voice laced with suspicion.

The man squirmed. "Little gunshot wound. Nothin' to be concerned about."

Asa's shrewd gaze never wavered. "Oh, I wasn't concerned. I just wondered why a man with a wound that hasn't healed properly is out chasing Indians."

The wiry volunteer swallowed hard. "Just couldn't stand the thought of them wily Sioux havin' decent white women. Thought I would help out."

"Where you from?" Asa pierced him with a stare.

"Granger's Point," the man answered. Noting the doubtful expression on Asa's face, he added, "Just recently from Granger's Point. 'Fore that I was in Chicago."

"Chicago? That's a big city. What brought you to Iowa?"

"Change of scenery. The wife died, and I needed a place to start over."

Mac was bothered by the fact that the man didn't blink, just chatted on nervously. Out here a man kept his thoughts to himself. To do otherwise could be dangerous.

He voiced his own question. "What'd ya say your name was?"

"Rathburn," the man answered. "Jeb Rathburn."

Mac went cold. Jeb Rathburn was the name of the man who had befriended Sadie on the wagon train. According to Sadie, Jeb Rathburn was the man Rowland and Harvey had buried with smallpox. Something was definitely not right.

Mac kept his voice level. "Well, Mr. Rathburn—Joe, Asa and I were just talking about our plans, since the trail has run cold."

The man leaned forward. When Mac offered no more information, he asked, "So, what's the plan? If you don't mind me asking, that is."

Mac smiled genially. "'Course not. We naturally thought it was best to stay together. We plan on talking to some people in the Dakota Territory, try to get a decent ransom together. We're hoping to keep the Army involved until we can get our women back."

Mac glanced at Joe and Asa, and was proud of the way they masked their surprise at his blatant lie. Finally, his gaze settled on the man calling himself Rathburn. For a split second he thought he could detect displeasure in the man's expression.

As suddenly as it appeared, the sour look disappeared, replaced by a cheerful grin. "Good idea!" the man enthused, a bit too brightly. "I'll bet you'd pay just about anything to have little Sadie back."

Alarm bells rang in Mac's brain. Sadie's name rolled too smoothly from the stranger's lips. He could tell by the slight paling of the man's features that he'd realized his mistake. "How did you know my wife's name?" Mac asked.

"I, ah, I heard you mention her."

Mac's jaw was like granite. "No, you didn't."

The little man laughed nervously. "Well, maybe I heard someone else say her name."

Mac's hand went to his revolver. He knew in his heart that this termite of a man was dangerous. The man saw the direction of Mac's hand and knew that Mac would have no compunction about shooting him through the head. "Whoa, mister! I just happened to know your wife's name! Let's not make this a bigger deal than it's gotta be."

Joe Thatcher intervened. "Cool down, Mac. You're just tired. We all are." Shooting a meaningful glance at Asa, Joe offered, "I'll take Mr. Rathburn here and get him a cup of coffee. Why don't you two walk it off?"

"Good idea, Joe," Asa said quickly before turning to the open field. "Come on, Mac." When Mac didn't budge, Asa hit him on the shoulder, hard. "Let's take a walk, my friend." More softly he added, "This lowlife is not worth dying over. Either you kill him in cold blood and rot in jail, or you rile him up till he shoots you in the back." He sighed a breath of relief as his words seemed to penetrate Mac's thick skull.

Mac kept his eyes trained on the back of the weaselly little man who walked away with Joe, but he answered, "I'm coming."

He and Asa had put a fair distance between themselves and the camp before either man spoke. The moon illuminated them like a party lantern. "What's going on, MacCallister? I've never seen you so ready to tear a man's head off. He knew Sadie's name. So what?"

Mac could feel the wet dew of the spring grass on his pant legs, could hear the frogs that were reclaiming Heron Lake. He hated to answer Asa until all the pieces of the puzzle fit neatly together in his own mind.

"So, what gives?" Asa demanded.

"It's not just that he knew Sadie's name. I don't know if I can explain it to you, but it was the way he said her name. Like he'd said it a thousand times before, like he was intimately familiar with it."

Asa let out a guffaw. Nothing about Mac had ever struck him as fanciful. This did. The man was losing his mind. "You didn't like the way he said her name?" He laughed again.

"Forget it!" Mac snapped, walking toward the lake. He had only taken a few steps when he added, "He's not who he says he is."

Asa ran to catch up with him. "What do you mean, not who he says he is? How in God's kingdom would you know that?"

"The man claims to be Jeb Rathburn. Jeb Rathburn was the name of the man who befriended Sadie on the wagon trail, the old man who stayed with her when she had to pull out to nurse Matthew. Rowland and Harvey buried him after he died of smallpox."

Mac looked Asa in the eye. "It's not a common name, Asa. I'm telling you, something doesn't smell right. Why would he claim to be someone he's not? Why would he join a rescue team shortly after being shot?"

"What do you want me to do?"

"I'm leaving before first light. You keep an eye on him."

The two men shared the silence as they returned to camp, each lost in his own thoughts. It was no secret that with each passing day their mission took on renewed urgency. The longer the women were gone, the less likely it was that they would ever be rescued.

Mac bedded down with his back to an outcropping of rocks and knew that morning could not come soon enough.

He rose at dawn under the pretense of answering nature's call. He looked for Asa, who had offered to take the final shift of guard duty. Asa was slumped against one of the boulders, his head bent to his shoulder, his rifle in his lap. Mac was glad Asa wasn't an Army regular who would be disciplined for falling asleep on the job.

He gathered his meager belongings and slipped away quietly. Mac didn't dare mount his horse until he was well away from the sleeping men.

He knew that he wouldn't breathe until he was on his horse, riding through the thick trees that shielded the north side of the lake. He stepped through the sparse grass, attempting to avoid a clump of leaves or anything that would give him away.

He never felt the feverish gaze of the eyes that were trained on his back. He never knew that as he endeavored to leave camp undetected, a man followed at a discreet distance, the cold barrel of a revolver nestled against his thigh.

Finally, Mac entered the dark sanctuary of the woods and sent a prayer of gratitude heavenward. The man followed him into the woods, pulling his weapon. He didn't care that the shot would be heard in camp. He didn't plan on sticking around to answer any questions.

Taking a deep, satisfied breath, the man aimed his revolver squarely at MacCallister's broad back. His finger itched to pull the trigger, but he wanted to wait for precisely the right moment. He waited for MacCallister to move that big horse a few feet further into a clearing. . . .

Eldon never knew what hit him. The impact to his head sounded like a ripe melon being thrown to the hard ground. "Oh, damn," he muttered as his skinny body slumped to the earth.

Chapter Forty-eight

"Would you look at that?" Abbie's face radiated wonder. "I think those dogs are more trouble than they're worth!"

Sadie couldn't help but grin. More Sioux had joined Inkapaduta's band a day earlier. Along with their women and children, the Indians brought their dogs—strong, healthy animals who served by pulling supply-laden travois.

The problem was that these particular dogs weren't much in the way of pack animals. They fought constantly. It was a wonder that any of them had fur left on their hindquarters, having been bitten there so often. At the moment, two Indian women were chasing a wayward dog that had taken off, full speed, after a rabbit. The dog did not care a whit that he was carrying all the women's worldly goods on the wildly careening travois.

Sadie watched in wonder as the women argued about how best to stop the animal. She looked around and noticed that the Sioux seemed to be as entertained by the sight as she herself. She looked at their relaxed brown faces, some that she knew she would have considered attractive under different circumstances. She wondered how long it had been since they had laughed.

It seemed that there were no winners on the frontier. The Indians were losing their way of life, starved out of their own homeland. The settlers lived in constant fear of attack. She questioned the wisdom of those who professed to have all the answers regarding the Indian conflict. The longer she was with the Sioux—even if these were considered renegades—the less clear any of it seemed. Who was right and who was wrong? Sadie wasn't sure.

The band began to move again, leaving the concern of the runaway dog behind. As had become her habit, Sadie checked the whereabouts of the other captives. Abbie trailed closely behind her. Margaret Ann was ahead, the Sioux child on her hip. Sadie found Lydia near the back of the migrating tribe. Something about Lydia's posture disturbed her. The woman who had always been so proud walked with her head down, her shoulders slumped. Sadie hurried to Lydia's side, although she wondered why she bothered.

"Lydia?"

"Isn't it funny?" the woman asked, sounding suspiciously like the sweet youth Sadie first met at the Gardners'. "Isn't it funny that Elizabeth had to die when she had Joseph waiting for her? I mean, if you think about it, it should have been me. My Alvin and John are both dead. My parents are gone. There's no one left who would miss me, but poor Elizabeth . . ."

Sadie stared at her. The woman's darkly tanned face was smudged with dirt and her black hair hung loosely down her back, but she was still beautiful. Sadie shifted the pack she carried to her right hip and reached out, offering Lydia her hand. She was surprised when Lydia responded by grasping it.

Sadie squeezed that hand lightly, praying that Lydia was working her way back from the brink of insanity. She wished that she had more time alone with her, but she could see Margaret Ann weaving her way back to them. Margaret Ann no longer had the child with her.

"Sadie," Margaret Ann said, her breath coming in short gasps. "They want us. They want all of the captives together."

Sadie's heart pounded wildly. "What's going on?"

"I don't know. One of the braves just told me to gather the rest of you together and to meet him by those trees," she said, pointing to a cluster of small trees at the base of the hill.

Sadie tried to control her emotions as she called for Abbie, then walked with the other three women to the specified location. She continued to hold tightly to Lydia's hand, hoping that she wouldn't convey her own nervousness. They were met by a small group of Indians.

Most of them looked familiar. They watched the captives with interest. For minutes they stood there at the base of the hill, saying nothing. When she could no longer stand it, Sadie asked, "What's this all about?"

One of the Indians laughed, but not unkindly. "I am Sounding Heaven and this is my brother Grayfoot. We are from the Yellow Medicine Agency, here to purchase a captive."

"Whom do you wish?" asked the Sioux who had served as translator.

The brothers took their time in looking the captives over. Sadie wanted to protest, but doubted the wisdom. After the brutality she had witnessed at the hands of the Sioux, she had to believe that whoever went with the brothers might be better off.

It suddenly occurred to her that she might be separated from Abbie. Hadn't she promised that she would take care of Frances's daughter? Sadie averted her eyes and prayed that the Indians would not choose her or the girl.

"Her." Sadie looked up, relieved to see that they evidently wished to purchase Lydia. Perhaps it would be best for Lydia's fragile state of mind to leave the group.

"Not on your life!" Lydia insisted, her voice full of fear. "I'm not going anywhere."

The one called Grayfoot smiled gently at the frightened young woman. "We do not wish to harm you. We are friends with the Indian agent Charles Flandreau. We will send you to him and he will return you to your family."

"No, a thousand times no!" Lydia screamed.

The Indian looked at her long and hard, then shrugged. He turned his focus to Margaret Ann. "Will you come with us?"

Margaret Ann turned to Sadie. Her dark eyes conveyed her worry and doubt. Sadie wished that she knew what to tell her. Resolutely, Margaret Ann turned back to the brothers. "I will," she answered simply.

The captives were given no time for goodbyes. The

brothers handed a gun, a pile of blankets, and a keg of gunpowder to the Sioux, and were on their way with the newly purchased captive.

It seemed odd to resume the march without Margaret Ann. Sadie realized how much she had come to depend on the woman's quiet strength during their journey.

Camp was set early. The captives were once again put in the same teepee. Lydia actually smiled at Abbie as the two worked at setting up the structure. Sadie wanted to hug Lydia, but didn't dare. She was beginning to hope that Lydia would survive.

They had just finished gathering wood when Roaring Cloud barked an order at Lydia. As was her custom, Lydia simply ignored his command. Roaring Cloud seemed especially agitated. He marched to Lydia's side and knocked the wood from her arms.

Roaring Cloud pointed to the wood scattered on the ground, then back to Lydia. It was clear that he wanted to watch her pick it back up. Lydia stood toe to toe with the brave. "Get out of my way, you stupid mule," she snapped.

Roaring Cloud wrapped Lydia's dark hair around his hand, twisting it cruelly. When she could stand the pain no longer, Lydia fell to her knees. Roaring Cloud repeated his order. Through clenched teeth, Lydia responded, "Not on your life, you baby killer!"

Without loosening his hold on her long hair, Roaring Cloud bent and picked up a sturdy piece of wood. With a sickening thud he brought it down on Lydia's head. Sadie heard Abbie's gasp and felt her own head begin to swim. Not again! They could not lose another!

Sadie knew that she was screaming as she ran to Lydia's side and tried to help her up. If she could only get her to the teepee, away from Roaring Cloud . . . Roaring Cloud pulled the stick he wielded and swung it across Sadie's chest, knocking her to the ground. She blacked out.

When Sadie awoke, she was in the teepee. Abbie leaned over her, her face a mask of concern. "Sadie? Are you all right?"

Sadie sat slowly. "I must have hit my head when I fell. Where's Lydia?"

Abbie's eyes filled with tears. "She's still outside. They wouldn't let me bring her in here. I had to drag you."

"You did well, Abbie. I'll go see about Lydia."

Abbie's small hand stilled her. "Sadie, Lydia is dying."

"But . . ."

"It was awful. Roaring Cloud wouldn't stop. He just kept hitting her."

"Where is she?"

"Just outside."

Sadie and Abbie sat in the dark teepee with only the sound of the wind over the prairie and what Sadie could swear was a moan. "She's alive! That's her crying!" Sadie exclaimed. Before Abbie could stop her, Sadie scrambled out of the teepee, feeling her way to Lydia.

She refused to allow her brain to register what her eyes were seeing. The woman she saw bore no resemblance to the beauty Lydia Noble had once been. Only Lydia's pitiful cries proved her human.

Sadie could do no more than sit by, crooning softly in the suffering woman's ear. She prayed for Lydia's death. After what seemed an eternity, Lydia cried no more. Sadie closed her eyes and tried to imagine that Lydia was at that moment being reunited with her beloved Alvin and John.

Tiredly, she made her way back to the teepee. She wrapped her arms around Abbie and cried. She cried for Lydia and Elizabeth; she cried for all the others who had died. She cried for Abbie, for her lost innocence. Finally, she cried for herself and the possibility that she might never hold Mac again or see her precious children.

But in the end, Sadie reasoned, all the crying in the world wasn't going to keep Abbie safe, and that had to be her priority. She went to sleep, determined that whatever else happened she would keep Abbie safe.

Chapter Forty-nine

Like bees confined to a jar, energy stirred through camp. Sadie exited the teepee, aware of the excitement that lit the air. Her blue eyes scanned the area, mindful of the brown eyes that looked back at her . . . and Abbie. Cold dread clutched her chest. Not again.

"What's happening?" asked Abbie, unable to control the quaver in her voice.

"I don't know, sweetie," Sadie answered resolutely, "but I intend to find out."

"Abigail Gardner?" a deep, booming voice called out.

Sadie and Abbie turned to see a middle-aged Indian dressed in an odd mixture of Indian and western clothing. "She is," Sadie answered in Abbie's stead. "What do you want?"

"Does the girl not speak? I had not heard she was mute," the Indian responded mildly.

"Yes, sir, I can speak for myself."

"Gather any belongings. You have been purchased by my associates and me."

Abbie looked wildly to Sadie. "But I don't want to go. I want to stay here with Mrs. MacCallister."

Sadie understood how the girl felt. They had been through a tremendous trauma together. Now though, she wanted to know more about this man who claimed to have bought Abbie. She asked more sharply than she intended, "What do you plan to do with her?"

The Indian seemed to be in no hurry. Something about his calm demeanor, the gentle expression in his eyes, filled Sadie with hope. He answered politely, "Forgive me. I am John Other Day. The Minnesota State Legislature has appropriated a ransom, and I have delivered that ransom to Inkapaduta. In return, I am to safely deliver Abigail to society. Her sister, Eliza, is most anxious to see her."

Sadie turned to her young friend. "Go with him, Abbie. Eliza must be worried sick about you."

Abbie nodded and allowed tears to escape. After a quick hard hug, she walked to John Other Day's side. The Indian smiled sadly at Sadie. "I am sorry that we only had ransom for the little one. One day soon, perhaps . . ."

Sadie nodded. As if in tunnel vision she watched Abbie ride away with John Other Day. For the first time in six weeks Sadie allowed herself to hope that Abbie would be safe. She had done all that she could.

The sights and sounds of camp drifted away as she allowed herself to fall into the memory of Mac's arms, of how safe and loved she felt there. Mac once promised to build her a larger home, but Sadie knew that if she ever made it back to the people she loved, she would never want for more than that simple cabin on the water's edge, that place where dreams were ripe for the plucking and wishes could come true. Where they had come true for a short time.

Sadie shook her head and noticed that the Indian women had begun dismantling their teepees. As she set about to do the same, Sadie realized that she had never been as alone as she was at that moment.

She recalled Margaret Ann's warning that, although they might survive this experience physically, the real challenge was going to be getting through it mentally. Sadie wondered how much longer she could hang on.

Chapter Fifty

Mac had never been a patient man. For days he had cooled his heels, waiting for the right moment to make a move—a very dangerous move.

Mac felt that it was by pure providence that he had actually stumbled upon the whereabouts of the Sioux. Even as he had parted ways with the rescue team, Mac was aware that the Sioux might have traveled in any direction. Sheer instinct drove him to follow a westward path into the Dakota Territories. It had taken days for Mac to realize that the tracks he picked up were actually those of the Sioux he was tracking.

Until that moment, Mac hadn't admitted, even to himself, how terrified he had been of letting Sadie down. Even now, he still could fail her.

Mac lay on his stomach, surrounded by thick brush, prairie grass scratching his body. He had lost count of how many hours he had been in that position, of how many plans he had formulated and discarded. He would have only one opportunity.

He had followed the band from a distance, well aware of the risk he ran. When it became clear that they were camping, Mac had tied his horse to a tree then walked a quarter of a mile to the spot where he now hid.

It wasn't until they began to erect their dwellings that he saw her. Even from a distance, his heart broke at the sight of his beloved Sadie. She was even thinner than when he first met her. She went about her duties with detached precision, never looking up. Gone was the spirited woman who had argued with him so vehemently, who had dared him into loving her.

Mac saw Sadie retire to her teepee as the rest of the Sioux ate their meal. He wondered if she had been fed at all during their long journey.

Where were the rest of the captives? What had become of the other women? Mac's stomach cramped at the thought of what the hostages must have endured. Could they all be dead? Was Sadie next? She certainly appeared to have little hope. After seeing the atrocities that had been visited upon his neighbors, Mac didn't doubt that Sadie was in grave danger. He had to act . . . tonight.

The sun took its final bow, leaving the earth closeted in moonless darkness. He felt a grasshopper crawl over his pant leg and slapped at a mosquito that tormented his neck. He knew that he would need light to spirit Sadie safely out of reach, so he settled in for the night and kept his eyes trained on camp.

As the pink of dawn came, a quiver of tension buzzed in Mac's belly. The camp had yet to stir, but he had no delusions. The moment the Sioux realized that he was attempting to rescue their captive, all hell would break loose.

Those and other ominous thoughts crowded Mac's mind as he crawled, elbow over elbow, to the side of camp just opposite Sadie's teepee. Remembering the story of Gideon he had learned at St. Catherine's, Mac decided that a diversion was their only chance.

He was so close to the camp now that he was afraid the Sioux would hear his heavy breathing. Mac froze. An ugly mongrel, its hair standing on end, stood over him, sniffing curiously. Mac tried not to breathe. When it became clear that the animal was not going to leave, Mac lifted his head and whispered, "Get! Go away!"

Evidently this was a sensitive creature. The dog began to bark wildly, pacing back and forth. A child's voice called to the animal. Mac pushed his big body down into the soft earth. He didn't care about a mouthful of dirt. The child, a boy of about ten or eleven, walked closer, coming within feet of Mac's hiding spot. Again, he called to his pet. The dog seemed confused. He looked at the man on the ground, then back to his master. Finally, he loped back to camp.

Mac rested his head on his forearm, took a deep breath and proceeded. He crawled farther down the row of teepees and waited for the boy to disappear back into his family's dwelling. With relief he saw a boulder he had spotted from his hiding place. He picked up his pace and reached the big rock seconds later.

Mac knelt behind the rock and pulled a packet of dried twigs he had collected the night before from the waistband of his pants. In record time he lit one of the twigs, watching it until he was sure the flame would survive.

Without a moment's hesitation Mac slid from behind the cover of the boulder. Quickly he piled the twigs next to a teepee and lit the entire pile. After several puffs on the burgeoning fire, he rushed back into the brush.

Half-crouching, Mac continued around the perimeter of the camp, his eyes fixed on Sadie's teepee. *God, he prayed, don't let that fire take off until I've made it around.* A man shouted. Dogs began to bark. Mac flattened himself on the ground. His heart beat furiously. The fire had spread to the teepee more quickly than he had anticipated.

Weary Indians began to file out of their dwellings, wondering at the commotion. It took almost no time for the inhabitants of the burning structure to vacate. Flames licked up the sides of buffalo hide.

Mac looked up. It appeared that no one had spotted him—yet. He knew that if Sadie left her teepee to join the crowd he would lose his chance to snatch her.

The camp went wild. Women yelled for their children, dogs barked, warriors looked for an unseen enemy.

In all the activity, Mac stood and ran. He slid down behind Sadie's teepee, lifted the stretched skin and slipped in. Sadie's shocked expression might have been comical if they hadn't been so close to death.

"Mac . . ." Her eyes were wide, her mouth open.

"Let's get you out of here."

His eyes settled on a small bowl. "See what's going on out there, will you?" he requested, pulling a small pouch and matches from his shirt pocket.

Sadie lifted, then dropped the flap. "Mac! They're coming to check on me."

"What's tying your hair back?"

Sadie looked him blankly. Mac reached behind her head and pulled a length of thin cord from the bottom of her braid. "Ouch! What are you doing?"

Mac didn't have time for answers. He pointed to the rear wall of the structure. "Get out," he ordered. "Now!"

With a worried glance, Sadie slipped from the teepee. She seemed stunned. Mac placed the bowl he'd grabbed in front of the flap. He poured the contents of the pouch into the cracked bowl, buried one end of the cord in the center, then laid a burning matchstick to the end. As soon as he was sure that the cord was burning, he dove out of the teepee.

Sadie stood just outside, waiting nervously. Mac grabbed his wife's hand. "Run! Don't look back, just run!"

"What did you do?" she asked, pushing to keep up with his long stride.

"It was gunpowder. Just enough to create a little flash, but maybe it will slow them down for a few seconds."

They had made it no farther than the top of a rise overlooking camp when Mac wished he had heeded his own advice to not look back. Below them the Sioux shouted, wildly pointing in their direction. Mac felt the whiz of a bullet pass his shoulder. More shouts.

"Keep down!" he instructed. "It's not much farther."

The ground was wet with morning dew. Sadie slipped in the grass, practically pulling Mac down with her. Mac saw his horse tied where he had left it hours before. He swept his wife into his arms and ran.

As he reached the horse, Mac pushed her onto the high saddle. Sadie held on for dear life, aware that pursuit had begun.

Mac untied the horse and, in a fluid motion mounted behind her. He wasn't going to allow her to take a bullet by exposing her back. His nervous horse tore across the open field, seeming to be aware that it was all that stood between its two riders and death.

In spite of their predicament, Sadie had to know. "The children?"

"Are fine. They hid during the attack. I'll fill you in later."

Sadie's chest burned. She sobbed into the wind. The children were alive! Mac had found her! Was it all a dream?

They continued at that breakneck pace for more than an hour. Mac knew that as fine an animal as his was, the horse was not going to survive at this rate for long. He could not see the Indians behind him, but he knew that they were coming. Why hadn't he thought to incapacitate their horses?

Fear for Sadie's well-being pushed him. The Sioux would not stop until they had their captive back. Mac would do whatever it took to ensure that never happened.

They came to a creek. Mac reined his animal toward shallow water and began riding upstream. Sadie looked over her shoulder, the question clear on her face. He explained, "They're going to expect us to either cross here or go downstream. This will buy us a little time . . . I hope." Mac softened the last comment with a wry grin.

He followed the stream to its origin, a small lake. "This is where we get off," he announced as he led the mount out of the quickly deepening water.

Sadie's legs were wet, but she'd didn't care. Mac had

come for her! He had brought her hope, proved that he cared! "We're going to continue north?"

"Northeast. They'll expect us to head south for home. By the time they figure out we didn't, we should make it to a town in Minnesota."

They rode all day. Sadie would never forget the feeling of Mac tenderly pulling her head back to his chest, of him urging her to rest. She had missed him so much that being with him again seemed unreal.

By evening they did come to a town, a small outpost really. People stopped to stare at the white woman dressed in a deerskin dress, but Mac and Sadie took no notice. They were focused on one thing—getting home.

Stars began to dot the sky before Mac suggested that they stop for the night. "Mac, this is beautiful!" Sadie exclaimed, as she admired the spot he had chosen. A ragged cliff dominated the rise overlooking another small lake. Beyond, dense woods stood like centurions guarding the water.

Mac built a small fire and unrolled the bedroll under an overhang of granite. Sadie sat on the hill, her knees drawn to her chest, her arms wrapped around her legs.

"Cold?" Mac asked as he sat down next to her.

She smiled up at him. "A little."

Mac wrapped his arm around her shoulders and pulled her to him. Sadie snuggled her face in his neck, breathing deep his familiar scent. "You came for me," she said in wonder.

Mac pulled away slightly and looked intently into her blue eyes. "You doubted I would?"

"Mac, there are things you don't know."

"I know that I love you," he answered, as though that was all that mattered.

"No, there are things I should have told you long ago."

"I know, Sadie," Mac said, his voice a low rumble.

She felt faint. Surely he didn't mean . . .

"I know that Eldon Pritchard didn't die at the bottom of a ravine." He watched Sadie's shocked reaction, the way her eyes widened. "I know that's why you pulled away from me before I left for Fort Dodge. You had just found out yourself, hadn't you?"

The relief was overwhelming. For better or for worse, the truth was out. She nodded sadly. "He showed up the first time you took Aaron and Matthew hunting." A terrible thought flashed through her mind. "How did you find out?"

The panic on her face touched him. Mac placed his warm hands on either side of Sadie's face. "He was with the rescue team from Granger's Point."

"What?" Sadie blanched.

Mac smiled ever so slightly. "You didn't have anything to do with a gunshot wound to his shoulder, did you?"

"I thought he was dead," Sadie said quietly. "I shot him twice."

"Wanna tell me what happened?"

"The day you took Aaron and Matthew hunting was the first time Eldon showed up. He told me that he killed two thieves along the trail and stole their money. He changed clothes with one of the men and threw him over the ravine, just so everyone would think it was him who had died. He's the one who left the note on the tree for you to find, so you would believe I had another man."

Sadie sucked in a deep, rattled breath. Mac gently massaged her neck and waited for her to continue. "I don't know what I thought, Mac. I couldn't bear the idea of losing you, and I didn't want to see the hurt on your face when you found out Eldon was alive. I guess I just hoped he'd disappear after picking up the money. But he came back, like a bad dream, right after you left for Fort Dodge. He threatened to hurt the boys, to hurt you, if I didn't go with him. I waited until we were away from the cabin and pulled his gun on him. I threatened him, but I wasn't sure I'd actually have to shoot him. He charged at me and I just pulled the trigger. . . ."

"You did the right thing," Mac said.

"I thought he was dead. There was so much blood."

"I think you did some significant damage. He still seemed pretty sore."

"How did you know it was Eldon?" Sadie asked.

"He spent too much of his time trying to ingratiate himself with me. Something about the way he acted put me on the defensive. Then he claimed to be Jeb Rathburn."

"Why, that low-life, belly-crawling son of a rattlesnake!" Sadie spat. "He isn't worthy to lick Jeb Rathburn's boots!"

"I don't think it occurred to him that you might have told me about the real Jeb, about how important he was to you. Using that name gave him away." Mac squinted into the darkness. "Then, sometime during the conversation he mentioned your name. I wondered how he could have known. Anyway, it wasn't so much that he knew your name, it was the way he said it, like he'd said it a million times before."

Sadie could only imagine what it must have been

like for Mac, wondering how this total stranger could be so familiar with his wife. "I am sorry," she offered. "Is that when you became sure of who he was?"

"Not quite. When he stood to walk away with Joe Thatcher, I noticed that he wore a unique knife, a Bowie knife with a spectacular ivory handle. It wasn't until I was on my way to the Sioux camp that I remembered you telling me about the stories Eldon used to make up about fighting the Mexicans and how proud he was of his knife. The pieces finally fell into place."

"But you came for me anyway?"

"Sadie, come here," Mac growled as he pulled her to her feet. "See those oaks over there? They need two things to say alive—sunlight and water." He turned her to face him, then ran his rough hands over hair. Sadie shivered as his touch ran down her arms and moved to her tiny waist. "You are my sunlight and my water. Without you I would wither and die. You make everything about me better."

"But what about—"

"Shh," Mac whispered in her ear. "We'll take care of it, together. Right now I think we have other things to take care of."

They moved to the bedroll, trailing pieces of clothing as they walked. Sadie laughed. "I thought that man at the supply store was going to have a fit when he saw me dressed like this."

Mac smiled. "I was proud of the way you walked in there, head up."

They lay together on the soft bedroll, facing one another. "Did they hurt you?" Mac asked, as he stared into her eyes. There was nothing in his tone that indicated that he would think any less of her. It was a simple question.

"No." She shook her head.

"Good, because I wasn't looking forward to going back and killing every man in that camp."

Sadie shivered, knowing that he would have done it. Knowing that Mac loved her so much that he would die for her was a revelation. He had, in fact, risked his life for her. Risked everything for her. And after he knew the truth. For the first time in her life, Sadie felt totally safe. It was an odd but wonderful thing.

"I've missed you," she said boldly. She kissed him, wanting him to taste her, wanting to taste him. She savored the warmth of his lips, the feel of his teeth on her tongue. Her tongue roamed his mouth, longing to revisit every corner.

Mac's hands molded to her body, ran over her breasts, down her waist, and back up again. He settled on her breasts until he could feel the nipples teasing his hand, calling to his mouth. He complied. Sadie arched up in ecstasy and wondered how such a simple act could cause such pleasure. She held his head to her breast, watched with growing desire as he caressed it with his tongue, saw the way the moonlight reflected off the wetness there. Sadie felt wet all over.

When he attempted to move down her body, Sadie pulled at his shoulders with remarkable force. She had waited so many long months for this moment, she thought she would go mad if she had to wait any longer. She needed him inside her.

Mac smiled tenderly before he thrust his body into hers, made himself part of her being. She cried out, not only with physical gratification, but with supreme emotional satisfaction.

They moved together, each seeking to bring the other ultimate pleasure. Mac kissed her and felt her contract, pulling him deeper into her body. Their sweat mingled, their moans sounded like music. His hair brushed her face. The jaw that had not been shaved in days scratched her cheeks.

And then their worlds exploded. Sadie saw tiny flecks of light, stars that hid behind her eyelids. She felt her toes and fingertips lose all sensation, as though the only nerve endings that mattered were concentrated in her womanhood. And in this greatest moment of joy, she watched spasms rock Mac. She had brought him to this. They had brought each other to this place.

In those following precious moments when Mac rested his big body on hers, Sadie looked into the wide Minnesota sky and admitted the truth. Something greater than either of them had made all of this possible. Long before she'd pulled her wagon out of the wagon train, long before she'd ever set eyes on Samuel MacCallister, this had been preordained. No matter what she had suffered, all was well. And Sadie knew that nothing this good could have happened by accident.

Chapter Fifty-one

Sadie sat straighter on the horse. "Mac, I can see water!"

Her husband leaned over her shoulder, humor in his voice. "It's Spirit Lake, Sadie. We won't see Okoboji till later today."

"I don't care! I'm in Iowa, and I'm only hours away from seeing my children." His arm tightened around her waist until she added, "Oh, yes, and I'm with the man I love."

"Well, thank you so much for that afterthought."

After weeks of doubting she would ever see it again, Sadie was anxious to be home. With a heavy heart she realized that nothing would ever be the same. "I can't believe all that has happened in the past two months," she said for the millionth time.

Mac leaned his mouth close to Sadie's ear. "Poor Joe Thatcher. I don't know what I would have done if I lost you."

"After Joe's had some time to grieve, I want to sit

down and tell him how brave Elizabeth was, how very much she loved him."

"You were all brave, Sadie."

Sadie thought about that for a moment. "There's nothing brave about wanting to survive. That's all I wanted, you know."

Mac stiffened, then calmly asked, "You up to another race?"

Before she had the opportunity to panic, he snapped the reins, kneed his horse, and announced, "They've found us."

Sadie didn't have to ask who. Somehow, the Sioux had followed them all the way through Minnesota. Or some had. Four horsemen bore down on them.

Mac's horse ran like a champion. Across the plains he tore, bearing the weight of two. "We should have bought another horse in one of the towns," Sadie yelled.

"You don't ride," Mac reminded her, his concentration focused on controlling the huge animal. One misstep and they were both dead.

Sadie knew that now was not the time to tell him about her first riding experience, the night she'd shot Eldon. But she vowed that she would tell him when, and if, they lived through the day.

Mac pulled the horse sharply to the right. "What are you doing?" Alarm rang in Sadie's voice.

"I know a shortcut." They ran full speed across the field. Sadie could see that Mac's goal was a heavily wooded area. She wondered if it would provide them enough cover to get home. Or at least to safety. Mac pushed her head down. "This is going to be tight," he warned.

Tasting a mouthful of horse's mane, Sadie felt tree

limbs tear at her arms and legs. She could only imagine the terrible injuries Mac was suffering.

The forest was dark, wet, and ominous. Sadie peered into its depths, and she understood the stories that originated in the woods. It was easy to imagine ghouls and trolls reigning over this domain.

"Are they following us?"

Mac gave a terse response. "If they are, the going is slow for them. I have the advantage of knowing these woods."

"I don't want them to follow us home. The children . . ."

"We'll stop at Thatcher's. I doubt Joe and Asa are back yet, but Morris Markham should be around. He'll help."

The trees thinned and forest turned to beach, and Sadie cried out in relief at the sight of Okoboji. She knew these waters. Sadie could not help but look around Mac's broad shoulders every few moments. So far, no Indians.

"There's Joe's place. Markham must have company—there's a horse tied in front."

Sadie drank in the sight of the cabin Elizabeth and Lydia had shared with their families. She tried not to look at the bark that had been stripped from the trees, or to remember the horror that had taken place there.

Mac dismounted, then reached up to help Sadie do the same. Her legs felt like rubber. She hoped that she could make it to the door without falling.

"I need to get you behind a locked door before those Sioux show up," Mac said. Then he shouted for Morris.

The door to the small cabin opened. Sadie backed

up slowly until she felt the warm coat of Mac's horse against her back. Eldon Pritchard stood in the doorway, an ugly grin on his face. "Why, this must be my lucky day."

Chapter Fifty-two

Mac's response was cold as ice. "What are you doing here, Pritchard? Where's Markham?"

Eldon laughed, his voice cracked and raw. "So, you know who I am, eh? Aw shucks, that takes all the fun out of everything."

"Where's Markham?" Mac repeated.

"Oh, he's resting," Eldon responded, opening the door just wide enough for Mac and Sadie to see Morris's big body sprawled on the floor.

Mac rushed for the door. Eldon pulled a revolver from behind his back. "I don't think I would do that if I was you. Back up," he ordered.

Fear choked Sadie. "Just do what he says, Mac. He will shoot you."

"Yeah, 'Do what he says, Mac,'" Eldon mimicked. He stepped out and pulled the door shut behind him. As casually as if he were entertaining guests, he said, "Like I said, this must be my lucky day. I came by here to kill Burtch, and I happen to run into the two of you. What do you know?"

"Why kill Burtch?" Mac wanted to keep him talking.

"That son-of-a-bitch hit me, that's why! Nobody gets away with hitting Eldon Pritchard."

"Why did he hit you?" Mac asked calmly, inching away from the house.

Eldon saw what Mac was doing. "Hey, don't you move till I tell you to, you got that?"

Mac held his hands up. "No problem," he assured the little man.

Eldon looked momentarily confused. "What did you ask me? Oh yeah, you wanted to know why Burtch hit me. I guess it don't matter none if I tell you now. The day you snuck out of camp, I followed you. What I didn't know was that Burtch followed me. That sneaky bugger pretended to be asleep!" Eldon looked genuinely surprised.

"I knew I could have all that I wanted if you weren't in the picture. Sadie girl would have your land and I would have Sadie *and* the farm. Get it?"

"I get it, Pritchard," Mac said.

"I guess old Burtch doesn't much care for the idea of people shooting his friends. He saw me taking a bead on you and bam, he let me have it. He took me back to camp trussed up like a pig and told everyone his version of what happened." Eldon spit onto the dark ground.

"I outsmarted him, though," he bragged. "I acted like I was hurtin' real bad, and they decided only one guy needed to guard me till they could get me to a town. I pretended to be asleep and then, *whack*, hit that guy like a Christmas goose and skedaddled outta there!"

"So, what are you doing here?" Mac asked.

Eldon's matter-of-fact tone chilled Sadie to the bone. "I'm gonna kill him. He messed with me, now I'm gonna mess with him. He ruined all my plans for staying around here." There was a whine in Eldon's thin voice.

"Why would you want to stay here anyway, Pritchard? You left Sadie and the boys. Did you suddenly decide you missed being a husband and father?"

Eldon's face flamed. "Enough questions," he yelled. "You two back right on up, hands in the air."

Mac and Sadie complied. Sadie backed across the sandy beach, wildly considering their options. "Throw your gun in the water, MacCallister," Eldon ordered.

Mac hesitated.

"Now, or I'll blow her head off!" Eldon trained his gun on Sadie.

"Don't do it, Mac!" she begged. "He's going to kill us both anyway!"

Mac's eyes met Sadie's. He tossed his gun into the clear lake. Sadie cried out as she watched their last hope disappear.

"Mac!"

Mac faced his wife. "I'd rather die with you than live without you," he said quietly.

"This is going to be more fun that I thought," Eldon crowed. He eyed Mac, knowing that in every way Sadie thought MacCallister a superior man. The thought rankled. "On your knees."

"No, Eldon," Sadie cried. "Don't do this. I'll do anything. I'll go away with you!"

"It's too late for that, Sadie girl. You shot me, remember? You gotta be punished."

Sadie faced the man who had made her life a living hell, hoping that she looked contrite. "I am so sorry about that night, Eldon. I was just scared. I don't know what I was thinking." She dared a look at Mac, noticed the deep, raw scratches that marred his beautiful face. Then to Eldon she said, "There's no reason why I can't say one last goodbye if you're going to shoot us anyway."

"No way."

"What are you afraid of, Pritchard?" Mac taunted. "You're the big man holding the gun, and you won't even let us share a simple hug?" Scorn was written on Mac's face. "You that scared of me?"

Eldon shook with rage as he moved off the porch and down the few stairs to sandy ground. "I ain't scared of nobody!" he yelled. "Say your damn goodbyes."

Mac walked slowly to Sadie, never taking his eyes off her. He wrapped his arms around her, felt her tremble. He held more tightly to her and put his mouth to her ear. "As soon as I let go of you, hit the ground," he said softly.

Sadie knew that it would do no good to protest. They were going to die at Eldon's hand anyway. She looked into Mac's stormy green eyes, and silently thanked him for all that he had done for her. Her life with him had been worth the few snatches of joy she had experienced.

Mac's jaw thrust out in the way that Sadie had come to love. Resolutely, he pushed her away from him and said, "Now!"

Sadie tasted sand, felt the warmth of it against her exposed skin. She looked over her shoulder and watched in horror as Mac dove for Eldon's legs. The butt of Eldon's gun made a sickening thud on the back of Mac's skull, knocking her beloved back. By the time Mac righted himself, Eldon had the gun aimed squarely at his forehead.

"Stay right there, MacCallister! You too, Sadie girl," he added as he noticed that Sadie was on her feet.

"Mac," Sadie said, longing to move to her husband's side.

"Stay back, Sadie," Mac answered. "Please stay back."

"Well, aren't you two sweet?" Eldon sneered.

"She *is* sweet, Pritchard," Mac growled. "She's also strong, smart, and incredibly brave. But you wouldn't know that, would you? You never really got to know Sadie. You never saw her when she was happy, you never learned how good it feels to hold her when she's scared, or to share a secret with her. I pity you, Pritchard, I really do."

Mac looked over his shoulder at his wife. "Every moment with you has been worth it, Sadie. I'd die a hundred times over if it meant a few hours with you. Promise me you'll never forget that."

Tears flowed freely down Sadie's dirty face. Never had joy and pain mingled so confusingly throughout her body. "I love you," she mouthed.

"Don't you feel sorry for me, MacCallister," Eldon interrupted. "I plan on having plenty of good times with Sadie after you're dead." Eldon smiled grossly across the sand at the woman who had been his legal obligation. "Yes indeed, Sadie girl, I'm going teach your body tricks you ain't even heard of."

A deep growl was the only warning. Once again, Mac went for Eldon's legs. Eldon raised his weapon, a murderous expression in his eyes.

Chapter Fifty-three

Eldon shook convulsively, shock stamped on his face. Like an oak being felled, he thudded to the soft ground. A long feathered arrow protruded from his bony chest.

The Sioux had finally found them. Sadie looked up to see a warrior lower his bow. With a start, she recognized him. It was the father of the boy she had saved from the Big Sioux River. He stood alone.

For what seemed an eternity, the Indian stared at her. With the slightest nod of his head, he jumped up on his horse and turned back into the woods. As though he had been an illusion, the brave disappeared into the dark trees.

Mac moved to his wife's side. "You all right?"

"He just saved our lives," Sadie said, as though she couldn't believe her eyes. She couldn't. "I saved his little boy from drowning, and he's repaid me by saving the man I love."

"There are good and bad among all of us, Sadie. That's a lesson I learned way back in Kansas."

The pair stood silently, trying to absorb all that had transpired. Mac finally broke the silence, "What do you want to do with him?"

Sadie looked at the sorry body of Eldon Pritchard and was tempted to tell Mac to leave him to rot. "We should bury him, but not because he deserves it. Aaron and Matthew deserve it, though."

"Let's get in the house and make sure Morris is okay."

Sadie pulled away. "I've seen too much, Mac. I don't want to see what Eldon has done to that man."

"Sadie, the other Sioux may come. Please come inside with me."

Sadie looked to the woods. "They won't be back," she said confidently. "I don't know what that brave will tell his friends, but I'm sure they won't be back."

When Mac didn't move, Sadie pushed him. "Go on. I'll tell you all about it later."

Chapter Fifty-four

Sadie was sitting on the stoop when Mac came out. "He'll be fine," he reported. "He's got a pretty nasty bump on his head, but Markham is a tough one. He's in there cussing a blue streak."

Without explaining why, Mac walked to the shed. He came out with a shovel and slipped into the woods. Sadie kept her gaze averted as he carried Eldon's body to its final resting place.

"You ready to go home?" he asked an hour or so later, after completing his task.

Sadie looked up at her handsome husband. "When I was very young, I used to dream of you—of this place. But I don't think I ever really believed someone like you or this place existed. I wished for it, maybe, but . . . I guess when you told me that you loved me my mind just wouldn't accept it. All I could hear were the voices from my past, telling me how worthless I am."

"And now?"

Sadie smiled softly. "And now I understand that we're all worthy. If there's one thing I've learned in the past few months, it's that every life is priceless."

"You know I'm forever, right?"

"Whether you want to be or not." Sadie laughed and rose to her feet.

Mac helped her back into the saddle, then mounted behind her. They were both quiet for a moment.

"It won't be the same," Sadie said, looking out across the water. "Rowland, Frances, Mary, Harvey, Elizabeth, Lydia—they're all gone."

Mac wrapped his arms around her. "No they're not, Sadie. As long as we're here to remember them, to tell their story, they'll be with us. The spirit of those who dared to settle here, to follow their dreams, will live as long as those blue waters continue to push to shore."

Mac and Sadie rode slowly along the shoreline of Lake Okoboji, meditating on all they had to be grateful for.

"Mac?"

"Hmm?"

"Remember that story you told the boys and me? The one about the handsome warrior and the beautiful maiden from different bands, the couple who could send wishes to each other across the water?"

"Yes." There was a smile in Mac's voice.

"You never finished the story. How did it end?"

Mac nuzzled his nose in his wife's hair. "Well, against tremendous odds, in spite of overwhelming obstacles, they found a way to spend their lives together.

And, *Mrs. MacCallister*, they lived happily ever after. Now let's go see our children."

It took a moment for his words to sink in, but when they did, Sadie smiled. Somewhere, she knew that Frances Gardner was smiling too.

Author's Note

One of several true historical figures in this book, Abbie Gardner did survive what is now known as the Spirit Lake Massacre, but life was never easy for her. She married a man by the name of Caswell Sharp a few short months after being ransomed. She lived long enough to experience divorce, poor health, and the death of her children. In spite (or perhaps because) of her troubles, Abbie never forgot her family. She never buried the memory of that March day in 1857.

In 1891 Abbie moved back to Lake Okoboji, purchased the land and cabin that had once belonged to her father, and opened a tourist attraction. Abbie wanted people to hear about what had happened in that cabin, wanted her family to be remembered. By 1895 Abbie had raised enough money to build a monument to the victims of the Spirit Lake Massacre. That monument can be found near the Gardner cabin at Pillsbury Point, Lake Okoboji, Arnold's Park, Iowa.

Sometime before her 1921 death, Abbie forgave her captors. She even began to collect Native American artifacts, displaying them in her cabin-museum. It became clear to Abbie that there are good and evil people wearing every color of skin. She chose to celebrate what was good and noble about her Native American neighbors.

By all accounts, Margaret Ann Marble was treated well by her rescuers. It is said that she was sad to leave them when the time came for her to reenter "polite society." Margaret Ann eventually remarried and moved to California. She died there in 1911.

Inkapaduta continues to be a controversial character in history. Nearly sixty years old at the time of the massacre and kidnappings, the man had a lifetime of resentment to purge. He had been part of a band driven out of the Sioux nation in response to their misdeeds, and he was resentful of the treaty agreements made in his absence.

Inkapaduta's hate for the settler Henry Lott was real, and probably well deserved. Lott not only sold whiskey to Inkapaduta's people, but he also stole their horses. Two years after being run out of northwest Iowa by Inkapaduta's band, Lott returned with his stepson to murder much of Inkapaduta's family, including his brother, Sidominadota.

Rather than take revenge himself, Inkapaduta reported Lott's crimes to the Army in Fort Dodge. At first it seemed as though the government would seriously investigate the Indian's claims. Then, instead, in full view of Inkapaduta's band, the prosecuting attorney nailed Sidominadota's head to a pole outside his home, leaving it there as the ultimate sign of disrespect. Henry Lott disappeared to parts unknown, and the Army took no interest in finding him.

While there's no arguing the fact that Inkapaduta and his band committed atrocious crimes during their 1857 rampage, it is easy to see how their frustration was fueled throughout the years by intolerance and prejudice.

Roaring Cloud, the son who beat Lydia Noble to death, was killed by troops from Fort Ridgley. Inkapaduta was never caught or prosecuted for his actions at Lake Okoboji. He was rumored to be with Sitting Bull at Little Bighorn the day George Custer was killed. Inkapaduta died in Manitoba in 1881, at the age of 84.